Two Face

L. Williams

This is a work of fiction. Names, characters, places, and incidents are the product of the author's imagination or are used fictitiously. Any resemblance to actual persons, living or dead, events, or locales is entirely coincidental.

All rights reserved. No part of this publication may be reproduced, distributed, or transmitted in any form or by any means, including photocopying, recording, or other electronic or mechanical methods, without prior written permission of the author or the publisher, except in the case of brief quotations embodied in critical reviews and certain other non-commercial uses permitted by copyright law.

Two/Face Copyright © 2024 - Author: L. Williams

Cover Design - @Chris_Covers_ & team (IG)

Year of publication - 2024

Playlist

Louis Armstrong – What A Wonderful World

KALEO – Way Down We Go

Bon-Jovi – Livin' On A Prayer

Jessie Ware – Wildest Moments

Frank Sinatra – The Way You Look Tonight

Christina Perri – Jar Of Hearts

Sugababes – Freak Like Me

Slipknot – Snuff

Muse – Madness

To all those who have waited patiently for this book...Thank you x

Chapter One
Summer ♥

My eyes remain focused on the street below, the hustle and bustle of tourists going about their evening. Taking in the immense city lights, the sea of smiles and cheers as the fountain below dances to the tune of *Louis Armstrong – What a wonderful world*. I close my eyes as a single tear trickles down my cheek, taking in those beautiful words that offer me little comfort. Inhaling a deep breath, my body screams in pain, but I hold my silence, refusing to allow him to win again.

Allowing my fingers to trace over the double scotch I poured myself, my gaze lands on the engagement ring, which now feels like a vice wrapped around my entire existence. I gently close my eyes again and hum to the peaceful tune, allowing the silent tears to fall further. Lifting the glass to my lips, I try to stifle my cries as the sudden pain shoots through my ribs. Slowing my movement down, I finally take a sip. Allowing the warm liquid to pass my lips, quietly numbing the utter turmoil in my mind and quilting over the pain surging through my body.

He said it wouldn't happen again; I smirk to myself. Knowing that man is a compulsive liar, I shake my head again at my stupidity for believing the deceit. The empty glass clinks as I set it back down. Bracing my palms on the table, I whimper. The pain courses through me once again as I try to stand. Shaking my head, I don't allow myself to fall back into the seat. I can't because if I do, I've admitted defeat. Once I do that, I may as well just let him kill me. The large engagement ring on my finger keeps catching the light as my entire body shakes and sweats with pain. As I go to take it off, I hear those cutting words.

"Why are you removing your ring? Is there someone else, you fucking WHORE? Who do you think you are? Without me...you'll die alone!"

I sigh heavily, glancing around the dark suite and moving slowly towards the bathroom. Switching on the light, the entire mirror lights up as I stare back at my reflection. Stepping closer, I lift my shirt and finally see the damage. Black bruises imprinted on my skin, a familiar reminder of what happens when I question Harry after a cocaine bender. I'm not too sure what sent him into a rage this time. It could have been because I wore a red dress to dinner and not a black one, or possibly because my mother decided to order champagne at the dinner table. Either way, it happened, and here I am. Looking back at a shell of the person I once was, the sad reflection looking back at me is a stark reminder that I'm alone.

I know what you're thinking. The day the person who loves you or claims to lays their hands on you, run. Run for the fucking hills and never look back. That would make a lot of sense if I had somewhere to even run to. My mother chooses to ignore her husband and Harry's awful behavior because they have money. Eric would never dream of laying a hand on his wife, but that doesn't stop him from enjoying the dancers at his clubs most evenings. As long as Rachel remains the good, dutiful wife, she'll remain lavished with designer clothes, luxury holidays, and a lifestyle royalty may even consider "extravagant".

My mother left my father around fifteen years ago, so long ago that I barely remember them being together in the same room. She took me away from New York and ran into the arms of Eric Stanton. A successful, well-connected, and well-known businessman from Los Angeles.

Men always seemed fixated on Rachel Harper. She'd always looked after herself and taken great pride in her appearance, her shoulder-length blonde curls were always perfectly set, and her immaculate makeup always showcased her high cheekbones, red lips and large hazel eyes. But there had always been something ruthless about her, too. She always got what she wanted. Whether that would be to throw a tantrum or wear those around her down, I never liked it.

I can't really complain. However, I had more than most growing up. Only in the last few years did I wonder what Eric did for a living. My mother claimed he was a "businessman". But a couple of nightclubs and strip joints can only take you so far, right? Then, a couple of years back, in walks Harry Maine. My stepfather introduced us. In the beginning, he seemed caring and attentive, sweet even. But it didn't take long for the demon lurking beneath that well-cut, expensive Armani suit to rear its ugly head.

Harry and Eric went into business ventures together, but that was when I noticed his behavior shift dramatically. He was angry, erratic, and on edge. The first time he hit me was when I found him snorting cocaine at a family dinner. He clearly didn't like being questioned, and that night, when we arrived home, he backhanded me so hard that I fell into the glass coffee table, which required stitches in my hand.

Fearing for my safety, I rushed back to my mother's house, bleeding all over her floor. Yet she didn't seem bothered, it turned out Harry had already called her and smoothed it over as a minor disagreement. I knew from that moment; I was on my own. My mother had chosen money and expensive gifts over her own daughter. I think that moment broke my heart more than Harry hitting me, I guess because deep down, I always knew my mother was a vindictive bitch, but I hadn't yet seen it for myself.

Switching on the tap, I pool the cool water in my hands, splashing my face. I hope it'll reduce the redness before I face my family tomorrow at breakfast. Part of me hopes Harry just stays out all night and stays the fuck away from me. Then the other part hopes he overdoses with one of his whores and dies in some seedy motel somewhere. As soon as that thought comes into my head, I shake it away. Trying to remind myself, one bad day doesn't mean a bad life. I need to be smart and push through this, or else it'll fucking eat me from the inside out.

I jump, hearing a firm knock ring through the hotel suite. I wince. Clutching onto my ribs, I turn the tap off and dry my face. Padding along the marble tiles, I reach the front door. Opening it slightly, my brows pinch in confusion as I'm face to face with my stepfather. His eyes are solemn, and his voice is almost gentle as he speaks.

"Could I come in?"

Blinking a couple of times, I open the door further as he whisks past me. The smell of cigar smoke and whisky woven into his evening suit. To avoid bringing attention to my current injuries, I move slowly into the vast living space, which overlooks the Las Vegas strip. Eric stands at the window, his hands firmly placed in his pockets.

"Eric, is everything ok?" I ask quietly.

His entire demeanor is unusual. If anything, he's usually brash and overbearing, very much like his lifestyle. Turning towards me, he looks down to the ground for a moment.

"I'm sorry, Summer, but your father is dead." His words are firm and clear.

As those words leave his mouth, I brace my hands onto the back of a chair before I lose my footing completely. A wave of nausea passes by, which I manage to work past. Taking a couple of deep breaths, my teary eyes meet his again as he rushes over, pulling me into a tight hug. The pain rushing through my entire body causes me to cry out. Eric backs away immediately and only offers a knowing look. Wiping the sweat from my brow, I manage to finally speak.

"How?" I ask as my tears roll down my cheeks, unable to meet his eye.

"He was shot. That's all I know. Your mother is very upset but wanted you to know immediately."

I nod my head, trying to process what the fuck is going on. A loud thud enters the living space. Eric's eyes meet mine once again as Harry's garbled, angry demands can be heard. He staggers into the room, his sandy blonde tousled hair looking messier than usual, and his grey suit is dishevelled.

"I don't know what the…." His bloodshot eyes darting between both Eric and I.

"I came by to inform Summer that her father is dead." Eric cuts him off immediately, likely so Harry can calm the fuck down and not make a complete fucking show of himself.

Harry visibly swallows as he turns to me. His rage-filled eyes somehow now replaced with sincerity and concern. I flinch as he takes a couple of steps towards me, but he plays the part of concerned fiancé well.

"Oh, baby, you poor thing. I'm so sorry." I wince as he pulls me into a tight embrace, the pressure on my ribs causing my breath to shallow, the pain shooting through me.

He knows exactly what he's fucking doing.

Eric eyes the scene before him suspiciously, yet he doesn't say anything. Mustering some courage from deep within, I step back, straightening myself up and ignoring the pain. I now stand defiant in front of Harry, but I feel safe enough to know he wouldn't say anything with Eric here to witness it.

"I'm heading to New York in the morning. I need to sort out my dad's affairs."

"Summer, we have lawyers for that. Don't worry yourself with that right now." Eric interjects.

I smile at his kindness, but I know this is what I need to do.

"That's kind of you, but I owe it to my dad. He doesn't have any other family."

I force a weak smile, turning my attention back to Harry. I see a flicker of anger as his eyes dart to Eric, then back to me. I swallow hard as I watch him slowly nod his head.

"You're right." Turning his attention to Eric, he wraps his arm around me, his fingers digging into my bruises as more tears prick my eyes. "I'll make sure she gets on the flight tomorrow morning."

"Very well, if you need anything whilst you're away, you know where I am."

I smile politely as Eric takes his leave.

As the door clicks shut behind him, Harry turns to me, gently tucking a piece of hair behind my ear. Leaning in, his lips trace the shell of my ear. In a sinister tone, he finally speaks. Feeling his hot whiskey-laced breath skate across my skin, I fight the urge to vomit all over the floor.

"Tomorrow morning, you'll change your fucking mind, you aren't running off to New York. You're mine, don't forget that."

I stand frozen, trapped, as those words repeat in my head. Distraught over the loss of my dad and all those unanswered questions, yet Harry playing his own sick part in this scares me far more. He plays the part all too well. On the surface, he's successful, caring, kind, attentive, but something almost demonic lurks beneath.

Chapter Two

Bhodi ⚣

Nodding to the patrolman, I ensure my NYPD shield is on full display as I slip under the crime scene tape. With my leather jacket pulled up close around my ears, I clutch onto the shit gas station coffee I managed to pick up on my way here. Passing one to my partner, Detective Strode, he looks at the cup, and his face contorts into disgust. His handlebar mustache droops, making him look like an unimpressed Hulk Hogan. The crisp night air rushing through me whilst we both stand in the street amongst the chaos.

"Couldn't have found a classier establishment, Grey?" He chuckles, taking a large gulp, followed by a scrunched-up face.

"Well, when they pay better over time, I may be able to afford a nicer coffee. But until then, that's the best you're getting." Taking a swig from the paper cup, I glance around at the on-lookers on the other side of the tape and the Crime Scene Team as they pass by. "What have we got? Another mafia shooting?" I chuckle as Strode slowly shakes his head.

"It's a blood bath in their kid, it looks as though the target was Michael Harper."

I freeze as the cup is part of the way to my lips. Lowering it, I look away for a moment.

"Are you sure?" I ask, curiously eyeing the on-lookers in the crowd.

Strode nods, placing the coffee cup down on the ground; he gestures for me to follow him into the club. Pulling out overshoes and latex gloves, we put them on and head into the dimly lit area. As the main area opens, the bar and dance area's lights are all on. CSU work in small groups across the area.

"Why is it all nightclubs look decent until the lights all come on? It's like the morning after a shit one-night stand. You never know what you're going to be faced with."

I politely smile and nod along with Strode. He's only fifty years old but currently working on his third divorce. Real charmer, as you can imagine.

As the coroners move past us with a body in a black zipper bag, I quickly stop them. Taking a deep breath, I pull back the zipper. As it slides down, revealing Michael's face with a large gunshot wound on his forehead. I just merely shake my head and allow the coroner to go on their way.

"You ok over their Grey?" Strode quietly asks with some concern in his voice.

Shaking myself from the trance I'm in, I nod. "Yeah, just seems Michael Harper was probably the least shady club owner in the city. An execution-style killing seems extreme."

"If there's one thing this city has taught me. One, never be surprised, and two, someone always has shit to hide." Strode comments half-heartedly before moving further into the club.

I shrug again, following him through to the office space. Analysing the blood-spattered over the wall behind the desk. It looks as though he had no idea the shot was coming. I chew on my lip, looking over the crime scene before me. The office is neat and tidy, with little paperwork or signs of a struggle. The safe on the far side of the room appears untouched. At the moment, we can rule out robbery as the motive.

"Woah, who's this beauty?"

I turn as Strode thrusts a picture in my face. I feel my heart skip a beat as I admire the beautiful sight before me. Almost white, blonde hair framing an angelic face. Big sapphire blue eyes against sun-kissed skin. Those plump pink lips curved into a smile as she shields the sun from her eyes. I don't know how long I've been staring at the photo before it's whipped away again. I feel my jaw tick slightly as my partner studies it.

"Girlfriend?" I ask innocently, trying to show little interest.

"Bit young, don't you think?" Strode scoffs.

"You told me to never be surprised?" I feign innocence and offer a shrug.

"There's hope for you yet, son." He laughs, patting me on the back before setting the photo back down, but part of me can't help but continue to steal glances at it.

"Excuse me, detective?"

We both glance over as a young patrol officer enters the room, holding out a piece of paper.

"Yes?" I take the paper from their hand, studying it as they speak.

"The manager at the bar mentioned Mr Harper has a daughter. He and his wife are divorced, but she was confident he and his daughter would keep in touch."

"Good work, thanks." I pick up the photo and show it to the officer. "Is this her?"

"Yes, the manager confirmed that was her."

I offer the officer a small smile as I read the small amount of information on Michael's daughter. Summer Harper, twenty-four years old. An address based in L.A and a cell phone number. Pulling out my phone, I type in the number and save it.

"I think someone has already contacted the ex-wife," Strode interjects.

"I know, but we'll need to speak with everyone in Michael's life."

I find myself catching sight of the framed photo once again, cocking my head to one side, still enthralled by Summer's beauty.

Michael didn't talk much about his personal life, so I guess it's no surprise he once had a family.

Shaking my head one final time, I head back to the precinct before my shift officially starts.

Chapter Three
Summer ♥

    Once the sun rises over the mountains in the distance, I watch below while the street sweepers clear last night's chaos from the sidewalk. The once lively strip now just appears like any other street. People are going about their day, heading to work, grabbing coffee or returning to their hotels after a heavy night, getting ready to do it all again tonight. Luckily for me, I won't be here to see it.

    After Eric left, Harry decided to go back out, but I haven't heard from him since. I used the time to pack my suitcase and check on flights to New York. Fortunately, there was one available at eleven am today. A taxi to the airport won't be hard to come by with rows and rows of taxis parked outside the many hotels on the strip.

    Teaming my yoga pants with an oversized hoodie, I slide on some trainers for the flight. I feel my stomach drop as I hear the door to the suite open.

    Oh fuck.

Sitting in the chair in the dining area, I try to steady the anxiety that's coursing through my entire being. I almost feel cold, frozen, even when Harry comes staggering into view, clutching onto a bottle of Jack.

"I didn't think I needed to repeat myself, Summer." He takes a couple of steps forward, reaching for his belt.

His tone is cold. When that sinister smirk I despise creeps across his face, he slowly shakes his head.

He slowly pulls the belt away from the loops of his suit trousers, sliding the leather against the fabric. The noise is like nails on a chalkboard, almost causing me to recoil because I know what's coming next, and I need to get the fuck away from here.

Standing only a few feet away, he launches the bottle at my head. I manage to duck out of the way, narrowly missing being hit as the glass shatters onto the floor. Falling to my knees, I scramble to my feet before being lashed with the belt, I cry out as the leather whips my skin once. Throwing my right arm up to protect myself, I feel the burning heat bloom over my skin. Staggering away, clutching my arm, I find myself standing with the table between us. He begins circling me like prey.

"Please don't do this, Harry." I plead.

He manages to launch himself over the table, pushing me into the wall hard and grabbing my throat. I clutch onto his wrist, digging in my nails as he applies too much pressure, restricting my airway immediately.

"I said no. Why won't you ever learn?" He snarls.

Pushing me to the floor, I land hard while he straddles me. As his belt comes flying down on me, releasing his hand, I throw my own up in defense again. I manage to stop a strike to the face, but the second strike to my arm causes me to cry out. Managing to kick out of his grasp and turning away. I begin to crawl, my nails clawing into the carpet, pulling myself away. My foot connects with his face and he flies backwards. A satisfying crunch is heard. When his hands fly to his face, he drops the belt onto the floor.

"You fucking cunt!" He screams at me.

With droplets of blood dripping from his nose, he shakes with uncontrollable anger.

Pulling myself up to the breakfast bar, lifting the vase idly placed onto the side, I weakly throw it, hoping he'll stop the attack. He laughs maniacally when it goes over his shoulder, shattering into pieces. Harry's face goes almost blank and void of any expression. Watching me try to keep myself upright and reach for the breakfast bar again, I manage to pull myself to my feet. As I turn around, his hand reaches my throat again, and his body presses firmly into mine. Tears prick my eyes and I struggle to breathe. My vision becomes blurred as he applies more pressure, forcing me to lean back.

My eyes widen as my fingers wrap around something solid. With one final push, I manage to swing it at Harry. A sickening thud bounces off his skull as we both fall to the floor. Coughing, I manage to push myself away from him. My back hits the bar again, taking in the scene before me. The pain that wracks my body from old injuries and new, leaves me in agony and crippled with fear.

Harry lays on the floor face down as tiny droplets of blood pour from the open wound on the side of his head. My hand flies to my mouth as thick tears blur my vision and fall from my eyes.

Oh god, have I killed him?

My mind races, my heart is pounding in my chest. Pulling my knees to my chest, I take deep breaths as I try to work out what the fuck I should do. Slowly reaching out my shaky right hand, I place two fingers on his neck. Closing my eyes and concentrating for a couple of moments, I fall back against the bar when I feel a pulse.

Oh, thank fuck.

Running my trembling hand through my hair, I pull myself up and steady myself. Wasting no time, I pick up the bottle and rush to the sink, rinsing off the blood and placing it back where it was. Removing all trace of me from that room, I glance around again as Harry lays on the floor out cold.

Let's hope he's too fucked up to realize I hit him.

The heavy weight on my left ring finger catches my eye, without hesitation I forcefully yank it off and throw it into the trash. Reaching for my suitcase, I slam the hotel room door behind me as I escape to New York, with no intention of looking back.

Later that afternoon...

Stepping off the flight, the late-afternoon autumn wind causes me to shiver. Pulling my sleeves down, I try to cover my arms as the goosebumps rise.

Definitely different from the desert heat in Las Vegas.

I shudder while walking through the airport, constantly checking my surroundings as I reach the luggage carousel. My heart skips a beat each time someone even looks at me. Keeping my head low, I finally spot my suitcase.

I spent most of the taxi ride from the airport to the hotel, clutching onto the door handle for dear life as the driver clearly had a fucking death wish. I don't wait for a porter when the taxi pulls up outside the hotel, instead throwing the car door open, I take a deep breath of fresh air and stand on shaky legs.

At the check-in desk, I catch the young receptionist eyeing me curiously, with almost a smugness behind her fake smile. Feeling self-conscious, I catch myself studying my outfit. I suppose it wasn't New York chic, but I doubt this little bitch has had to flee a second attack from her shithead ex.

"Can I help you miss?"

"My name is Summer Harper; I have a reservation for two nights."

She nods, but I feel my petty side rearing its ugly head whilst she taps away. I decide to go for an upgrade.

"I may be here slightly longer than anticipated. Please could I get a suite if there is one available?" I force a smile, which the receptionist matches.

"Oh, I'm sorry. The only suite available is the Venus Suite, that's two thousand dollars per night." Her drippy sarcastic tone gets even more patronizing.

Taking my credit card from my purse, I slap it down on the desk, sliding it over to her.

"That's fine."

Blinking a couple of times, she now appears flustered. As though she thought I would just waltz up to the hotel reception desk, ask for a suite, and not have the means to pay for it?

Fucking idiot.

"I'll take this from here Jen." A woman with dark auburn wavy hair and kind smile approaches.

The young girl I now know to be Jen looks visibly embarrassed, her neck almost snaps when she turns in the direction of the other women. Appearing flustered, she does eventually move from the desk and I eye the name tag.

Pamela.

Pamela takes over, she studies me for a moment, a sadness falls over her face for a brief second, but it's only fleeting. If I wasn't paying attention, I would have missed it.

Hesitating, she offers me the card machine to confirm my numbers. Hitting enter, I pass the machine back to her.

Jen stands behind Pamela, observing the situation. Her shoulders seem to visibly sag as the machine confirms the payment was accepted.

What the fuck is her problem?

Managing to gain some composure, I look between the two women confused, the entire situation from Jen wreaks of nasty unprofessionalism and outright bitchy behaviour.

Pamela smiles and slides a key card over the desk to me.

"Here's your card. The elevators are down the hall slightly and to the right. You'll be on the top floor. Will any guests be joining you?"

As I hear those words, I turn to her. My eyes widen as an overwhelming wave of fear passes through me, and I feel the sweat gathering at my hairline. She hesitates slightly as I begin to fumble my words. Shaking my head frantically in response, her demeanor changes instantly. She quietly nods, jots something down on a piece of paper, and slides it over to me along with my key card.

Politely nodding, she proceeds to busy herself at her desk, turning to Jen, I assume to reprimand her for her bad attitude. Stepping toward the bank of elevators, I admire the warm marble and subtle gold details while patiently waiting for the elevator to open. As it does, I enter. Pressing the button for the top floor. The lift rises, allowing me to lean back onto the wall. Looking down at my hands, I begin to read the note passed to me by the receptionist. I feel tears well in my eyes as I read the words scrawled.

Your reservation is under Amy Jones. If you need anything, call reception and ask for Pamela.

Shaking my head, I kick myself for acting like a bitch during the whole situation. The elevator doors eventually open, moving into the hall and placing the keycard against the handle, I step inside and observe the large suite. Dropping my case down and shutting the door behind me, I kick off my shoes and sigh when my feet sink into the soft plush carpet.

TWO/FACE

Taking a drag of my third cigarette, I stand on the sidewalk. Content Summer has checked into her hotel for the evening and won't likely leave tonight.

It's good to have someone on the inside.

I feel my phone buzz with an incoming message. Pulling my phone from my pocket, I read a message demanding a meeting as soon as possible. Rolling my eyes, I take another drag of my cigarette. I tap a reply as I exhale over the screen. Shaking my head, I look towards the hotel. The events over the last twenty-four hours weighing heavily on all of us.

The team feels twitchy. I've told them we have nothing to worry about. We can't be exposed if no one knows us or what we do and there is no record of it anywhere. We haven't gotten away with it for all these years by being lax and sloppy. Do I enjoy killing? I do. Watching the fear in someone's eyes, it's like fireworks going off on the fourth of July. It gives you a sense of wonder and excitement, and then once it's all over, you will have that feeling of accomplishment.

Stepping back into the shadows, observing as the busy New Yorkers go about their evening. With the sun beginning to set and the cold autumnal wind blowing through the tall buildings, I take one last look at the hotel before heading down the street.

I can become acquainted with summer tomorrow. I'll let her rest for now. She'll need it.

Chapter Four

Summer 🖤

Slowly rolling over in the large plush bed, my body feels weak and heavy. Each time I stretch, I feel my muscles ache and tense up. Gently pushing myself up in the unfamiliar bed, I glance around. Rubbing my eyes, I quickly remember where I am. Pulling my knees up to my chest, I allow my gaze to fall on the bright New York skyline.

I have no idea where to start with all of this. As soon as I entered the room, I stripped my clothes off and crawled into bed, hoping some rest would clear my head and offer a clearer perspective. If I'm being honest, it hasn't. I've come to New York, but for what purpose? I have no idea what my dad's affairs are if he even has any. That's just what you hear people say in some soap opera. Even though we spent time together in my adult years, I don't feel like I really knew him. I know he owned some successful businesses throughout the city, but that's it really. My mother made spending time together difficult during my childhood, but I never blamed him. He knew what she was like and never made me suffer because of it.

Laying my head back onto the pillow, I stare at the ceiling, trying to devise a plan. I don't even know who to speak with? I mean, are the police needing to speak with me? I hadn't seen my father for around six months. I was due to see him for Christmas, where I was going to tell him about my engagement to Harry. I was preparing myself for the disappointed look on his face. Part of me hoped he would ask me to come and stay with him so I could escape Harry's relentless abuse, but now I'll never know. The alarm clock beside the bed catches my eye, my shoulders sagging as I realise it's only one am.

I shouldn't have crashed when I walked in here.

Feeling my stomach grumble slightly, I throw my duvet off my body. Gently placing my feet onto the floor, I throw on my clothes from earlier and make my way through the hotel in search of food and some fresh air.

When the hotel doors open, I feel the chilly New York wind pinch my cheeks. I smile as I can see my breath for the first time in years. I love the cold; I don't know why? Something about it is so comforting. The heat in L.A. and the heat was initially fun when I first arrived, but eventually I grew tired of it. Partly because I was trapped with my materialistic, intolerable mother.

With my mother on my mind, I pull my phone from my purse. I raise my eyebrows as I realize it's still off. Holding the buttons down, I watch as the Apple screen lights up. Casually looking ahead, I spot an open McDonald's, feeling my stomach grumble once again. I head with purpose for the entrance, allowing my phone to update.

Once inside, the warmth engulfs me as I join the queue. I stare up at the boards, deciding what to order, but right now, everything looks amazing. The queue moves quick, I order my food and pay, settling for a Big Mac meal with coke and large fries.

Stepping away, allowing the next customer to order, I patiently wait for my food. However, feeling a slight shudder run up my spine, I instantly turn around, spotting a man staring at me from the corner of the restaurant, dressed in heavy dark clothing. Quickly looking him up and down, his beady eyes meet mine for a moment before he abruptly turns and walks out of the main entrance making sure to obscure his face, but I manage to catch a glimpse of some intricate facial tattoo's.

Squinting, I watch intently as he walks away out of sight, luckily in the opposite direction of my hotel. I stare for a moment longer, contemplating whether I should leave and head back to safety, that brief five second meeting leaves me feeling nervous and on-edge.

Feeling a gentle nudge on my shoulder. I jump and turn back to see the member of staff holding out my order to me. Offering a polite smile, I waste no time in heading back to my hotel, constantly checking over my shoulder every few steps and picking up the pace as it nears.

The long ride up to the suite feels agonizing, nervously chewing on my lip, I slam the door shut behind me as soon as I hear it unlock via the keycard. Throwing the bag down onto the coffee table, I dig into my food, taking large slurps of my drink between bites. After twenty-four hours without food, I put my heightened anxiety down to low blood sugar. I eventually feel myself beginning to feel a little better, I suppose a good meal does help.

Once finished, I throw away the trash and sink further into the sofa. Spotting the familiar Netflix logo on the TV apps and settling for a crime documentary, I lay my head onto a large fluffy cushion and pull the warm blanket over my shoulders. Curling myself into a ball, my heavy eyes becoming heavier.

Bhodi ⚥

Rubbing my eyes, I stare at the multiple statements from last night's homicide investigation. My stomach turns, taking a sip of my fourth coffee.

Whoever made this needs to be fucking shot. It's burnt and tastes like shit.

Launching the cup into the bin, I glimpse the clock on the wall.

Eight am, thank fuck.

I've been on this now for around twelve hours and have achieved fuck all. I left two messages on Summer's phone regarding an interview and sent LAPD officers to her mother's residence, but a neighbor informed them they had all gone on a vacation. For some reason, her phone was off by the time I called. I can only hope she already knows about her father.

Feeling my eyes begin to let me down, I pick up my badge and keys. Feeling the brisk morning air hit me as I leave the precinct, I head for my car.

I can't get fuck all done if I'm exhausted.

Sticking the key into the ignition, I listen as the car roars to life. Before I can even pull out of the parking lot, my phone rings. Quickly glancing down at the screen, I groan. Hitting answer, I bring the car to a stop before lifting the phone to my ear.

"Strode," I grumble, hearing a slight chuckle down the line. Watching the lucky victims of the parking lot make their escape.

"Summer Harper called the precinct; she's coming in at midday for an interview." My ears prick up slightly at the thought of meeting Summer in person.

"I'll be back in ten, I need a fucking decent breakfast first." Throwing my phone back down, I pull out onto the busy city street.

Chapter Five
Summer ♥

Wrapping the warm fluffy towel around myself, I ring out my long hair, allowing the residual water to be swallowed down the plug. Wiping the excess water from my face, I step out of the shower, heading for the bedroom. Picking up my phone, I check the time. Luckily, I still have a few hours before my interview with the NYPD about my father's murder investigation.

Murder investigation.

Feeling my stomach drop, the tears blur my vision and the waves of cold shivers run across my skin. Wrapping my arms around myself, I run my palms against my skin, hoping the coldness will subside.

Sitting on the edge of the bed and batting away the tears, I allow my head to fall back slightly, trying to relieve the tension in my neck. I sigh heavily, knowing that I can't offer them any help in his murder. I wish I could. I can't understand why anyone would want to hurt him. I'd never heard a bad word said about him. Well, apart from my mother, but she speaks badly of anyone just because she can.

Spending the remainder of the morning getting ready, I lose myself in the whirring noise of the hairdryer and a true crime podcast, mentally preparing myself for the day ahead.

Pulling out fresh clothes, I check the weather on my phone for the day. I give a lopsided smile as it'll be chilly for most of it, but luckily the sun will be out. Opting for some black super skinny jeans and a cream roll-neck jumper, I slide on my heeled black ankle boots. I run a brush through my loose curls before giving myself one final nod in the mirror. Picking up my purse, I ignore the constant buzzing from my bag as I head to the precinct.

Harry, you can fuck off. Like I'm going to speak with you.

My inner thoughts may seem confident, but the idea of him trying to contact me or even find me scares me. I saw an opportunity to escape, and I took it. I have no intention of ever going back. It wouldn't upset me if I never saw him or my mother again. Between them, they have made my life miserable whenever they felt like it.

A short taxi ride later and I'm stepping into the precinct, the warmth causes my cheeks to burn. Feeling a slight sweat develop on my back and the smell of burnt coffee causing me to recoil slightly. I shrug my coat off as I'm taken to an interview room, the door opens, and I take a seat at the table. Interlocking my fingers, I rest my elbows on the table and catch my reflection in the two-way mirror, just staring back.

The past twenty-four hours hitting me hard, even though I've escaped one hell, I've been thrust into another. Anxiety settles in my gut; I've never even planned a funeral before. I have no idea where to start, what my dad's wishes were, or how to even deal with his estate.

I feel myself begin to nervously chew on the inside of my lip, trying to gather my thoughts and work out how to handle everything with my dad's best interests and with confidence that I know I currently lack.

My eyes snap to the door, it swings open as two men enter. The older of the two carrying a folder in his hand and he wears a confident smile, but as my eyes narrow and the more I look at it, the more it appears to be a smirk. I feel my sweaty palms clench slightly at the thought of this man smirking during a time like this. My eyes boring a hole into his forehead, the silence in the room becoming uncomfortable. The younger man begins to speak, but I can't hear him. The rage building within me feels as though I'm taken to another dimension.

"Is something funny, detective?"

My tone is clip, almost defiant towards an authority figure. I hold eye contact as he finally looks me in the eye, he manages to hold it for a couple of seconds before his façade falters. His shoulders sag whilst he runs his hand over his stubble and his eyes avert my gaze.

"No, ma'am, I apologise." He shakes his head.

To my surprise, he doesn't jump to his own defense. With my small triumphant win in my pocket, I sit back in my seat, letting out a low breath and running my hand through my hair.

"No, Detective, I apologize." My eyes wander to the two-way glass behind them. "It's been....an odd twenty-four hours." Feeling my eyes fill with tears and quickly swiping them away, I take another deep breath before shrugging.

"I'm Detective Grey, and this is Detective Strode." Detective Grey gestures between them both, holding intense eye contact with me, as my gaze eventually locks with his.

Whilst his voice is smooth and deep, I can already feel the heat crawling up my neck and rising to my cheeks. I swallow hard and slowly nod, unable to tear my eyes away from the man before me.

A gorgeous, tanned complexion, a strong nose, sharp chiselled jaw, inky dark wavy hair all wrapped up in a leather jacket and sitting with only a couple feet of space between us. My skin feels hot, as though his gaze leaves an imprint on me everywhere he looks. There's no denying he holds an intensity, that stare manages to pull me into a trance after a mere few seconds.

"You've been in Las Vegas for the past three days?" Flipping a piece of paper over, Detective Grey continues. "It says here you were staying at The Bellagio?"

"That's correct." I nod. Pulling myself back into the present and trying to shake off the trance I've been pulled into.

"What were you doing there?"

"My stepdad wanted to take us away for a few days. I think he and my former fiancé were celebrating some business deal going through."

I feel both sets of curious eyes on me, and my heart rate picks up a little. I look between them both.

"I ended the relationship during the trip." Trying to remain confident, I take a deep breath. Deciding to elaborate further. "I ended the relationship before my flight to New York. Things haven't been good for a while. With my dad passing, staying somewhere where I was unhappy didn't feel right." My voice begins to crack, and each gaze shifts away.

"Has your father ever discussed his business here within the city?" Detective Strode asks.

His tone is much kinder. Almost reminding me of a warm fatherly figure, but I shake my head.

"No, I just knew he owned and ran some businesses here. There was never an indication when we saw each other or spoke, that there were any issues. He didn't really like talking about work much, but when we saw each other, he was more interested in how I was and how school or work was going."

I notice how Detective Strode nods and gently smiles.

"And how often was that?" He asks as he jots down some notes on a notepad.

I feel myself deflate, trying to focus on the last time we spoke, but the sadness of not seeing him as often as I'd like feels like it's eating me from the insides. Placing my elbows on the table, my head falls into my hands, staring down at the table Infront of me. My body begins to shake, a thick knot of guilt forms in my throat and I can feel my mind beginning to shut down, the pressure of the situation becoming too much to handle.

"Can I get you some water?" Detective Strode leans in and asks calmly.

"Yes, please." Not moving, I weakly answer.

Squeezing my eyes shut, I try to gather my thoughts and maintain my composure, but it's so fucking hard. Once the cup of water is placed in front of me, I take a sip, watching as my hand shakes.

The interview carries on into the early evening. The room has no clock, but I can see it's begun to get dark outside. Both detectives continue to ask questions, but after some time, I feel flat. I can't offer them anything about my dad's murder, which breaks my heart. I'm here, but I'm fucking useless to them, and I want to help, but there's nothing that has ever stood out about him or his lifestyle which could indicate why anyone would want to hurt him.

Sliding my coat back on, Detective Grey abruptly leaves the room. He said very little during the interview, which made me uncomfortable. I noticed how each time I answered a question which gave little information, he visibly became more frustrated. Detective Strode asked most of the questions, but I could always feel those forest-green eyes on me. Stealing a few glances here and there, his expression never changed. No smile, no nod of the head. It was as though he was a fucking robot. But the more he stared, the more I wanted to ignore him.

Detective Strode walks me out, passing Detective Grey on the way. He doesn't look up, instead he remains focused on the notebook in front of him. His dark, tousled hair obscuring his face slightly. But that doesn't mean as I pass, I don't feel his white-hot gaze on me as I walk away. I roll my eyes as the exit nears; the sulky persona doesn't work for me, and it never has. I just hope I don't have to deal with him anytime soon. He makes me feel guilty, even though I've done nothing wrong. I don't like being silently accused. That chapter of dealing with difficult men is definitely over for me.

Stepping out into the cold winter night, I see my breath instantly. Pulling my coat tight around my body, I turn back to Detective Strode as he speaks.

"Are you sure I can't get you a ride home?"

I shake my head, looking up at him as I take a few steps down the street.

"I think the fresh air will do me good. No offense, it's fucking roasting in there."

His hearty laugh takes me by surprise, handing me a card.

"Here, if you run into any issues or remember something, anything. Just give me a call, ok?"

"Thank you." I nod, heading down the steps of the precinct.

Chapter Six
Summer ♥

    Feeling the tense muscles in my body begin to loosen with each step, I feel an odd surge of adrenaline rush through my body but, at the same time, an unbelievable exhaustion that I've never felt before. Putting it down to the intense day, I continue down the street. After a few moments, I begin to look at my surroundings. Quickly realizing I'm lost, I look around the street, hoping to see something familiar from earlier, but it's no use.

    As the dark evening has descended, the entire street looks completely different. Letting out a frustrated sigh, I pull my phone from my purse, admitting defeat and searching for an Uber. As the app opens, I feel a presence approaching, but before I can turn, I feel myself being shoved into the adjacent alleyway. Losing my footing I hit the concrete floor with a thud. Blinking a couple times, a large silhouette stands in the entrance of the alleyway. Spotting the knife in their hands, I beg.

    "Please just take it." I throw my purse onto the floor in front of them. "Just take it."

My pleading words appear amusing to the figure as they chuckle. I squint a couple of times as they lift their balaclava off, revealing a familiar tattooed face from the McDonalds last night. Moving from my side, I sit on my ass, trying to ignore the pain and blinding fear.

The figure takes a couple of steps forward, and squatting down, he reveals a crooked smirk. His facial tattoos make him appear more than unsettling. I study his face, but he seems to be taking his time with his mugging.

Shit has he been following me?

Every hair on my body stands up on end as the thought of him raping and killing me here in this alleyway sends my soul into a spiral. Shuffling back slightly, he allows the light to reflect off his knife, drawing my attention to the shiny blade.

"You're in big trouble, Summer." His tone is haunting and sarcastic. His sinister smile stays etched on his face, whilst he continues. "You can't just walk away from Mr. Maine without repercussions."

I swallow hard as my hands dig into the dirt. My eyes don't move from the man while he blocks my exit from the alleyway and continues his taunts.

"What do you want?" I ask with fake confidence, knowing as the figure cocks his head to one side that he can see right through my façade.

"Well, it's kind of my choice."

I blink a few times, trying to process his chilling words.

"Mr Maine kinda left it up to me. If I teach you a lesson, he's happy."

"A lesson?" I ask hesitantly as my lips quiver.

He nods, focusing on the long blade he holds between his fingers.

"Maybe if I cut that pretty face, those scars would be a constant reminder of who not to fuck with." I feel my blood run cold through my veins as he continues. "Or maybe, I could destroy that sweet cunt of yours. Mental scars can be crippling."

I feel the bile rise in my throat; a cold sweat begins to run down my back. My eyes dart in between the two buildings, and cars whizz past every few seconds, but I know no one would hear my screams back here. I would be found days later, mutilated by some fucking monster.

A monster paid by another monster, because he's too much of a fucking weak coward to come and get his own hands dirty. Pushing off the floor, I slowly rise to my feet, the stranger follows. His large frame looms over me, standing at what feels like a foot taller than me. As my entire body shakes with fear, I have no escape plan. My eyes dart around, but there's no weapon to hand. I feel truly lost for this moment, with no glimmer of hope in sight.

Taking a step towards me, I take two back. His large hand surges towards my throat, wrapping it around my neck tight. Stumbling in my boots, I feel my body being slammed into the stone wall, and a garbled cry escapes me in the process. His body pressed into mine, shuddering when I feel his disgusting hot breath on my ear.

"We're gonna have some fun, Summer. You'll never forget our time together."

I squeeze my eyes shut, feeling the strength this stranger has. I'm thrown back onto the floor even harder than before, causing me to skid in the dirt. My skull bounces off the hard surface, laying on my side, and my vision is blurred. A high-pitched noise rings in my ears, unable to focus on anything else. Feeling disorientated, I see his silhouette begin to approach me with my shaky vision, but it's the figure standing behind him that causes me to scream.

   Spotting a heavy pair of black boots approach, I lift my head enough to look past a stranger threatening me. A large, hooded figure stands behind the stranger, but he's wearing a black mask as he raises his head. The attacker turns immediately, and like a caged animal, I faintly hear him speak, slowly raising his hands in defense.

   "Woah, this is a fucking mistake."

   Before he can say anything further, I see the blood fall from his body, splattering at his feet before he drops to his knees. I watch in horror as he falls to the floor, a garbled moan escaping his limp body before he stops moving altogether.

   Taking a calm step over the body, the masked man halts in front of me. All dressed in black, it's like having the grim reaper staring down at me, holding my life in his hands. I fight with everything in me to run, but it's no use. The feeling of falling washes over my body before my mind gives up. The noises from the street drowning out my internal screams, and the cold night air consuming me.

Chapter Seven

TWO/FACE

The hospital is busy, and the smell of disinfectant is overbearing. With my hood pulled low over my head, I observe the busy doctors and nurses running between different patients. Even through the chaos, I manage to spot her. The harsh hospital lights shining down brightly on her blonde curls, her limp body lying in a hospital bed while the nurses treat her wounds. I know she'll be ok, likely just a bump to the head, but I still don't fucking like it.

My fists clench as the blood and dirt from her fall stains her sun kissed, delicate face. I feel my jaw tick and anger simmering, as the fucking monster who did this to her now lies hidden in the alleyway. Whilst he's not dead yet, when I'm fucking done, he'll prey for death. But first things first, I need to know why he targeted Summer. She's been in New York for less than twenty-four hours, and if he was some scum that just snatched purses, he would have taken it and run. But no, this fucking animal was taking his time, and I want to know why. I can't promise him freedom for his honesty, but I can offer a quick death.

A message on my phone pulls my focus from the hospital bed, letting out a sigh, I get ready for my next appointment.

Glancing between the exit and the entrance to the A&E department, I take one final look towards Summer. Letting out a low breath, I contemplate staying a little longer, but I know I don't really have the luxury of time on my side right now.

Moving swiftly towards the exit, I pull my hood down low as I disappear off into the night.

Summer 🖤

The voices around me are quiet yet calm. Slowly opening my eyes, I take in my surroundings. Luckily, the lights are dim, but all focus is on me once I wince. The pounding in my skull leaves my head feeling heavy.

"Here, let me help you." A young woman approaches dressed in scrubs; she gently places her arm around me, allowing me to lean on her as I pull myself up.

"Where am I?" I ask, scanning the dimly lit room. Allowing my body to relax into the firm pillow she places behind me; her kind eyes meet mine.

"You're in the hospital summer." Her voice remains soft. "Do you remember what happened?"

Blinking a couple of times, my hand flies to my mouth as tears fall from my eyes. I feel myself shake, yet I can't get the words out. I frantically shake my head as she pulls up a chair to my bedside, resting her hand on my arm.

"It's ok, Summer. You're safe." She speaks softly, yet firmly, as I feel my mind begin to spiral, when the memory of the attack begins to flood back.

"Did...did he rape me?" I manage to choke out before sobbing loudly, pulling my knees up to my chest and trying to curl myself into a ball.

"No, he didn't. You took a nasty bump to the head, but aside from that and some bruising, you'll be ok." She reassures me.

I frantically nod when relief washes over me. The young nurse holds my gaze, still offering me her calmness.

"There are some detectives outside. Are you okay with talking to them?"

Nodding, I accept the water passed to me. Taking large gulps, I'm so empty I feel the water passing through me. Wiping the droplets from my mouth, the nurse leaves the room. She looks back for a brief moment but doesn't say anything before closing the door behind her. Trying to gather my thoughts, the door opens after a couple of moments, and Detective Strode and Grey both enter.

Detective Grey remains stoic, his cold demeanor not faltering as I sit in the hospital bed. Detective Strode immediately passes me another glass of water before pulling his chair to my bedside, his eyes filled with concern when he spots the small cuts on my forehead.

"Summer, the hospital found my card on you when you were brought." I nod, trying to concentrate on his words and ignoring the pains and aches rushing through my body. "What happened after you left the precinct?"

Leaning back into the firm pillow, I close my eyes for a moment, trying to remember everything. Looking at Detective Strode, I speak softly.

"I didn't recognize where I was, so I pulled my phone out to call an Uber. I felt someone throw me into the alleyway, and I landed hard on my side. But then I'm not sure. I think I hit my head."

I swallow hard. I try to argue in my head that I'm not lying, but I don't want either of the detectives digging into my past with Harry, and I don't want them giving him any confirmation of where I am or that I've been hurt. I know what I saw in that alleyway, but who the fuck is the second masked guy? I don't want trouble. For some reason, he didn't kill me, so the best thing I can do is not mention that part.

He did save me after all...

Detective Strode gently pats me on the hand, giving me a subtle nod.

"Ok, Summer, do you need me to call anyone?" He asks.

"No...I mean, no thank you, detective."

A wave of panic rolls through me and I look away, feeling rude, but neither of the detectives say anything. They don't press further, and both take their leave from the room. Feeling my head rest back into the pillow, I allow my eyes to close gently as the threat of weariness continues to linger over me.

Bhodi ⚥

"Excuse me, detectives?"

The young nurse treating Summer approaches us quietly, checking over her shoulder before gesturing for us to follow her into a private room. I eye Strode curiously before entering.

"Is everything ok?" I ask the nurse as she nervously chews on her lip.

"The young girl, Summer?" She begins.

"What about her?"

"I think she's suffered abuse before the mugging." Her gentle voice cracks slightly.

"What makes you say that doc?" Strode asks with some concern, taking a step closer to the nurse.

"When we examined her, the bruises from the attack are consistent with her fall. But there are some older ones along her rib cage and arms, which look to be in different stages of healing."

"Are you sure?" I ask, trying to remain calm.

"Pretty sure. She seems withdrawn, which isn't uncommon in her state, but I just wanted to let you know." The nurse offers a polite nod before leaving the room.

I see the cogs turning in Strode's mind. I know something he can't stand is men beating on women, something from his childhood that haunts him to this day.

"What should we do?" I ask curiously, wanting to see his reaction.

"She mentioned her former boyfriend earlier. We've both seen the lengths bastards will go to when a relationship ends." He sighs before rubbing the back of his neck. Seeing the toll the long day is taking on him, I decide to call it a day.

"Go home, get some rest. We can start this fresh tomorrow. I'll check on Summer, but she's safe here."

He sighs again before nodding. Patting me on the back, we both leave the hospital room. As we break off in the hall, I watch as he heads towards the exit. I find myself wandering back to Summer's room, knocking on the door before entering. When there's no answer, I gently nudge the door open.

Allowing my eyes to adjust to the dim light, I sit at her bedside whilst she sleeps soundly. Her delicate features rest peacefully, but the sight of the small cuts and growing bruise on her forehead causes my fists to clench.

Leaning back in the chair, I allow my head to fall back. I remain focused on the ceiling as my mind reels over her attack. I need to dig into Summer's past, I know she's hiding something. Whether it has anything to do with her father's murder or not, I'm going to find out.

Chapter Eight

Summer ♥

Moving slightly, I feel the aches and bruises reawaken all over my body. I do a double take, propping myself up in bed, Detective Grey sleeps in the chair opposite me. Leaning to one side, with his head resting on his hand, I allow him to sleep further. Sliding out of bed, I go in search of a bathroom. I could hear the nurses in and out of my room most of the night. I could ask one of them where the bathroom is, but at the moment, I just need to stretch my legs and not feel like a burden to anyone.

"How are you feeling?"

My head snaps to the voice that sits towards the end of my bed. My wide and confused eyes meet his once again. Blinking a few times, I try to speak but can't form any words. Taking a step back into the room, I take a seat on the bed.

Why do I feel like it's some kind of accusation when he asks me a normal question?

As my jaw tenses, I look away. Trying to regain some confidence in front of him.

"I'm fine," I respond coldly, refusing to look his way.

I feel his stare burning holes into my head, but I hate how he looks at me, and quite frankly, I'm sure I hate him right now, but I'm not sure why. Whether it's the arrogant attitude he gives off or because his questioning yesterday left me feeling like I was meant to be guilty of something, either way, I don't have to put up with it.

"I'm heading back to my hotel. If you need anything from me, then I'll be there."

Before he can respond, I hastily throw on my clothes which lay on the chair next to me and head for the exit. The thundering footsteps behind me give me a reason to pick up the pace. With every muscle in my body screaming at me to stop, I head for the taxi rank.

"Summer, wait!" Halting at his command, my body internally thanks me for the break. "Let me give you a ride back. You shouldn't be going anywhere alone right now."

I eye him curiously, chewing on my lip. I hate to admit it, but he's right. The last thing I want to do right now is get into a taxi alone; I don't want to be alone at all. The feeling of being alone leaves me with a gnawing feeling of unease. Looking between Detective Grey and the waiting taxis, I eventually nod and follow him towards his car. Once I get in and clip in my seatbelt, I focus on the road ahead.

The drive back to the hotel remains silent. With my hands in my lap, I nervously twiddle my thumbs. Detective Grey doesn't speak, and neither do I. The tension in the car is rife, and I just want it to be over as soon as possible.

Glancing towards the time and to my surprise it's only two am. It feels strange to see somewhere so busy at this time of the morning, but it's very rare I'm ever out this late.

Eventually I feel my eyes stealing wandering glances towards Detective Grey. In the late-night passing lights, his face is much clearer. His deep forest green eyes now appear light, almost kinder. His tanned complexion compliments his rugged and incredibly handsome features. But it's not his strong jaw or inky black hair that draws my attention closer. It's the scar I hadn't noticed before that starts on his forehead and travels in a half-moon shape around his right eye. While it's not obvious in the beginning, it's clearly been well-stitched.

As the words leave his mouth, I feel my entire body want to crawl under the seat.

"It's rude to stare Summer."

My brows pinch slightly as I blink a couple of times, processing his words. I feel the heat creep over my cheeks, and I kick myself for even looking in his direction. Lowering my head, I turn my focus back to my hands placed in my lap.

"I'm sorry, detective, I didn't mean to…"

"It's Bhodi."

My head snaps to my left as I study his expression. The mentioning of his name takes me by surprise, offering an odd level of familiarity to an unfortunate encounter, but I merely nod, turning my focus to the passing traffic as we head back to my hotel. Letting out an involuntary yawn and wiping my eyes.

"You should probably get some rest when you get back. You'll probably feel tired for a couple of days after what happened."

Cocking my head to one side, he finally looks my way analyzing the puzzled look on my face, then turning his attention back to the road ahead.

"Will you find the guy that…" My voice trails off as I try to think of the best way to end the sentence without telling him about the masked man. "You know, that attacked me?"

Bhodi sighs and continues to stare at the road ahead. Rubbing a hand over the stubble on his chin, he shakes his head.

"Probably not. Without a description, it would be difficult."

I nod without pursuing the question further, a chill sweeps up my spine, causing me to shudder.

Yeah, because the guy is fucking dead, killed by someone else in a fucking mask.

Lost in thought, the car eventually halts on the curb outside the hotel. Hearing Bhodi's faint voice in the distance I finally look his way. With my attention pulled to his extended hand in front of me, he passes me a card.

"That's my card. My number is on the back. I'll call the hotel if I get any news on your father's case."

Taking the card, I nod, sliding it into my back pocket. "Thank you."

Looking away, I feel the heat rise in my cheeks again, Bhodi's deep stare almost able to pull me into a trance as the busy New York traffic flies past the vehicle. Shaking it off, I give one final nod before exiting the car and heading back into the hotel.

After a few minutes of extending my stay at the hotel down at reception, avoiding Pamela's concerns about my appearance and getting a new keycard. I finally enter my room. Allowing my back to fall against the door, breathing a sigh of relief as the peaceful silence of the suite brings me back to a level of calm. Taking a couple of moments to gather my thoughts, I manage to push myself off the surface and head to the bathroom.

I find myself glancing over my shoulder as the hairs on the back of my neck stand on end. When I see nothing but an empty hall, I feel a shudder run up my spine again. With this and the waves of exhaustion running over me, I decide to shrug it off and put it down to my frayed nerves.

Finally, I step out of my clothes and feel the hot water rush over my skin. I let out a low groan as the heat begins to soothe all the aches, pains, and stress.

After a few minutes pass, I begrudgingly shut the hot water off and reach for the large warm towel. Wrapping it around myself tight, I avoid the bathroom mirror and opt to head straight into the bedroom. Sitting on the end of the bed, I feel my blood run cold, and jaw falls open as my purse sits on the dresser in front of me.

What the fuck?

TWO/FACE

For someone who's been through a traumatic event, Summer's lack of awareness of her surroundings fucking infuriates me. Without even turning the lights on or checking the suite first, she didn't notice me sitting in her living room or even notice the cigarettes being smoked. I will punish her for being so blasé. I thought that after what she had been through, she would at least try to protect herself in some way.

I know she's seen the purse placed on the dresser, and I thought she could probably do with it, but at the same time, I like the idea of fucking with her. The gasp that escaped those rosy, pink, plump lips left me hard, causing a smirk to creep across my face. Whether it's the head injury or lack of concern for her safety, she's been asleep for an hour or so, leaving me to watch her from the corner of the room.

Slumped in the chair, I watch as her chest slowly rises and falls. In complete silence, I glide through the room, placing myself on the edge of her bed, still watching her peacefully sleep. She's blissfully unaware of the demon that's watching.

While I know it's wrong, I can't help myself. I watched her in the shower earlier as the water cascaded over her tanned skin and slipped over those perfect curves. I knew I wanted her more than when I first saw her. But right now, I need to know where those bruises came from. They're not fresh, and I want to know if I should cut someone's hands off and feed them to the cunt who dare put their hands on what will be mine.

The guy from the alley was just a local paid thug. He didn't know who paid him or so he claimed. He was just contacted yesterday by an unknown number, shown a photo of Summer and was told where to find her. I knew he was lying, but I didn't really need or want his clarification. I can find that out on my own.

I feel the white-hot anger simmering under the surface, and I gently graze the back of my hand over her cheek. A smile tugs at my lips as she slightly twitches and her eyes slowly open. I see the peacefulness escape as her gaze lands on me. When her eyes widen with recognition and fear, I slam my hand over her mouth with force, leaning in closely, my voice calm and low.

"You won't scream, Summer. If you do, I will punish you. Do you understand me?"

I watch her fear of the mask replaced with a confused familiarity and a flicker of curiosity. After a moment, she nods, and her rigid body relaxes slightly. Removing my hand, a mere whisper escapes.

"I saw you." Her voice is breathy, yet she doesn't appear too surprised.

"You did." I confirm.

"The police didn't mention the mugger…..What did you do to him?"

Summer speaks quietly, her eyes refusing to meet mine as she looks away.

"I think we both know he wasn't a mugger, Summer."

Her eyes instantly snap to mine, her brow furrows processing my words. I watch as the cogs turn in her head before her eyes widen again. Scrambling back towards the headboard, the fear is back.

"What did you do?" She asks again in a shaky voice.

"I did what any sane person would do when someone places their hands on something that's not theirs."

She swallows hard, staring as the duvet bunched at her waist. Her bouncy tits are constricted by a tiny tank top as they rise and fall with each breath. I watch intently as she lets out a deep sigh, which is weighing heavy on her soul.

"You killed him?"

A slight chuckle escapes my throat, reaching out and cupping her chin. Bringing her entire focus back to me.

"Of course I did. I took him with me, I cut off his fingers one by one, and then once he told me who he was…..I fed them to him. Because he touched what was already mine, I made sure that wouldn't be possible again."

Her jaw falls open as her body begins to shake, the shock and fear in her eyes bringing an overwhelming happiness to my dark soul. I continue to smile under the mask that she sees.

"What do you want from me?"

Reaching out, I gently tuck a piece of hair behind her ear as she continues to sit as close to the headboard as possible. Exposing that angel-like face once again in the New York moonlight, there's no denying her beauty. Bracing myself from the bed, I stand over her, leaning in. This time, my voice sinister and full of warning.

"You'll find out soon enough, Summer. I'll get the answers I want from you." Craning her neck to look at me, her eyes water slightly as the fear remains etched across her features. Softening my tone, I continue. "But for now, you need some rest."

Pushing myself from the bed and turning away, I leave the suite. With the vibration from my pocket, I pull my phone out, studying the message. My scowl soon replaced with a smirk.

Duty calls.

Summer 🖤

I don't know how long I've been lying in bed for, scared to even move or look toward the door. I've spent the remainder of the night with my focus remaining on the ceiling above while my heart thunders in my chest. I heard the door open and close but can't guarantee he left. I clearly did eventually fall asleep, once my eyes open for the last time, I'm still lying in the same position. I can see the sun poking through the curtains.

Slowly sitting upright, my eyes scan the room. With no masked man in sight, I manage to push the duvet off myself, rising on shaky legs to search the remainder of the suite. Passing my purse, which is still placed on the dresser, every hair on my body stands on end as I exit the room. My eyes still frantically scanning the area with each weary step I take.

After a few moments of checking behind every door, in every cupboard, and locking my hotel room door from the inside, I finally take a seat in the small kitchenette. With my elbows placed on the counter and head in my hands, I take a couple of deep breaths, trying to process what this man could possibly want with me and how he knows me.

It must have something to do with my dad, surely? I have no friends or family here. No connection to New York at all apart from him.

My head snaps to the hotel door when a knock rings through the suite. Slowly pushing myself from the stool, my curiosity takes over as goosebumps slide over my arms. Reaching for my large hoodie, still discarded over the chair, I throw it on and anxiously wait at the door. Looking through the peephole, I let out a low breath as Bhodi stands on the other side of the door. Nervously chewing my lip, I unlock it and swing the door open, instantly feeling on display as his eyes roam my bare legs, up my entire body before those intense green emeralds meet mine.

"How are you feeling?" he asks quietly.

I nod my head, taking in his dark jeans and leather jacket. His dark, wavy hair now slightly obscuring his scar. Raising his right hand, he gently scratches his brow, causing me to look away and internally kick myself for yet again staring.

"Better, thanks, a bit sore." I shrug, pulling my eyes from his broad frame and leaning against the door.

"I came by as your dad's attorney visited the precinct. He wanted to speak with you regarding his estate and the funeral. Here's his card."

Passing me a business card, I gently take it reading the curled letters printed on the ivory paper. My shoulders sag as I realize this is happening, but I know I must be brave and do the right thing. Nodding, I look to Bhodi, who is feigning a small smile.

"Thanks, I'll get in touch today." I say, moving back into the suite, ready to close the door.

Before I can close the door, I feel his hand gently blocking it. My brows knit in confusion as we silently stare at each other, the warmth dancing across my skin is back as he visibly swallows, searching my face once again.

"I did some digging last night, Summer. I know you said you've ended things with your fiancé, Harry."

My stomach plumets, even the mention of his name leaves me in a tailspin. I feel my mind and body spiralling, and tears fill my eyes, as I frantically shake my head. I've managed to ignore any attempt him or my mother have made to try and contact me.

"NO….No…Please!" Wiping the fallen tears from my cheeks, while gripping the door handle for support. "You can't speak to him. Please don't tell him where I am."

Bhodi's calm expression is now replaced with concern, he gently places his arms on my shoulders, steadying me. My entire body shakes with fear as I try to catch my breath and focus on his words.

"I'm not going to say anything, but you should know what kind of person you're dealing with."

Blinking a couple of times, the shaking begins to subside, and I nod.

"He's not a good person." I mutter.

My voice weak and pathetic as the shame of the abuse rears its ugly head so soon.

"No, he isn't, but I need to ask you if those bruises were from him?"

Bhodi

Heading back out to my car, I shake my head in frustration as the door swings open, and I slide in. I know, without a doubt, Summer has fucking lied to me about Harry and is choosing to protect him. Slamming my fist onto the steering wheel, I run my hand over my face as I stare at the street. I know how people who have suffered abuse want to forget about what has happened and move past it, but when my gut feeling tells me that he could have had something to do with the murder of her father. I can't just let it go.

But with no proof, it's a tough theory to prove. Pulling out my phone, I search my contacts for a familiar name, someone who can dig into Harry's personal life. Once the message is fired off, a call comes in immediately as Strode's name crosses the screen.

"Yeah?" I answer abruptly.

"Our friend looks as though he's just landed, at the airport."

With my blood bubbling away under the surface, I close my eyes, contemplating my response.

"Follow him. I want to know where he's staying. Call me when you know."

Ending the call and throwing the phone into the passenger seat, I speed off into the traffic. My body tense with crippling rage and anger.

Chapter Nine

TWO/FACE

    The long drive back into the city is something I've always liked about what I do, allowing me to compartmentalize that aspect of my life and leave it in one place for now. However, with Summer being in the city the two are beginning to bleed into one, I knew exposing myself to her so soon in the alley could have been a mistake, raising more questions for her, but it helped with my understanding of what we are all up against.

    Michael was someone I considered a friend and mentor, his death was a fucking knife in the heart to us all, and I will do everything I can to find out who did this and make them suffer.

    I've taken charge for now. While not everyone is happy with that, I don't give a fuck. I'll handle this in my own way and how I see fit. With news of Summer's former fiancé arriving in the city, he's now in my den. While his little stunt with the paid thug may give him the idea of having the upper hand, he has no idea what I have in store for him when the time comes. I found out the man's name was Jack, but I couldn't get a last name. By then, the shock had begun to take over, but he claimed he didn't know who hired him. It's hardly a coincidence that Harry is now here, though.

Deceit and lies are at every corner of what we do, and trust is not something that comes for free and must be earned for all those involved. The rules are very simple, don't draw attention to yourself, be wise, and of course, be fucking good at what you do, or else you could end up dead. Ridding the world of scum gives me an odd satisfaction. Killing someone who is bad anyway, who's going to miss then? No one.

As the lights of the city near, I take a different route. Summer has been given the keys to Michael's apartment after the police no longer consider it a crime scene. We knew nothing would be found there. Anything considered evidence was moved weeks ago once he began to consider there was a chance someone was watching him. Anger churns in my gut that we allowed him to carry on as normal, but he was a fucking stubborn son of a bitch at the best of times. He wouldn't listen, nor would he take our advice.

His lack of care for his own well-being causes my grip to tighten on the steering wheel. Whilst I know we are all clever and abide by our rules, it doesn't make us infallible, there's always a fucking risk, and when you're dealing with violent criminals, there's no limit they won't go to for revenge.

Pressing the key fob, the large shutter doors open to reveal an underground car park. Slowly driving in and parking up, I spot the service elevator to the penthouse. While Summer is safe in her father's apartment, she wouldn't be aware that I installed the security system there and I feel it's only right she's punished for her recent behavior. She was offered help to stop Harry by the police, yet for some reason, she refused, and now he's roaming my city a free man, well for now anyway.

Unlocking the trunk and pulling out a black duffle bag. I study the desolate parking area before heading to the service elevator. Turning my key, I slide on the mask as it ascends. Not to my surprise, the code for the main door remains unchanged. Rolling my eyes, I slowly enter the darkness.

Taking a few steps inside, the familiar surroundings pull at my dark heart a little. But the sound of the running water and the steam seeping from the bathroom, instantly replaces that with want and wicked desire to see what's on the other side.

Gently pushing the door open, I stand for a moment yet again, allowing my eyes to roam Summer's naked, wet body. The water gathering on her back and then sliding over her round ass before hitting the tray sends the blood rushing to my cock. Taking a couple steps forward, I stand at the steamy screen, her arms raised above her head as she rinses the suds from her hair and exposes those bouncy tits. Still unaware of the show I'm enjoying, I watch with joy as she stops for a moment, and her eyes wander to the screen. Turning to face me, a gasp escapes her lips, my joy is replaced with anger as those bruises are once again revealed.

Instantly shoving the shower screen away, my hand bangs against the tap, turning the water off. Stepping into the shower, she backs up to the tiles, her back hitting them after a couple of steps. As the droplets continue to hit the floor, her eyes are once again filled with wonder as her nipples harden and my body presses to hers. Towering over her, I lean in.

"Oh Summer, tsk tsk tsk. You haven't been telling the truth, have you?"

Summer ♥

I feel exposed, and I'm mentally kicking myself for how my body has chosen to react. Wetting my lips slightly, my words are stuck in my throat. I want to scream down the entire place, but my morbid curiosity towards him stops me.

Fucking fantastic.

With my back pressed into the cold tiles and his large frame pressed into my chest, I feel trapped, but I don't feel threatened. Part of me wonders if I should. This is the third time we have come face to face, yet he's never even laid a finger on me, and is it wrong that I want him to?

I watch as he raises his arms on either side of my head, caging me, leaning closer, his gloved palms flat on the tiles. I bite my lip slightly as I look at the matte mask covering his face. Unable to speak, he repeats himself. This time, his voice is dominating and rich, and a chill rushes up my spine when the goosebumps pepper my body.

"You haven't been telling the truth, have you, Summer?"

My brows knit for a moment, my mouth falls open, but the words are still stuck in my throat as I process what I could have possibly been lying to him about.

"I...I...haven't said anything."

"You haven't, and that's the point." The confused look stays etched on my face. "When the police asked you about your bruises, you didn't tell them it was Harry. Why is that?"

My bottom lip quivers, and I suddenly feel more exposed than before. As my head lowers, he leans in closer, so close I can feel the heat radiating from him.

"How did you know?" I whisper.

"Because one thing you should know about me, I always find out the truth. One way or another."

"I don't want the police to speak to Harry. I don't want him near me ever again or to know where I am."

"Bit late for that, isn't it? He sent come cunt to kill you." The sarcasm is rife.

I nod in response. Unable to look at him, but his sinister presence brings an odd comfort and feeling of safety to me.

"Who are you?" I finally speak, swallowing hard as he pushes off the tiles.

Looking away for a moment, the mask eventually turns back to me as his head cocks to one side. His gloved hand reaches out, gently running a leather-clad finger along my jaw.

"You can call me…..Two/Face."

His finger runs along my skin, I can't help but allow my eyes to flutter close. His words are like velvet, but once my eyes open, my brow furrows at his response.

"Two/Face?" I repeat back, but he just nods. "Why?"

"Because that's what I am, Summer." He shrugs.

My eyes search his mask before I swallow hard, the tension in the bathroom is thick as the steam clears. Taking a step forward, I reach for the towel placed on the towel rail, but before my I can reach for it, his hand snaps around my wrist, tugging me closer.

"What do you think you're doing?" he growls, with our faces inches apart. I freeze as he shakes his head. "You've lied, Summer. Liars don't get rewards."

With his hand still clamped over my wrist, he pulls me forward and out of the shower. Losing my balance slightly, I skid along the wet floor. Leading me from the bathroom and into the living room, he stands behind me, placing his hands on my hips and moving me towards the full-length window.

"What are you doing? People might see me!"

"That's the idea, Summer. People below can see you naked in the window while I make you come."

My head snaps to his and my mouth falls open.

"Place your palms on the glass…. NOW!" The demand causes me to jump, but without questioning him, I slowly raise my palms flat against the glass.

I feel a single warm finger run a trail down my spine, causing me to shudder as a warmth spreads across my skin. Lifting my head slightly, I stare at our reflection in the window, our eyes meet in the dark glass as his finger moves to my ass, reaching beneath my cheeks. I part my legs instinctively, unable to pull my gaze away, the anticipation builds. As his fingers graze across my wet pussy, my eyes flutter shut at the sensation as my heart rate begins to rapidly increase once again.

"Eyes on me, Summer." His voice is dark, a soft drawl that tempts me.

My eyes snap open, feeling his hot gaze on my entire body as his fingers move back and forth, spreading my wetness to my clit.

He pushes my hard nipples into the cold glass, causing me to gasp.

"You're so tight and wet already, Summer, makes me think you like the danger."

Those velvet words drip from his mouth as he continues to slowly spread the pleasure with each stroke. As moments pass, getting lost in the euphoria, I feel my fingers trying to clutch into the glass. My body begins taking over my mind, letting out an involuntary moan. I feel him lean in closer before plunging two fingers into my pussy. I cry out as he still works my clit, the sensation beginning to build deep within the pit of my stomach as I rise to my tiptoes.

"Are you going to come for me, Summer? Are you going to be a good girl?"

I frantically nod my head as the glass steams up. My teeth biting down onto my lower lip, I try pulling my eyes away from the mask but can't. It's like he can see into my fucking soul as he works his fingers. I feel my legs begin to shake.

"Oh fuck…."

I manage to mutter, finally allowing my head to drop onto the cool glass. I feel my orgasm building, beginning to move my hips and working my pussy over his fingers just where I need it. In an instant, he pulls his hand away, slowly lifting my head from the glass. Our eyes meet once again in the reflection, but he just stares at me. I watch him move in closer, leaning towards my ear. His voice is low.

"You're not coming."

Blinking a couple of times, I go to turn my head but feel a sharp tug as he grabs a fistful of my hair, holding me in place, pressing me further into the glass. I gasp, feeling his warm breath skate across my neck.

"See…I lied to you, Summer. Not nice, is it?"

After a moment, he releases me. I stand frozen, firmly placed against the glass, watching him turn away from me. As the door opens, I feel a coldness descend over the apartment. My shoulders sag and I turn to the front door stealing one last glimpse of his large frame cloaked in black, leaving me alone once again. I stand facing the door open-mouthed at what's just happened.

I need to know who he is. This is fucked.

Stepping away from the window, I can't help but turn back, looking at the only proof he was really here. As the condensation disappears, I can only see my fading handprints in the glass as the city continues below, as though nothing ever happened.

Chapter Ten

Bhodi ⚤

Finding myself standing outside Michael Harper's lawyer's office, I wait for Summer to finish her appointment. With his body now being released, Strode called her earlier, letting her know she could begin to make the funeral arrangements. The murder investigation isn't going anywhere. With each lead being exhausted, it sends me right back to Harry Maine. But with no proof and it just being my gut instinct, I can do little about it right now.

The leaves scatter along the street as the wind sweeps through the city. I find myself looking around making sure he hasn't followed Summer here. It can't be a coincidence he's just appeared in the city, and I know it isn't. A man like him wouldn't give up on someone like Summer so easily, while I've been cold towards her, there's no denying that she's devastatingly beautiful, and the more I see her, the more I want her, but that's a line I know I could never cross. Probably because it would end badly for both of us. I've never been one to shy away from trouble, but with Harry still lurking, I know Summer isn't safe.

The door to the brownstone opens, I turn as she begins to descend the stone steps. Our eyes meet and I see the flicker of curiosity as to my presence. As she nears, her loose blonde curls bounce gently with each step. Unable to pull my gaze away from her long legs, I feel the feral need to have them wrapped around my waist as I devour those soft plump lips. With my cock straining against my jeans, I shuffle slightly as I turn to face her fully.

"Is there any news on the case?" she asks eagerly with a hopeful look, but I just shake my head.

"No, I just wanted to check up on you."

It's not a lie. I wanted an excuse to see her again. She has a light and warmth that seems brings a glimmer to my emptiness.

Looking a little taken back, she offers a small smile, pulling her coat tighter around her.

"Oh, I'm fine, thanks. It looks like the funeral can go ahead in a week or so, so I'll need to make a few calls." I see the smile falter as she finishes her sentence.

"Do you want to grab a drink?" As the words leave my mouth, I inwardly kick myself for even fucking asking. But before I can shrug it off, she smiles and nods.

"I'd really like that, thanks." Tucking a piece of hair behind her ear, I see the tension leave her shoulders. "Lead the way. You know what's around here better than me."

Walking side by side, I see the look on her face as she takes in the views of New York. A small smile etches on her face as we pass the large buildings and hot dog stands, seeing the city through new eyes is refreshing, after living here all my life and seeing the dark side regularly of what the city has to offer it's hard to look at it with wonder. For me, it's rife with crime and murder daily, but Summer seems almost intrigued by her new surroundings.

Leading her into a small bar. As the door opens, the smell of stale cigarette smoke is pungent. Eyeing the bartender, he just shrugs. Heading to the bar, I order two Jack and cokes, whilst Summer sits in a nearby booth. Scott, the bartender, gives me a knowing look as he spots Summer. He's never seen me bring anyone here, so he's taken back when I pass her a drink.

Taking a seat in the booth, I watch as she runs her fingers up and down the glass, lost in thought. But it doesn't stop me from wanting those hands on my cock. Shifting once again, her eyes turn to me as she smiles.

"Thanks for this. I was going a little mad at the apartment."

Pushing my thoughts aside, I nod taking in her lost expression.

"How so?" I ask, taking a sip of my drink.

"Oh …you know, it's quiet." I watch as she shuffles uncomfortably in her seat but refuses to look my way.

Deciding not to press the situation further, Summer sips her drink, gently licking her lips as she places the glass down on the table.

"Have you lived in New York long?" She asks curiously, changing the subject, but it's not the question that causes me to stiffen in my seat.

She's eyeing my fucking scar again.

As her eyes flick to mine, I watch as she sinks slightly. Knowing she's been caught staring at the scar, I feel my jaw tick. Leaning in, I can't help myself as I lower my voice.

"It's rude to fucking stare Summer." My eyes pierce into her sapphire blues before she looks away as the blush creeps up her cheeks.

Tucking a piece of hair behind her ear, she softly speaks.

"I'm sorry, I shouldn't have...."

"It's fine." I cut her off.

Allowing my fingers to move across the half-filled glass in front of me, the feeling of darkness descending further over me as I hear the screams of my past ringing in my ears. The memory begins to subside, I catch Summer by the wrist as she tries to leave. Her eyes snap to mine as the crimson stays planted on her delicate face.

Movement in the corner of the bar catches my attention as I pull her back to me. As the figure moves closer to the bar, my grip tightens on her, pulling her closer.

"Bhodi, what is it?" She looks down at the firm grasp.

That's not a fucking coincidence.

When both men turn toward us, a sinister smirk creeps across his lips as he spots Summer next to me. Feeling the rage building deep within me, he begins to approach. As my eyes dart to the exits, I know I can't get Summer out of here, so I accept the situation.

"Summer?" He speaks in a mock surprise, approaching the table.

With Summer still focused on me, I see the recognition and fear run through her as her eyes snap to the voice.

"I thought it was you."

That fucking smirk isn't moving as Harry stands at the table. His devious eyes roam Summer's body as she inches closer to me. I watch as her hands shake, unable to get the words out.

Briefly looking between them, I stand, pulling Summer with me. Placing a protective arm around her, I pull her close. Harry's eyes momentarily flicker with anger as she finally speaks.

"What are you doing here, Harry?"

"Well, I have some business in the city for the next few weeks. I tried to call you."

His eyes move towards the healing grazes on her forehead, but without hesitating, she pulls away from me and practically flies out the door. Leaving both of us in a stare-off, he looks me up and down before smirking again. His words drip with sarcasm and a cock sure confidence.

"She'll come running back. She always does."

"Think so? She doesn't seem to be too interested." My own mocking tone allows me to gain the upper hand when I move a step closer. His smirk now replaced with anger. "If you come near her again, I will kill you."

I watch as his mask falters for a moment. It's likely no one ever stood up to him. As he goes to speak, another familiar face approaches and interrupts, pulling Harry away and back to their table. Spotting a few other men waiting for him.

As he finally turns away, the associate he's with sends me a death glare. Fortunately for them, there are too many witnesses here, but I know his face. Luca Bernardi is known to the precincts in New York. He's a fucking criminal, but unfortunately for us, he's fucking good and rarely gets caught, but it doesn't stop people from talking, yet nothing ever sticks. I smirk back, as Harry's just given me a way into investigating him for Michael Harper's murder.

Harry looks at the door Summer's just exited from, pulling out his phone. Not wasting time, I move through the exit and back onto the busy street. Checking up and down, but I can't spot her.

"Fuck." I say through gritted teeth before hailing a cab back to her apartment, hoping she'll already be there.

Summer ♥

Bursting through the apartment's front door, I slam it closed as I lean back into the door. With tears falling down my cheeks, I quickly wipe them away, trying to steady my racing heart with deep breaths. I watch through blurred vision as my hands tremble, moving toward the kitchen. I slide a stool out, dropping myself onto the seat, allowing my head to fall into my hands as my elbows rest on the breakfast bar.

I have no idea how long I stare at the marble in front of me, lost in thought. My mind racing over coming face to face with Harry since I fled for New York. Part of me wonders if he even remembers the fight, but with the conniving look plastered all over his face, I'm sure he remembers it well.

With my dad's funeral scheduled for next week, I can't even run away and not look back. Not attending the funeral to say my goodbyes is out of the question. I owe it to my dad to be there for him during those final moments, and without any suspect in custody, his killer is still walking free. I sigh as my mind reels over the day, silently screaming to run as far away as possible, but my stubborn side rears its ugly head.

Squeezing my eyes closed, an eerie feeling of being watched causes the hairs on my neck to stand on end. My head snaps to the living room. Immediately pushing myself from the chair I lurch into the open space, hoping to see a familiar sight. Scanning the empty room, I proceed to search the remainder of the apartment, but he's nowhere to be seen.

Before the disappointment can register, I jump as a loud hammering on the door rings through the quiet apartment. Standing frozen, I crane my neck as a low voice can be heard. Taking a few steps closer, I feel myself reaching for the nearby lamp as I approach, I begin to lower the lamp in my hands as a familiar voice speaks.

"Summer, it's Bhodi. Are you in there?" Letting out the breath I was holding in, unlocking the door I pull it open. his wavy hair is windswept as his chest rises and falls heavily. We stand facing each other, his eyes full of concern as the tears begin to dry on my cheeks. Wiping my face, I step back inside the apartment, gesturing for him to come in. As he steps inside, I close and lock the door behind him.

"Were you followed from the bar?" I ask nervously.

"No, he went back to his meeting when you left. I couldn't see you, but I thought you'd come back here." He shrugs, but I can only nod in response.

"I can't even run away." I manage to squeak out as a sob escapes me.

I look at Bhodi as his jaw ticks, and he straightens his posture, appearing taller than before. Taking a couple of steps towards me, he gently cups my cheeks, those emerald, green irises staring deep into mine before he speaks.

"You aren't going anywhere, Summer; I'll look after you. He won't be allowed anywhere near you."

His words are full of sincerity and warmth, allowing my eyes to close as more tears fall. Placing my hands over his, I open my eyes once again. As we stand in a trance, I can't help but take a step forward, inching closer and closer as our lips almost touch.

"We can't Summer."

"Why not?" I ask, my voice breathy and full of need.

"Because I won't be able to stop."

"Then don't."

With a low growl, Bhodi pulls me close as his lips crash onto mine. His strong hands dig into my hips as our bodies remain flush. I allow my hands to roam through his hair and grab fistfuls as he backs me to the sofa.

Hooking his hands under my knees, he spins us around, dropping himself down onto the seat below, letting out an involuntary moan. Feeling his cock growing beneath me, I can't help but slowly grind down, seeking that friction I desperately desire. Feeling his hands roam up my back, pulling my top down and exposing my neck, I feel his lips and teeth kissing and grazing over my sensitive skin.

I brace my hands onto the back of the sofa before he captures my lips once again in a frenzied kiss, allowing our tongues to battle for dominance. Eventually pulling away, his forehead rests on mine as we both pant, his fingers grazing over my skin in small circles as we remain locked in our embrace for a moment longer.

As his eyes meet mine, he searches my face before rising from the seat and placing me back on shaky legs. Taking a step back, he runs his hand across his mouth, shaking his head.

"I shouldn't have done that." His words are monotone, "Fuck!"

I look at him wide-eyed, before he turns away and starts heading for the door. Standing in the living room dumbfounded, I watch as he leaves, slamming the door behind him with a harsh thud, which causes me to jump.

The stillness in the apartment sends an unwanted chill through me, as I stand in the darkness. My swollen lips still tingling from the kiss, that I now instantly regret.

Chapter Eleven
Summer ♥

My eyes are firmly planted onto the ceiling above, and I watch through stinging eyes as the shadows dance across the plaster. Tears soak my pillow as the weight of, yet another fucking mistake crushes my soul that little bit more. Rolling to one side, I stare out the window, the moonlight illuminating the room as the curtains stay parted, hoping that sleep will eventually take over.

No such luck. Glancing at the clock on the bedside table, two am nears. Letting out a frustrated sigh, I pull myself up in the bed. Throwing my head into my hands once again, the confusion and frustration of the entire New York stay continues to eat me from the inside. After Bhodi walked out without another word, I stood in the living room again, like I had twenty-four hours previous. Shame racking my body, yet I had hope that he would return, but if he had returned, for me, the damage was done.

The damage has already been caused by my own warped fascination with the man who calls himself Two/Face. Even as he crosses my mind, I feel my body ache with desire and need, yet my head is screaming at me to fucking run away. I mean, seriously, who the fuck fantasizes about a man in a mask who has already killed once and enters your home without permission to 'punish you'.

The same person that stood naked at a window while he finger fucked me. The same person who wanted him to carry on and also the same fucking person that's craved that touch ever since.

I crossed a line I shouldn't have.

Pushing the duvet off with a frustrated huff, I swing my legs off the bed and head through the kitchen. I pull out one of the barstools and take a seat. Pulling the paperwork from the attorney, I force my eyes to glance over the funeral arrangements.

If I can't sleep, I may as well try and be fucking useful.

Pouring a large glass of red, I get lost in the arrangements I need to follow up, making a couple of notes here and there, but the silence of the apartment is eerie, feeling the hair on the back of my neck rising once again, my eyes remain on the documents.

Glancing across the hall, I see my dad's bedroom. The door has stayed shut since I came here. The idea of going through his things just feels like too much right now. I know I'll need to go through his belongings eventually, but It's something I know I'll put off for as long as I can.

Refusing to acknowledge my feeling of uneasiness, I persevere at the table, but with the words beginning to move around the page and the constant shivers running over my body, I shunt the paperwork away, leaning back in the chair.

My eyes snap to the door as three sharp knocks grab my attention. My brow furrows, looking between the door and the large clock in the kitchen. My stomach drops and the knocks repeat, sliding from the stool and quietly moving towards the door. I eye the door curiously, but it doesn't take long for a familiar voice to send me into a silent frenzy.

"Summer? Baby, I know you're in there." At first his voice is sincere, almost kind.

After he knocks again, the monster that lies beneath begins to stir.

"I fucking know where you are. I will gut you, you fucking slut. I'll slice those pretty lips from your face."

The maniacal laugh seeps through the door. His sinister voice is low as I stand frozen on the spot a few feet away with only a door between us.

My eyes fill with hot tears, and my entire body trembles. Leaning against the wall for support, my fingers clutching onto the paint as the feeling of helplessness consumes me.

Oh god, how did he find me? What do I do?

"I'll make sure Detective Grey watches while I fucking claim what's mine." He continues to speak, "I'll be seeing you very soon."

I slide down the wall as silent sobs rack my body, dropping to my knees the sound of retreating footsteps thud through the hall, eventually becoming non-existent as I huddle in a frantic mess on the floor.

TWO/FACE \

The city never sleeps, and neither do I. Launching the glass across the room, it shatters into pieces, scattering along the floor. But I can't pull my eyes from the screen. White hot rage pulses through me as I watch helplessly with the situation that unfolds before me. My hands tremble, watching him lean close to the door, his sneering taunts pulling Summer further into the darkness.

That fucking cunt, I'll saw off your fucking head off while you watch.

Grabbing my phone, I immediately hit call. With each ring, my blood boils, my fucking eyes boring holes into the screen. Hitting silent on the keyboard, Harry's words are silenced for a moment while I unleash the fucking demon.

"What do..." his nonchalant answer immediately crushed by the anger I can no longer contain.

"You told me that fucking building was secure. That fucking cunt is at her door, find out what the fuck has gone wrong, or I'll be over to soak you in fucking acid!"

Not waiting for a response, I slam the phone down, causing the entire IT system to bounce off the desk. Hunched over the monitor, my eyes remain laser-focused on the hallway and Michael's apartment. Shaking my head, I watch Summer approach the door.

Don't fucking do it, don't you fucking dare.

Letting out a low breath, I watch as he turns to leave, heading down the hall and eventually out the exit and into a waiting car. Jotting down the number plate before it speeds off, I move my attention to Summer, a surge of adrenaline courses through me when I see she's safe and hasn't moved. But Harry has cemented his fate. I'm going to fucking kill him and make her watch.

Grabbing my car keys and black duffle bag, I storm out of the apartment, slamming the door behind me. Taking a deep breath, the icy night air sweeps over me, but the rage doesn't subside. I know what I fucking need to do.

The drive to the apartment is intense. Each time I replay that cunt's words in my head, the grip on the steering wheel becomes tighter and tighter. Once the door to the underground parking lot begins to rise, I waste little time speeding in. The area is desolate at this time of night. Slamming the door closed with my duffle bag in hand, I head for Summer.

Summer ♥

Once the footsteps had gone silent, I managed to get to my feet. Glancing at the clock in front of me, I've been standing in silence for the past twenty minutes, aimlessly staring at the wall in the kitchen. I feel my body begin to sway, becoming lightheaded as the adrenaline rapidly wears off.

Feeling my soul leap from my body, heavy footsteps thunder back to the front door. As my head snaps to the hall, the door crashes open, bouncing aggressively off the wall. Like a bat out of hell I manage to reach for the knife rack as the dark figure comes into view. Clutching the knife in my trembling hand, the familiar mask approaches with a purpose.

My eyes widen as I round the kitchen island. Applying distance between us, he finally speaks. His chest heaving, slamming his fists down on the table, causing glasses to fly off. Shattering to the ground, whilst my heartbeat thunders in my ears.

"Put that knife down unless you know how to fucking use it." He spits out at me, and my eyes dart between him and the butcher knife that shakes in my hand.

As soon as my focus moves from him, he pounces, swiping the knife from my hands as it flies across the floor. The large hand reaches out, gripping my throat hard, pulling me to his chest. My body smacks forcefully into his, and I feel his warm breath across my skin as our eyes are in a deadlock. The anger is rife, and his grip fierce as he pulls me through the apartment. My feet barely touching the floor as the bedroom door is thrown open, and I land with a thud on the bed.

Unable to push myself up, I feel him crawl over me. His broad body leaning so heavily into mine. A large blade glimmering in the moonlight catches my eye before it's brought to my throat. A thin layer of sweat seeps from my skin as the blade is pushed against my sensitive skin.

"I should fucking cut you! He fucking followed you!" His harsh exclaim causes me to wince. "Arms above your head."

Without hesitating or arguing, I obey the demand, allowing my arms to slowly rise above my head. As he reaches into the bag and pulls open the zip, he turns back to me. The sharp flexi cuffs tug on my skin, as he tightens them. Managing to look up and unable to pull my arms away, my wide eyes fall back to the mask with a fearful, questioning look.

"Wh-what are you doing?" I ask, my voice a merely audible whisper.

Tugging gently on my restraints, I feel the morbid curiosity creep over me. Watching him in awe, he finally turns back to me, holding a piece of black material.

"Doing something I've wanted to do since I first saw you, Summer. I want to see you fall apart, crying out and letting go of those fucking demons you seem to hold on to." He leans in, as the material nears my eyes.

Blinking a few times, I process his words. The anger is still stitched into his words, but I'm not scared of what he'll do for some unexplained reason. It's wrong, it's so fucking wrong, but I'm drawn to him. His presence gives me a feeling of safety, something I haven't felt for a long time. In recent times, I've lived in fear of abuse and violence and walked around surrounded by a black cloud that could swallow me at any moment.

Once the blindfold is secured, my head relaxes on the pillow below. The darkness consumes my sight. My ears are alert and listening to every movement or creek in the room, but the feeling of his body sliding over mine once again sends warmth all through me. I feel his breath on my lips, gently ghosting across mine.

"Do you want this, Summer?"

I swallow the hard lump in my throat.

"Yes."

"You don't even know what I'm going to do?" I feel his smirk graze my lips as I gently chew my bottom lip.

"I want to forget." I say, a weight beginning to lift from my soul.

"Good." Leaning in, he gently presses his lips soft lips to mine.

I feel the electricity shoot from my toes, traveling the length of my body. But as soon as I do, I feel the warmth move away. His fingertips gently grazing my stomach and gripping the waistband of my silk shorts, and I feel the need flood my core. When the waistband is gently pulled from my skin, a loud shearing sound rips through the room, causing me to gasp as the torn fabric is pulled with haste from my body.

"Shit." I manage to squeak out when the cool air glides across my bare skin.

The bed shifts, holding my breath as his body slides down mine. Pushing my top up, his soft lips leave a gentle trail of kisses from my neck down my stomach. My breath hitches in my throat, feeling his strong hands push my knees apart before traveling back up, fisting the soft cotton vest top before another shred is heard, allowing my top to fall on either side of my body.

The thundering in my chest rapidly increases as I lie naked and exposed. My nipples harden when a gentle breeze ghosts across my tits, and my entire body is on fire. A shiver runs through me as the sharp blade is gently dragged from my wrist down to my thigh, leaving goosebumps in its wake. His lips crash down onto mine, and I fight the restraints to pull him closer, the plastic digging into my skin, causing it to burn. Lifting my head and allowing his tongue to sweep into my mouth, the kiss is aggressive and needy before he pulls abruptly away.

"You're so fucking perfect." He growls in my ear.

The bed shifts once again, feeling the warmth of his body sweep down mine. I lie frozen as a gentle blow of air skates across my inner thigh, causing me to jolt the restraints again. A low chuckle escapes him before his strong grip forces my knees further apart.

A loud groan escapes my throat, feeling his soft tongue glide over my soaked pussy, circling my throbbing clit immediately.

"Oh god!" I gasp while he continues in delicate circles before sliding two fingers into me. Arching my back, I cry out. "Fuck!"

His soaked fingers slide in and out of me as my needy moans fill the dark apartment. Gripping onto the restraints hard, I push myself down the bed, needing to feel closer. When the pad of his thumb connects with my clit, his fingers continue with the rhythmic thrusts when I feel his eyes on me, watching me fall apart, falling into a deadly trap.

"Come for me, Summer, come fucking hard on my tongue while I fucking enjoy the show."

The darkness in his voice sends my eyes rolling into the back of my head and I feel his tongue once again on me. Driving his fingers into me harder and harder each time, I can't hold back. Stretching me and pushing me to the fucking hilt, I cry out. I cry hard, allowing my orgasm to rip through me. My back arches and my entire body spasms while I lie at his mercy.

Panting hard, his fingers move away, leaving a feeling of want and emptiness. Gliding them up my body, I feel my arousal smeared across my heavy tits before landing on my throat once again, gripping me hard his lips ghost over mine before he speaks.

"Once the funeral is over, you'll leave this city and never return. No good will come to anyone if you stay here."

My mouth falls open at these cold words, my heart sinks, and the entire room drains of any warmth.

"And stay the fuck away from Detective Grey. I know what you did, and you're playing a fucking dangerous game, that I know you won't win."

His sinister demanding tone sends a chill through me, he releases my throat before shoving me back into the pillow.

The blade slices through the restraints, and my weak arms drop. Pushing the blindfold off quickly, the sight before me is dark. Two/Face looms over me like the dark reaper he is, the mask back in place while he stares down at me. Tears prick my eyes, and I lie frozen on the bed as the harsh reality of his words breaks what little hope he just offered.

I close my eyes and hear him move from the room and out of the apartment. Once the door closes, I allow my tears to fall. Loneliness and emptiness consuming me, like I knew it eventually would.

Chapter Twelve

Bhodi ⚥

Stepping back into the precinct the following morning, I avoid eye contact with anyone who passes by. I don't want fucking small talk, or for anyone to even look my way, each time I think back to last night, I fucking hate myself for allowing my vulnerability and want to cloud my fucking judgment on this whole fucked up situation.

That look on her face as I pushed her away was devastating. I took a vulnerable girl and used her without any consideration for her feelings, and it showed. Even though I stopped before it went further, it doesn't mean I didn't want it to. It took every fiber of my being not to pull her into bed with me while I tore off her panties and drove my cock so deep into that tight pussy, she'd forget everything for the moment, even the though the thought makes me rock hard as my mind wanders to the fantasy I know I could never delight in.

"Grey!" My eyes snap to Strode, approaching my desk with a purpose. He leans in with a fire behind those denim-blue eyes. "In the office now."

I rise from my chair and follow him into the small storage space, but before I've even managed to close the door behind me, he reaches for my jacket, balling the leather into his fists, and slams me against the glass. The rage in his eyes isn't something I see often, but I already know what this is about.

"Are you fucking stupid, Grey?" He speaks through gritted teeth, but I remain unfazed. "We're investigating her father's murder, and you're more interested in getting your dick wet."

Pushing him away, he staggers backward, slamming into the table before I step forward, squaring my shoulders.

"You fucking followed me?" My voice sinister and almost threateningly low as my eyes bore holes into his. But he doesn't back down, instead choosing to move closer.

"I was following Summer like we fucking agreed. I couldn't trust that Harry wouldn't try something as she was roaming the city alone. Then you fucking turn up, what the fuck are you playing at?" He bites back, throwing his hands in the air.

My jaw ticks for a moment. Looking away, I contemplate my response before I speak. Something I can't do is lie to Strode, one because he's my partner and we need to have trust, and two because we've both seen the destruction this city has to offer almost daily, and I've been sloppy. I've been caught out.

"It was a lapse in judgment. It won't happen again." My voice is monotone, allowing his eyes to search my face for a moment before he sighs, moving away and running a frustrated hand over his face.

"Kid, I care about you like a father does a son. You're messing with something very fucking dangerous right now. If Luca Bernardi is indeed tied to Harry right now, we need to watch our backs, or else this won't end well for anyone."

My eyes snap to his at the mention of Luca. "How did you know?"

"Once you left the bar, I was outside. It didn't take long for Harry and Luca to leave. I followed them for a while but eventually lost them in city traffic." I nod slowly as he continues, "I checked Harry's whereabouts during the time of Michael's murder, and he was in Las Vegas, but I can't find anything on Luca."

"And we won't, he's too fucking clever." The venom spilling through my tone, knowing that Michael Harper's murder may never get solved, ending up propped on a shelf and branded a cold case until the day they put me in the fucking ground.

"I called Michael's lawyer; he confirmed the date for the funeral. If we go, maybe we can arrest Luca and Harry for something and bring them in." The comment almost seems hopeful.

"Fucking seriously?" I Scoff, "As soon as we bring him in, that rat attorney will scurry in and have any charge we have dropped. He'll be walking out of here by happy hour."

"Then what do you suggest, Grey?" He eyes me curiously, but I avert my eyes, knowing there's fuck all that can be done when you're dealing with corrupt scum like Harry and Luca.

"We'll attend the funeral. Have a couple of squad cars nearby, too, in case either of them tries anything. He's following Summer. There's no way him ending up in that bar was a coincidence so we must assume he's got more people on his payroll, feeding him information."

Strode nods before leaving the room, his disappointment in my behavior all too obvious. I can't blame him; my actions could have cost me the case and potentially my job. Swinging the door open and taking a seat back at my desk, it doesn't take long before the tapping of heels pulls my attention to the main door of the office.

Immediately averting my eyes back to the paperwork in front of me, I avoid her usual gentle gaze. Yet this time, I can feel the burning holes boring into the side of my head, but I don't look up. I don't need to see the hurt look on her face to make me feel more of a fucking bastard than I already do. Strode approaches with concern, clearly alarmed by the wild look in her eyes after spotting me.

"He came to the apartment last night." I hear her squeak out, pulling my attention to the hushed conversation.

"Grey! Interview room…now!"

My jaw ticks, and my eyes narrow at Strode's order, but I comply. Pushing my chair out, I follow as he leads Summer into the interview room where we first met. Taking a seat opposite her, her eyes no longer steal glances my way. The angelic sadness I once saw is now replaced with a steel-like determination.

"What happened, Summer?" Strode leans in, his tone calm and comforting.

Taking a deep breath, she finally speaks, moving her eyes from the table to Strode. "Harry came to my apartment last night; I don't know how he got in, but he followed me. No one knew where I was apart from my father's attorney, James Kressler, and Detective Grey."

Her eyes refuse to look my way, but I immediately feel the side eye from Strode. Whilst he thinks I could have led Harry to the apartment, I know I fucking didn't. He's got eyes everywhere and there's little people won't do it in this city to make a quick buck.

"You do realise, Summer, if he's threatened you in any way, I need to bring him in for questioning."

She nods a couple of times, leaning slightly closer toward Strode. "He threatened...Bh...Detective Grey, too."

As Strode leans back in his chair, running his hand across his face. I keep my eyes focused on the table in front as my blood begins to simmer under the surface. The rage beginning to ring in my ears as the severity of what I've caused hits like a falling tonne of bricks.

"I wasn't entirely honest with you both." Summer looks away, sighing heavily she runs a shaky hand through her hair.

"What weren't you honest about?" I eye her curiously, hoping she'll finally tell us what Harry did. Even though we already know the type of person he is.

"Harry would hit me a lot." She stands from her chair and slightly lifts her jumper, exposing the fading bruises on her lower ribs. Eventually, she sits back down, and I hear Strode let out a heavy sigh, slightly rubbing his brow.

"Initially, he wasn't abusive, but once he got comfortable in the relationship, then beating me was almost fair game. I lied because I didn't want him to know where I was. We had a huge fight before I left Vegas, and I hit him hard with a bottle to get away. He was knocked out, so I don't know If he even remembers the fight. I just didn't want to be hit again. I just wanted to help my dad."

The tears fall from her eyes. She leans forward onto the desk. Her head rests in her hands as she sobs through her pain. Both Strode and I look between each other and know she was only trying to protect herself. Eventually, she looks up and wipes her eyes, sniffing hard, her shoulders sag as she continues.

"The man from the alley said that Harry paid him to attack me; he had a knife, and apparently, he could do whatever he wanted to me. Harry left it up to him." Summer shudders, gently wiping the corner of her mouth. "I don't know what happened to him, though. I just remember how blurry my vision was."

Once the conversation ends, we leave the room, and I watch Strode leave, taking Summer back to the apartment for now. The want and need to feel close to her clouded by the threat that now looms over both of us. Of course, he threatened me. Cowards like him always do when there's no one round to stand up to him, but he'll learn I don't back down.

Summer 🖤

Stepping into the apartment, I turn back whilst Detective Strode lingers in the doorway. The detective I once assumed to be an arrogant asshole is now the one, I feel I can trust.

How fucking wrong was I?

Allowing my mind to swallow me in thoughts of Bhodi, Detective Strode takes a step forward before speaking.

"I know this is an awful time for you, Summer. We're doing everything we can to find the person who killed your father." He hesitates for a moment, averting his eyes slightly before returning them to me. "Whatever is going on between yourself and Detective Grey cannot continue; there's too much danger, and someone will end up hurt. I don't want it to be either of you, do you understand?"

I swallow hard as the heat rushes to my cheeks. I can't argue with him. He's right. We're putting each other in danger and the thought of anything happening to Bhodi sends an ache to my heart. I simply nod, the shame plastered all over my face.

"I am proud of you, though, for telling us what really happened with Harry. It's never easy to talk about abuse."

Detective Strode nods and turns on his heels before closing the door behind him, leaving me with my own thoughts. I stare at the door for a moment, the sincerity in his words making me think there's another meaning behind it all.

Sitting in the living room hours later, I watch the sunset. Lost in the beauty of the pink and orange hues before the darkness of the night sky blankets the city. The same city that I once considered beautiful. My eyes travel to my phone on the coffee table as it buzzes, turning to the side I sit upright on the sofa, my bare feet firmly placed on the soft carpet, watching as the phone shuffles along the glass.

Eyeing the 'unknown number' that lights up the screen, I briefly hesitate before slamming my wine glass on the table and answering the persistent call. Holding the phone to my ear, I listen intently as that familiar shiver runs up my spine. Chewing my bottom lip slightly, I finally speak.

"What do you want?" My tone clip, listening for an answer.

"Well, I deserved that. I'll let you off...for now." His voice drips with velvet threat, sending the ache straight to my core. Slamming my thighs together, hoping the ache subsides.

"Well?" I ask impatiently, rising to my feet and beginning to pace the living room. Hoping it'll take my mind off my sinful needs.

"As Harry gained access to the building, I've had the access code for the service door and the code for the apartment changed. I'll text them to you now. They'll be active immediately."

My brow furrows, "But how did..."

Before I can finish the sentence, he abruptly hangs up. My eyes scan the entire apartment, anticipating his sudden appearance leaves me on edge. Yet after a couple of moments, there's no sound, no movement, and no Two/Face anywhere in sight.

Sinking back into the sofa, allowing my head to fall back. I get lost in the moment, staring off into space before a thought crosses my mind, causing me to sit bolt-upright upright, scanning the room once again.

How did he know?....What if he can see me?...Oh god, did he kill my dad?

The entire thought sends bile to my throat. Sitting frozen on the sofa the entire apartment feels like a fucking vice. Clutching my phone in my hand, I bolt from the apartment, grabbing my coat, before slamming the door behind me and making my way down to the street below.

Gasping for air as the doors finally open, I lean against the railings as the cool night air consumes me. Glancing up and down the road, I feel my feet beginning to carry me off, and I don't argue.

Chapter Thirteen

TWO/FACE

Stepping into the smoky room, all eyes turn to me.

"The fuck are you looking at?" I ask, eyeing Axe.

Pushing himself from his chair, he slowly approaches. I lift my chin slightly as the massive fucker has a couple of inches on me. His jaw ticks, and his eyes narrow before he speaks.

"It's been almost a fucking week, and we're still walking around with our thumbs up our fucking asses."

Allowing my gaze to move to Jimmy, he sits by the log burner. A glass of whisky between his fingers as he gazes deep into the flames. Michael's death hit us all hard in our own ways. Even though we were a team, we were also friends who relied on each other and worked towards the same common goal.

"We don't even know if this was an attack on us Two!" Axe continues, turning away and dropping back into his chair. His head in his hands, shaking his head from the sheer frustration we all feel.

"Without proof, you know we're not going after Harry; we don't do that shit!" I relay the point once again. "If we do, we're no better than the rest of the people we take off the streets."

Lifting his head, the anger begins to radiate from his entire body. "

So, we just fucking wait? By the time he does slip up, he could be long gone."

Keeping the rage at bay, I listen to Axe's concerns. Whilst he's correct, at any moment, Harry could leave and disappear if he chooses to, and we can't allow that, but at the same time, we aren't fucking mavericks. Everything we do is carefully analyzed, risks are weighed, and everyone knows what each mission result should be. Michael was in charge. He kept our egos in check, weighed up the risks, and planned for anything. We're now missing an important cog in the machine, and it feels like any good thing we have ever done is now overshadowed by the want and need for revenge and the inability to think clearly.

I feel my eyes moving away from Axe's intense gaze, not out of fear. But because I know he's fucking right, and I hate it. Trying to keep everything together won't work if we all have our own agendas. My gaze falls on Jimmy. He was always Michael's right hand, the sensible one, the thinker and the one to set everything in motion to ensure we always reached our target. Right now, I see a man who's lost and without a purpose.

"How's the funeral coming along?" I ask, taking a seat by the log burner. Reaching for the whiskey and pouring a large shot. He momentarily pulls his eyes from the flames to look at me before turning back to answer.

"I passed Summer all the documents. The funeral is planned for this coming Tuesday." I nod, listening intently, whilst he continues speaking into the fire. "Michael left her his entire estate, which we knew. I'm guessing she'll plan to leave once it is all over. As you requested, I said I could send her the paperwork whilst she's on the road to sell the businesses if that's what she chooses to do."

"She fucking better." I spit out. Catching myself, I feel Jimmy's gaze on me. He blinks a couple of times, studying my expression before leaning in.

"We have fucking eyes, Two. Whatever you're playing at with her, stop. You're watching her each night like a fucking stalker. You disappear. We both know where you'll end up going."

Throwing his arms up in the air, I feel his frustration over my behavior. But the truth is, I have no idea why I'm pulling her close and then pushing her away. Maybe because I can? Because she makes me feel things that haven't surfaced for a long time, or maybe because she's so fucking beautiful and full of hope, my own sickness wants to make her a dark and lonely shell like me.

Maybe I'm jealous?

"Those cameras were set up in Michael's apartment for safety, you're fucking using them like a private cam show." Jimmy shakes his head in disbelief, and he isn't far wrong.

The tension in the room is suffocating as the eyes continue to look towards me. The crackle of the wood fire is the only thing keeping the room from utter deafening silence, I feel myself slipping further into my own internal chaos as each moment passes, but I know I need to address my obsession with Summer before it fucking kills me or I lose the chance altogether.

"I got a call this morning about a job," Jimmy finally speaks, as we all turn to him, eager for the details and something we can take our pent-up frustrations on. "This one came via a different channel though," Axe and I both feel our gaze meeting for an initial moment, but we need this right now.

Summer ♥

    I allow my feet to wander the cold dark streets as a numbness continues to wrack my body. Only a few days previous, I looked at the city with wonder and hope, but now, with the secrets that are lingering over me, it just gives me nothing but fear and concern for what's to come.

    As my feet continue to move, I find myself moving towards Dad's club, standing on the sidewalk, I gaze up at the tall building, I've visited multiple times before. Usually, it was during the day, dad would pop in to check on things and make sure the staff had everything they needed for the night, have a quick meeting with the managers, and we would head off to spend the remainder of the day, sight-seeing, catching a show or heading for lunch.

    Those great times now feel like a lifetime ago; I wish I had stayed longer or never even left at all. Maybe if I had stayed, things would have gone very differently for both of us.

    Lost in nostalgia, I wipe a single tear from my cheek as the icy wind blows through the street. The odd stillness, leaving an imprint on my ongoing sadness. Pulling my coat tighter around myself, I can't help but shudder. Stealing glances around the empty street, there's nothing but the occasional passing car or the rustle of the crisp leaves across the concrete floor.

    Pulling out my phone, I blink a couple of times realizing it's only seven pm. The quiet street now makes sense. I guess people don't go to the clubs until much later. I know the right and sensible thing to do would be to hail a cab back to my apartment instead of wandering the streets alone, but the thought of returning there makes me feel sick. With the fear that Two/Face could have been behind my father's murder causes the bile to rise in my throat and leaves me feeling lightheaded. But that doesn't stop the fucked up feelings I have towards the masked man peeking through and tearing me in two. The conflict I have, like as though someone has wrapped my heart and brain in barbed wire and keeps tightening it every few seconds.

I can't help but sigh as my conflicted brain just can't seem to move past the strange pull I have towards him. Sweeping my hair from my face, I move towards a small bar that I've visited with my dad a few times before, I'll take a small amount of familiarity from a bar than heading back to a dark cold apartment right now.

Pushing the door open, the warmth instantly pulls me into an inviting hug. I offer a half smile to the bartender as I approach. Glancing around, I see that it looks fairly quiet, mainly small groups of people and couples enjoying a quiet drink after work. Pulling out the barstool, I take a seat and drape my coat across the back as the bartender stands opposite, offering a warm, friendly smile. The sincerity in his chocolate brown eyes compliments his olive complexion. I almost feel myself leaning in before he blinks, and I realize I've just sat there staring like a fucking idiot.

Shaking my head a couple of times, I try to laugh it off. "Sorry, what did you say?"

"Rough day?" he retorts.

I feel the smile drain from my face while my shoulders sag. Briefly avoiding his eye contact, I finally reply. "Yeah, you could say that."

Pulling a glass from above the bar, sensing the immediate shift in moods, he pulls a bottle of Jamesons from behind him and pours two measures before sliding one to me.

"To a shit day." He says, holding his glass in front of me. Lifting it, we both clink and knock our drinks back simultaneously.

As soon as the hot amber liquid travels down my throat, my face contorts before leaving a small amount of warmth in my stomach.

"Same again?" he asks.

"Please." I smile, sliding the glass back over to him.

As he pours another measure, I catch him stealing small glances my way. Knowing he's been caught looking, he eventually asks the lingering question that's been on the tip of his tongue since I walked in.

"So, you're not a regular here, so what brings you to this little bar?" he asks, placing his elbow on the bar, lowering himself to my level.

Swirling the second drink in its glass, I get lost in the orange liquid as it flickers in the dimly lit surroundings. Looking back up, his intense gaze is still fixed on me. Shrugging, I finally answer his question. "I'm here for a funeral."

"I'm sorry to hear that. Was it someone close to you?" Taking a sip of my drink, I just nod as my eyes stay fixed on the bar in front of me. Taking a deep breath, I lift my head, meeting his eyes once again.

"My dad."

As his eyes widen in surprise, he takes a couple of steps back. "Shit, I'm really sorry to hear that."

I smile, taking another sip. "Thanks, but it's not necessary." Trying to move past the awkward pity he's offering.

"I thought that murder down the road was bad...." Before he can finish the sentence, the bartender senses the uncomfortable shift between us. I halt as the glass stops mid-way to my lips. He throws his hand over his mouth, shaking his head slightly.

"Summer?" he asks curiously as my eyes snap to his. My brows knit together slightly as the usual uneasy feeling rises in my gut. I can only nod my head before the surprise takes over his expression.

"Shit, sorry! That was rude...I .. I knew your dad."

"You did?" I ask curiously.

He nods, offering a small smile before busying himself, wiping a small spill from the bar. "Yeah, he'd come in here a couple times a week for lunch, getting away from the office. We'd chit-chat here and there." He hesitates for a moment before continuing, "I'm sorry we met like this. I was really shocked to hear what happened. Your dad was a good guy. I'm Alex, by the way." Extending his large hand out to me, I accept. Giving it a small shake as my small hand gets lost in his.

Feeling the tears fill my eyes, I blink a couple of times and let out a small laugh, trying to shrug off my emotions. "Thanks, he was the best."

Lifting the bottle, he tops up my glass before excusing himself. Glancing around the bar, it begins to get a little busier with men and women dressed in work attire. The soft jazz continues to play as I feel the warmth of the whisky running through my veins. As my heightened anxiety begins to subside, I continue to sip my drink and enjoy an odd feeling of normality in the city. The warm décor of the bar compliments its slight rustic country feel as I smile, watching patrons laugh and joke with each other.

The buzzing in my back pocket pulls my focus away, and as "withheld number" lights up the screen once again, I shake my head and hit the ignore button. Right now, I just want to enjoy a drink in peace without any worries, but that's easier said than done as the second incoming call appears. Rolling my eyes, I do the same as before. Giving him a swift fucking ignoring as the confidence of the liquor begins to take over.

"Hey, we have karaoke starting soon if you fancy making a night of it?" I look between Alex and the karaoke stand, smiling, but my gut is definitely telling me three drinks was enough.

"I'm good, thanks." Taking the last gulp of my drink, I place some cash onto the side before reaching for my coat, but before I can turn, I feel the same strong hand grip my wrist. As my eyes snap to his, the person looking back at me, doesn't have the same warm, inviting smile he had earlier. Right now, it's drenched in desperation; his wide eyes have a sinister slant, and I feel every hair on my body stand on end.

Trying to pull away, his grip gets tighter with each tug, but he doesn't let up. We stay fixed in a deadlock, with the burning sensation on my skin beginning to sting.

"Let me go." I speak through gritted teeth, refusing to back down.

Alex shakes his head as a deadpan look creeps across his face.

"I can't let that happen, Summer, I'm sorry."

My face contorts into that of confusion.

"Sorry for what?" I ask.

I follow his gaze towards the bar's main door; in that moment, I know I've walked right into a trap. As my breathing becomes heavier, sweat forms all over my body, leaving me feeling like I'm on fire. My eyes dart around me, looking for the source of the trap. A loud bang pulls our attention to the main doors as they burst open.

"Finally, there you are!"

Relief washes over me, Detective Strode enters the bar, a large jolly smile on his face as he approaches us.

"We were meant to meet down the road, Summer!" he says smiling before turning his attention to Alex, who now luckily loosened his grip enough to allow me to slip away and move towards the detective.

Eyeing the money on the bar, he looks to Alex. Even with a smile on his face, his tone is full of authority as Alex begins to sink slightly behind the bar.

"Well looks like we're all squared up here. Have a good evening." He politely nods, not allowing Alex to interject.

Pulling the door open, the suffocating I feel begins to fade as we step into the street. Gripping my elbow tight, he begins leading me in the opposite direction towards a car parked on the sidewalk. With his phone in one hand, he holds it close to his ear whilst scanning the area around us.

"I think Harry's got to the staff at O'Reilly's bar. It's about fifty yards from Michael's club. I'm taking Summer elsewhere. I'll call you when we arrive."

Without even questioning him, I pick my feet up and match his pace with my heart rate rapidly increasing at his voice's urgency. Approaching the car, I finally speak as Detective Strode opens the passenger door.

"What's going on?" I ask, turning to face him.

"Get in the car, Summer, I'll explain on the way."

He pushes me into the car, I don't have a chance to argue before the echoing of gunshots rings through the street. Ducking out of sight, I throw my hands over my head as the bullets ricochet off the bumper and bonnet. Unable to see where they're coming from, I try to throw the door open, hoping to see Detective Strode, but it's no use. The spray of bullets is relentless as I lie across the two seats, huddled into a ball.

The sound of tyre's screeching, a black car tears past without acknowledging the carnage in its wake. As my whole-body shakes, I hesitantly peer above the dash as a crowd of people move cautiously towards us from the nearby bars. Kicking open the passenger door, I manage to sit up before my eyes land on the crimson liquid soaking into the concrete. Throwing my hand over my mouth, a blood-curdling scream escapes my mouth as I fall from the car, landing on the street with a thud as I crawl over to Detective Strode.

"SOMEONE PLEASE HELP! CALL 911 PLEASE!" My screams bounce off the tall buildings. "HELP!...HELP!" Sobs rack my body as I throw my hands across his torso, trying to stop the bleeding. "The police will be here soon, I promise." I whisper as the light in his eyes begins to fade.

I continue to shout and plead with people and eventually they begin to move quicker, as they catch sight of us lying in the street.

I feel someone pull me away as they continue to stop the bleeding, but my eyes move to Alex. My cold stare meets his as he stands with a wide-eyed expression outside the bar. That fucking prick probably thought he could palm me off to Harry and get paid. My heart is thundering in my ears, but I don't pull my focus away as he begins to move away from the bar and makes his way towards the end of the street. Before rounding the corner and disappearing altogether. The rage consumes my entire being as I stand in the street, the sound of sirens near us, but I can't pull my focus from the corner.

I will make you fucking suffer, one way or another.

Chapter Fourteen

Bhodi ⚧

The emergency room doors fly open. The loud crash pulls everyone's attention to me. Immediately spotting my captain talking to the doctor, I approach.

"Captain I..."

"Grey, this isn't on you. Strode followed Summer to the bar. No one knew he was there." Captain Dean speaks with authority, trying to keep calm in the busy hospital waiting room.

"But.."

"All I know is that he called in an immediate response from patrol officers when he saw a commotion inside the bar; they were on their way when he was shot."

I swallow hard as the floor feels like it's moving beneath me. Wiping my hand over my face, I stare at my captain but can't form the words. The fucking earth-shattering rage is clouding any reasonable thought. Pulling me towards a chair, he gestures for me to sit. Captain Dean follows suit as I do, placing his hat on the chair next to him. I lean forward, with my head in my hands as I try to process what the fuck could have happened in a few short minutes.

"Do we know who it was?" I numbly ask, trying to remain professional.

"No, I've sent Detective Wallace to interview Summer, but she's in a bad way."

My head snaps to his, "Was she…?"

He shakes his head in response.

"From what I can gather, she was in the car when the shooting began. Once the car left, she tried to stop the bleeding and called for help. Eventually, an off-duty nurse attended as they were waiting for the EMT's."

"Let me talk to her captain." I plead.

As his eyes move to the passing doctors and nurses, I feel the answer is one I won't fucking like.

"I can't allow that, Grey. If Strode was a target, then so are you. I cannot allow it."

I narrow my eyes slightly, trying to ease the tension in my fists, but I know I can't lose control right now. That's for later when I find out what the fuck really happened.

"What happens with the Harper case?"

"Right now, you can stay on it. But if you and Strode were right about Luca Bernardi being involved in this, we'll have to investigate other avenues."

My face contorts to that of disbelief, as the one person who knows what it's like to stare down the barrel of fucking mafia threats just backs down and rolls over like a fucking puppy before rising from his chair.

"He's in surgery. Once I have news, I'll let you know. But right now, I need you at home, and that's an order, Grey."

"Yes, sir," I mutter before pushing to my feet and heading back into the night.

Like fuck I'm going home. Prick.

Storming back through the hospital, I avoid the pity glances from the brass as I make my way to my car, I don't engage with anyone, whether I work with them or not. Pulling my phone from my pocket, I again listen to the voicemail. With no partner available and likely the captain has already warned everyone not to speak to me until we know if Strode will make it, I hit call and await an answer.

"If you're still in the city, meet me at O'Reilly's bar right now. I think I know how we can get around this little issue we have."

Desperate times indeed.

Summer 🖤

Thinking fast, I turn to the detective who's sat in the small hospital room with me, idly scrolling through his phone. While I know tensions are high now, this young man seems unfazed by the goings on, and I shamefully use it to my advantage.

"I really need to use the bathroom." I say in a weak, pathetic voice.

He looks up, awkwardly managing to avoid rolling his eyes.

"This way." he sighs before I stop him.

Clutching onto my stomach, I awkwardly look away.

"I'd really appreciate some privacy; I'm not feeling too good." I look his way and shrug slightly.

"Fine, hurry back." He doesn't even argue before sliding back into his chair and scrolling through his phone.

Well, that wasn't fucking hard.

Pulling the door open. Luckily, I manage to avoid any passing doctors and nurses who are too busy with their rounds and other patients to pay me any attention. Putting my head down, I manage to pass the police captain while he's deep in conversation with other members of the police department. As I leave the ward, I give one final look, confirming I'm not being watched or followed, before picking up the pace and heading for the parking lot.

He only left a minute before me; he has to still be here.

Scanning the area, I don't see him, and it doesn't fucking help. I barely remember what car I'm looking for. Eyeing the exit sign, I consciously decide to head there in the hope he'll see me before he leaves. I'm assuming Detective Strode called him before he was shot, so Bhodi knows exactly what happened. With the situation just happening, no one had a chance to speak with me. They wanted a doctor to check me first, but I didn't have time to waste. Bhodi needs to know that Alex is the one who caused this.

Finally reaching the car park exit, I eye a black Mustang as it begins to move through the lot. Squinting, I begin to move closer to the vehicle.

"What the fuck are you doing?" I halt in my tracks as the headlights shine bright, causing me to throw my hand up.

"Bhodi?" I ask, slowly lowering my hand.

He stands by the running car, taking a moment to observe my blood-stained clothes. I watch as any hint of warmth seems to leave his body, leaving nothing but a cold scowl as I stand only a few meters away.

"Go home, Summer."

"I can't do that; I saw what happened." I plead, moving closer until he's within reaching distance. "I know who it was. You need me right now."

Running a hand through his hair, the conflict etched across his face. The silence fills the parking lot. I finally let out the breath I was holding as he nods, gesturing for me to get in the car. Pulling open the door, I slide in as he tears from the parking lot and back onto the main street.

Weaving in and out of traffic, I clutch onto the seat. My fingers dig into the leather as drivers jump on their horns. Side-eyeing Bhodi, he seems unfazed by the anger from other drivers, and all things considered, there are a lot more pressing issues to discuss.

As the lights ahead turn red, the vehicle begins to slow before coming to a halt. I manage to relax a little, watching him pull out his phone and typing a quick message before we speed off again. We continue our silent drive with my back pressed hard into the leather. After a few moments, I turn to him with a questioning look when the familiar surroundings of the street ahead come into view.

"What the fuck are we doing here?" I snap, looking up at my father's apartment.

"You're gonna tell me what happened, then head into your apartment and lock the door like a good girl." He speaks with a sarcastic coldness that makes me want to slap him hard across the face.

Feeling the anger building within me, I push the door open and move for the apartment as fast as my legs will carry me. I faintly hear him call out, but he's the same as the rest of the cops from today. That silent look of blame and disapproval towards me because of what happened.

Slamming my fist onto the button for the penthouse, the doors for the elevator open immediately. Launching myself into the confined space, I catch sight of Bhodi approaching fast in the mirror before eagerly pressing the button again, allowing the doors to close. Leaning back into the hard surface, I breathe a sigh of relief as it begins to carry me to the top floor. I look up, counting all the passing floor before mine nears. Once the doors slowly open, I dart to the front door of the apartment before punching in the new code and shoving the door open. Silently thanking Two/Face for the new codes, else this would have been more fucking awkward being locked out and stuck with a pissed-off Detective Grey.

As the second elevator doors open, I manage to slam the door shut as his pissed-off face appears. I take a few steps back and watch the door as the footsteps approach. I feel a pang of want run through my body as he eventually knocks, but my irritation doesn't allow my feet to move forward.

As he knocks again, I find my memories taking me back to a few hours earlier. The moments when I was screaming in the street for help and pleading with people to call an ambulance. The guilt washes over me, forcing me towards the door and swinging it open. Still unable to meet his gaze.

"What happened?" he asks numbly.

Taking a deep breath, I look to the ground.

"The guy at the bar was Alex. He got angry when I tried to leave the bar. When Detective Strode pulled me out of there..." Wiping away my hot tears, I continue. "That's when the shooting started. I couldn't see who it was, though. But I know he had called Harry and let him know where I was."

Managing to look into his eyes, the darkness is back. He doesn't blink. He shows no emotion. He just reaches for the door and pulls it closed. As the light from the hall fades, I stand alone, only hearing his retreating footsteps head for the elevator.

Bhodi 🧿

A shadow passes the doorway of the isolated warehouse. Sliding on my leather gloves, I don't bother looking to the person standing a few feet away. As the material glides over my skin, I flex my fingers, stretching the fabric. I don't want a fucking audience; I just want answers. I know Alex will sing like a fucking canary. Pieces of shit always think they'll get away with their underhand actions unscathed, but this time he won't.

"I'll do this alone." I say, moving from the old, abandoned workshop and into the main area.

The only noises around are the slow dripping from a nearby pipe and Alex's pathetic whimpering as he sits bound to a chair in the centre. Rolling my eyes, I slowly approach, watching with amusement as his head darts all around, trying to locate the source of the footsteps.

"Please, I didn't do anything…. you have the wrong person!" His snivelling pleas of innocence echoing off the walls.

Without hesitation, I backhand him hard enough that he falls, falling to his side with a thud as he continues.

"Please, I'll tell you anything."

I smirk again, pulling the chair upright and ripping off the blindfold. Crouching down, I study his face for a moment as he looks at me, his eyes widening in fear.

"Who…Who the fuck are you?" He stutters as the sweat forms on his brow.

"I want to know why you called Harry Maine today?" I ask calmly.

His chest heaves and his eyes wander to the bench a few feet away filled with tools. As his eyes land on a large meat cleaver, his fearful gaze is snatched back to mine.

"Are you….Are…..Are you going to kill me?"

"Should I?"

Tears begin to fall, and his face contorts as the snot begins to pour from his nose.

"He came to the bar the other day. He said he'd pay anyone five grand if Summer came by. All we had to do was keep her there long enough for someone to come and pick her up…. but I swear I had no idea why."

Gripping his chin tight, I lean in close, spitting venom as his lies pour out.

"You had no fucking idea? Are you that fucking thick, you didn't think maybe he was a dangerous man? Seeing as her fucking father was just murdered?" Shoving him away, the snivelling continues.

"I didn't know he was going to hurt that cop!"

"How'd you know he was a cop?"

"Harry was talking about it when I asked him for my money."

"So, you even went after him for payment, even though you didn't fulfil your end of the deal?" I ask sarcastically. "You really are a special kind of thick cunt aren't you?"

Cocking my fist back, I land one right on his jaw, causing the chair to fly back.

Before he can react, I pull the chair back up and continue the assault over and over. Once the blood begins to slide down his cheek and his eye bulges, I momentarily step away. Moving to the workbench filled with tools, I glance over the array of steel and blades. Allowing my fingers to glide over each item, I find my hand landing on a pair of secateurs. Lifting them into the light, I study the item as my lips curl into a half smile.

"Oh god...NO! PLEASE.....FUUUUCK!"

Turning back to Alex, I shake my head. Throwing my hands in the air, I can't help but laugh.

"No one can fucking hear you, why else would you be here?"

As his eyes drop to the floor, he finally spots all the dried, smeared blood that's soaked into the concrete over time. I watch with joy as the cogs turn in his tiny incompetent brain, piecing it all together.

Moving back towards him, I look into his eyes. He sits like a rabbit in the headlights, and as I reach for his hand, he tries to fight me, but there's no point. As I manage to get the first finger between the blades, I halt for a moment, holding his gaze before squeezing tight. The crunching of bone pierces my ears, followed by a satisfying shriek of agony.

"Next time, when you try and make a quick buck, don't hitch your wagon to a cunt like Harry Maine, do you understand?" I lean in, almost whispering in his ear as his entire body convulses in pain.

He nods through the pain, squeezing his eyes shut as the sweat and blood pours from his body.

"Right, so we'll try this again."

His eyes snap to mine once again.

"Wait...What?" The panic spreads across his face, but I squeeze hard on the second finger before he can register. This time, vomit sprays from his mouth, spattering on the floor as I take a step back.

"Now, what did we learn today, Alex?"

His shrieks of pain continue to echo off the walls, his garbled words begin to morph into incoherent shit.

"If you can't remember, we'll only have to do this again." I warn him.

"Don't trust Harry Maine." He cries out.

Cocking my head to one side, I shake my head.

"No, no, no, you see, I said, 'Next time, when you try and make a quick buck, don't hitch your wagon to a cunt like Harry Maine', you're not very good at this, Alex, and you only have eight fingers left."

"NO…NO…. NOOOOOO!!!!!!"

As the third finger lands on the cold concrete floor, followed by more vomit and other bodily fluids, I shake my head in disapproval.

"I think you need a break. You clearly really have a bad fucking memory" Pushing myself back up, I move back to the workbench, drowning out the retching and sobs coming from behind me.

"She's just some dumb fucking slut! Let him have her!" he spits out. Clearly, adrenaline is beginning to kick in for him.

Turning on my heels, I stalk over. Leaning forward, I quietly ask.

"What was that?"

"If he wants her so fucking bad, let him have the dumb slut! She fucking …"

Before he can finish the sentence, I drive the butcher knife into his throat. His eyes go wide, and his entire body shakes as he struggles for breath. Pushing the knife in further with great force, I feel the blade cutting further through his flesh and windpipe.

Studying the sight before me as the life begins to drain from his eyes, I lean in close.

"I didn't ask for your fucking advice."

Slowly pulling the blade out, I watch with intent as his face changes from red to purple, blood pooling down his shirt as his pathetic attempts for breath continues. Shaking off the blade, the thick crimson liquid spatters along the floor, and I wait patiently while the warehouse returns to its previous silence.

After a moment, I toss the knife back down onto the bench. Throwing the gloves into the metal drum nearby, I slide my phone from my back pocket. Pushing open the heavy doors, I take in the night sky as the phone rises to my ear.

"Yeah, I'm done." Before hanging up.

Summer 🖤

Sitting on the sofa, I lean forward. My elbows placed on my thighs; I nervously pick at my thumb with my forefinger. My mind lost in the darkness behind Bhodi's eyes. A Look I didn't recognize, a numbness consumed him. I anxiously slide my phone over, but as soon as the screen lights up, there's no message, no calls, and no word at all about what's going on.

Detective Wallace eventually tracked me down and berated me for leaving the hospital, nothing to do with the fact he was likely scrolling through Tinder for hours before realizing I hadn't come back. Using the situation to my advantage, I explained I was in shock and went home as I didn't feel safe. He must have felt bad after that. He took a small statement and didn't stay long. However, he did remind me not to go anywhere.

Like I have anywhere to even go.

I sigh. A knot the size of a rock sits in the pit of my stomach. Taking a couple of deep breaths, I force myself from my seat. Aimlessly walking around the vacant apartment, my mind swims through what Bhodi could be doing right now, where he is, and whether he found Alex. Unable to process a reasonable thought, I brace my palms onto the kitchen island. The ongoing chaos feeling like an overwhelming permanent nightmare I'm stuck in.

He's right, I need to stay away from Detective Grey.

Two/Face's words sting my ears, and guilt consumes me. The fear of what could happen to Bhodi is just like detective Strode. Glancing down at my clothes, my heart sinks. Bunching the stained wool in my fists, I stretch the fabric out and look to the blood which dried hours ago.

Dragging my feet towards the bathroom and flicking the light on, I see the full extent of the dried blood smears that mark my clothes. Frantically pulling my dress over my head, I throw all my clothes into a pile on the floor, the suffocating fabric feeling like a vice wrapped tight around my entire body.

Stepping across the cool tiles, I slide the shower door open. Pulling on the chrome taps, I step back, allowing the water to hit the shower tray. Once the steam appears, I gently run my hand under it, checking the temperature.

Standing under the water, I allow the warmth to engulf my body. Glancing down, I shudder at the water that runs down the plug hole, a gentle shade of pink. Pulling my gaze away, I reach for the soap. Lathering it in my hands, I allow my hands to gently roam my body, trying to remove any trace of the last few hours. Reaching for the shampoo, a click snaps my head toward the bathroom door.

A chill fills the room. Slowly rising my hand to the screen, I wipe away the steam. As the figure appears, I gasp. Sliding the door open, I see the vacant look. Wiping the water from my face, I quietly whisper.

"Bhodi?"

His eyes meet mine, and a chill sweeps over me in an instant. Taking a single step forward, he doesn't speak. Spotting the blood stains over his clothes, my eyes widen. My heartbeat increasing rapidly, and looking back at him, my brow furrows.

"Whose blood is that?" Keeping my voice low, I move a little closer.

He shrugs and I feel my body pushing me to get even closer. Reaching out, my shaky hand cups his cheek. I watch as he leans into my touch. A moment of warmth flickers across his cold, gorgeous features. But he just shrugs again. The unanswered question lingers in the air.

I continue to search his face, a vulnerability stares back at me. My gaze wanders his frame. Stepping onto my tiptoes, I push his leather jacket from his shoulders. As it hits the floor with a jolt, I reach for the hem of his t-shirt, but it's too late. I feel his hand snap around my wrist, pulling me closer, our bodies colliding. A gasp escapes me as my body is pressed into his.

Bhodi's lips crash to mine, his strong hands grip the back of my thighs, while his tongue dominates mine. Lifting me, I wrap my legs around his waist, my already aching core gently rubbing onto the zipper of his jeans. His large erection strained against the denim. I moan, grinding for more friction. The kiss turns frantic. My hands run through his hair as he walks towards the sink. Feeling my ass land on the sink unit, the feel of cool marble against my flesh takes me by surprise.

Releasing me, I pull again at the hem of his t-shirt. Pulling it over his head, throwing it to one side, and frantically kicking away his boots, Bhodi reaches for the belt of his jeans. Taking a step closer, my thighs are spread wide, gently leaning back on my palms as his broad frame moves over my body. My breath catches in my throat; he doesn't speak, but the once cold look in his eyes is now ablaze. His eyes never leave mine. Pushing his jeans and boxers past his muscular thighs, we both stand naked in the bathroom.

Reaching for my wrist, his fingers lace around my skin, guiding me towards him. Laying the thick hard flesh in my hands, my eyes widen when my fingers wrap around him.

Jesus fucking Christ....

My jaw falls open, but Bhodi's face remains unreadable. I swear, briefly, I could see his lips discreetly curl into a quick smile. With my fingers laced around his thick cock, any other thought just completely fucks off from my mind. He's big, really big. So big I can barely wrap my hand around him entirely. But that doesn't stop that dull ache between my thighs, begging for some relief. The curiosity that swirls around in my mind, wondering what he'd feel like buried deep inside me and his large frame overtaking mine.

When my hand slides up his thick shaft, I watch as his chest rises and falls. The dried blood smeared over him should scare me, but it doesn't. I know what he's done was for the right reason. I can't say I wouldn't have done the same given the chance. Even if I'm yet to find out, what he has actually done.

The feeling of his palms sliding up my thighs sends another shiver through me; my back arches, and my thighs slide open wider than before. Guiding the head of his cock to my slick pussy, rolling my bottom lip between my teeth, I lean in, taking a gentle inhale before allowing my eyes to flutter to Bhodi's.

"Fuck me." I plead in a breathy whisper.

When his palms slap to my thighs, jerking me forward. I cry out. I cry out hard. My head falls back into the mirror, and my eyes roll back as the intense sensation surges through me. I can't form words. Only a garbled animalistic sound of pleasure can escape my throat. Bhodi's palms snake around my waist, sliding me towards him. I wrap my legs tight around his waist as the second thrust comes. Jerking me forward, I cry out again. Once he's fully inside me, he stills for a moment. Adjusting to his size, I pant.

There's a momentary stillness between us, and a silence quickly falls around the space. With his fingers pressed into my thighs, he roughly slides me off the cool surface. Snaking my arms around his neck, he turns and heads for the running shower.

When my back hits the cool tiles, my head falls onto his shoulder. Shuffling my hips, I try to adjust to his size further. Everything fits so painfully, yet so beautifully. With my hands on his firm, strong shoulders for guidance, the water cascades over us, washing away the dry blood off his golden skin. As my hips roll, I grit my teeth as the intense pleasure surges through me, pushing me to carry on.

Straightening my back, my nails digging into Bhodi's shoulders. He leans in closer, and when his eyes flutter open, the darkness resumes.

"Harder!"

I still at the command, but the want and dominance in his tone sends a jolt of confidence through me.

Tightening my thighs around his waist, using his shoulders for support. I allow my hips to roll over and over, as the bathroom begins to fill with each cry of pleasure. Each passing moment begins to send me into a frenzy, picking up the pace I hear him mutter as my head flies into the tiles, my eyes squeeze shut as all the sensations coursing through my body begin to collide.

"Fuck…" Bhodi slams his palms into the bathroom wall, his body rigid as I continue to ride him hard.

When the deep aching sensation begins to whirl in the pit of my stomach, I pick up the pace. My nails leaving deep red marks on his shoulders.

"Shit…I'm…I…" I can't get the words out, my body carries on, and I'm unable to stop or even allow myself to finish the sentence.

My orgasm crashes through me so fucking hard, my arms fly around his neck, holding on for dear life as my cries likely flood his ears. I feel my pussy contract, clamping down hard, but I can't stop. It's just too fucking good. In a euphoric daze, I hear a low growl when his palms clamp tight around my thighs.

"I can't hold on…" Bhodi's voice is breathless, almost pained. Each thrust is hard and rough when my back connects hard into the tiles. His fingers squeezing into my skin so tight, I look forward to the purple bruises I'll see tomorrow, reminding me of a night when I felt normal for once.

Feeling him come deep inside of me, the deep roar that escapes his throat elicits something in me that I can't explain. Maybe the feeling of being wanted? Maybe even desired? Whatever it is right now, I'll grab it with both hands and accept it willingly.

As my forehead falls to his, Bhodi's movements stagger. I feel us both sliding down the shower. As we land in the cool tiled floor, the water continues to rain down on us. He pulls me close, placing a gentle kiss on my forehead. Through each shaky breath, my eyes flutter close as he gently whispers to me.

"Thank you."

I lazily nod, his strong arms pulling me close, getting lost in our own peace.

Chapter Fifteen

Bhodi ⚥

Feeling a slight movement next to me, my eyes snap open immediately. Already on high alert, my eyes scan the dark room. I forget where I am or how I got here for a split second. But as my gaze lands on the blonde curls fanned across the pillow, I feel my heart rate settle. Last night's memories flood back instantly as I allow my head to gently fall back onto the soft pillow.

Laying on her side, Summer sleeps peacefully. I watch in awe as she breathes gently, lost in a warm slumber. I had no intention of staying, hell I don't even know why I fucking showed up. I just knew I wanted to see her, get lost in her, and forget the terrible things I had done. But that doesn't mean I regret killing Alex, I'll never regret that. Someone like him needed to be stopped without question.

I left the mess in the warehouse for someone else to sort out. I knew if I had stayed, I'd begin to feel myself spiral, second-guessing and questioning myself, and I don't need that right now. I can't deny Summer does something to me. From the first moment

I saw her picture in Michael's office, I felt a pull I couldn't explain. I'd never had that before, the desire to be near someone. The bright smile from the photo seemed to offer so much hope and wonder, that I couldn't seem to pull my eyes away.

Growing up, I had no friends. There was nothing wrong with me as a kid, but when your mom is a drug addict along with her abusive boyfriend, it's not something you want banded around school. Kids can be cruel, and I didn't need them having that ammunition. Instead, I chose to read. I'd climb a tree near my mom's place and get lost in a book for hours. There's something about your imagination that makes you believe anything is possible at that age. Back then, I had a slither of hope that maybe one day she would change, break the habit, get herself cleaned up, and become the parent I always wanted.

Life doesn't give you what you want most of the time and the dull ache in my heart begins to feel unbearable as I lay on my back. My gaze fixed on the ceiling as the hideous memory passes through my mind. I feel a tight knot form in my throat, and my eyes blur with tears as the screams pierce my ears. My guilt consumes me...

I should have done more...

That small phrase haunts me. Each night I close my eyes, it rears its ugly head, taunting me further, and makes sure I never forget what a terrible son I was. Maybe that's why I've chosen the path that I have, taking bad people off the streets so they can never torment and terrorize another soul again. But even I know all the good in the world cannot forgive my own mistake, I was only fourteen when it happened. My entire world crashed at my feet, but guilt doesn't have an age restriction. It eats at your soul, gnawing away like a curse.

Unable to sleep, I roll onto my side. Whilst the bed is incredibly comfortable, I know my mind is far too alert and on edge to allow me to sleep. I know Alex's death would never be traced to me, and that doesn't bother me too much. What bothers me is the same question that I ask myself over and over.

Will I ever have a normal life?

For ten or so years, the career path I chose has been hectic, long, and drawn out. My childhood years were full of misery and abuse. My teenage years weren't much better, but as a teenager, I filled out a little and learned to look out for myself. I became street smart which helped with my NYPD career. But I'd always had this dream of walking into my home. My wife would turn around with a bright smile because I was home, and we'd dance slowly to Frank Sinatra in the kitchen as we prepared dinner.

The thought always brought a glimmer of hope to me, hoping one day I could have exactly that. Someone could show me how to love, show me affection, kindness, and warmth, something I'm all too aware my dark soul lacks. My biggest fear of all, is that once everything is said and done, I'll end up alone. The only thing keeping me company is fading memories of the horrific acts I've committed, along with the screams of so many who dared to escape justice.

Some may say that's perfect; you've made a difference and should be proud. Maybe so? But not me. I know there's far more to life than what I have right now. I just have to work on it and not allow myself to fall down a black hole where I lack empathy and love. A few weeks ago, this wouldn't have crossed my mind. I would have just carried on, because I didn't know any different. But with Summer walking into my life, even under the tragic circumstances, I just can't seem to allow this to pass me by, no matter how anyone else feels about it.

Taking one final look towards Summer's peaceful form, I savour the moment. Making a note of each freckle on her nose, how her delicate features are resting, how she sleeps with one arm under the pillow, and how, even when she's in a deep sleep, she's so breathtakingly beautiful. It is so delicate and so peaceful, and I feel a warmth pull at my cold heart. As though someone is trying to remind me that it is still, in fact, there and beating.

Sliding from the bed, I briefly turn back to ensure I haven't woken her up. Moving through the apartment I find my clothes strewn across the bathroom floor. Quickly getting dressed, I pull my phone from my pocket, but to my surprise, there's no messages. My shoulders sag slightly when there's no news on Strode's condition yet, knowing I've been told to go home and stay there for now, I doubt they would have sent anyone to check on me.

Turning in the mirror and spotting the blood that's still stained on my T-shirt, I opt for heading home and burning it all. As my mind begins to swarm, I know the best thing for me to do right now is leave. I feel my fists clench at my own fucking stupidity, thinking with my dick and not my brain. I've now done exactly the opposite of what I told Strode. I've crossed that fucking line and made things far more complicated. How stupid was I to ever think this could end happily, she's about to bury her father for fuck's sake and all I've done is send mixed signals because I'm incapable of functioning like a normal human being.

As my head falls back, I let out a heavy sigh. Shaking my head, I move quickly from the apartment and back towards my car. Unable to shake the guilty feeling that follows me.

Summer ♥

When my palm connects with the cool bedsheets, my eyes flutter open. My brows pinch, spotting the empty space beneath my hand. Pulling myself up into the sitting position, I can't help but feel disappointed that I have woken up alone. Letting out an exaggerated huff, I fall back onto the pillow, unsure what I'm disappointed about right now. The fact that Bhodi has left, or the fact that I allowed myself to open up for a brief moment of intimacy that I wasn't forced or guilted into.

Either way, I feel it. I feel unbelievable disappointment and confusion all rolled into one, gliding right over my soul. As my eyes focus on the ceiling, I shake my head, knowing if I allow this to consume me, it'll do exactly that, and right now, I don't have the time for his games, and I don't need them. Taking back some control, I reach for my phone off the bedside table. Scrolling through my contacts, I opt for making plans today instead of wallowing. Tapping on Jame's name, I open a new message.

Hey, are you free for lunch today? Sorry it's short notice. I understand if you have plans.

The response comes after a few long minutes. Opening the reply, I feel the smile pull on my lips.

Morning Summer, sure thing! Come by the office around midday. I know a good place.

I don't know if that's what James meant by *"Call me if you need anything."* But right now, I really need a friend. Plus, it'll give me a chance to discuss a couple of lingering topics that I have been on my mind since I found out about my dad's will.

Feeling a little more positive about the day ahead, I head for the shower. Tapping the coffee machine on the way, I begin to play some Guns and Roses loudly as the water falls over me. Refusing to be a victim to anyone any longer, I make a mental note here and now that this is where it ends.

With my new positive mindset in full force, I finish getting ready, spraying some hairspray into my freshly styled loose curls, giving them a little tussle and zipping up my boots. Applying a fresh coat of nude lipstick onto my lips, I take a step back. My cozy, warm outfit suiting the chilly New York weather perfectly.

Over the knee, black boots, thick warm leggings, and an oversized black jumper. Giving a little spin in the mirror, I reach for my long, thick grey wool coat and purse, heading out into the busy street. As the wind blows, I gently push the hair from my face.

When my gaze wanders to my surroundings, my feet pick up the pace, walking to James's office with a purpose. With the weight of my own misery beginning to lift a little off my shoulders, I allow myself to smile for a change. I'm not in New York for a good reason at all but being here has allowed me to escape cruelty and abuse that I may have been stuck with else, and this is what I need to focus on right now. Doing right by my dad at his funeral and not allowing myself to ever go back and fall into the never-ending trap of fear.

For a moment, I grant myself that little bit of happiness, making a note that I'll never allow myself to be treated in such a way and never allow someone to do it. Finding a good pace, I eventually reach James's office just as he's locking the door behind him. Waiting at the bottom of the steps, I quickly glance around the street, preying nothing throws me off.

"Right on time!" James beams at me as he descends the stone steps of the well-presented brownstone. His navy blue suit and camel trench coat perfectly set off his sandy hair and hazel eyes.

"I felt like I needed the walk." I reply, smiling, as he pulls me into a quick hug.

"Well, I'm glad you called, it can't be easy in the penthouse alone. No matter how well appointed it is." He shrugs, but the comment leaves the hairs on the back of my neck on end.

I suppose the idea that people who I barely know, knows what the penthouse looks like. The thought on its own isn't a red flag, but a masked stalker just letting himself in without question and knowing how to change the codes causes that uneasy feeling to rise in my gut again.

"Hey Summer, are you ok?" James asks with concern, halting in the street for a moment.

Blinking a couple of times, I finally turn to him and pull myself from my mind. Nodding gently, I force a smile.

"Yeah, sorry. I guess it still feels strange being there when dad isn't." The left-hand side of my lip curls a little in a sorrowful gesture.

James's face instantly softens. Looking away for a moment, I also see the sadness in his eyes. But he merely nods, looping my arm in his, and he pulls me close. A smile pulls at his lips as he looks ahead.

"I understand, but you know I'm here to help you in any way I can. You aren't alone. I'll accept a lunch date with you whenever you need it." The words are kind and sincere, almost causing a knot in my throat at how warm someone you barely know can be towards you.

"Thank you, James. You really don't know how much I needed to hear that." I say, gently bumping his shoulder.

Stepping into the restaurant, we're quickly seated at a table by the window. I watch intently as amazing burgers are carried through to different tables, catching me following their journey. James lets out a small chuckle, causing my gaze to move to his.

"Hungry?" He asks, quirking a brow. Right on cue, my stomach grumbles.

As the slight blush creeps over my cheeks, I nod.

"I guess I've been skipping meals."

James blinks and looks away. When he turns back to me, his face is sombre and full of concern.

"I heard about Detective Strode Summer. I'm so sorry about that." Letting out a heavy sigh as he continues. "Do you know if he's ok?"

I shake my head no. But James leans in a little closer, lowering his voice. I feel myself lean in, too.

"What happened?"

Scratching my forehead, I briefly look out the window, trying to piece the evening back together without giving too much away. Remembering the gunshots and screams that flood the dark street, followed by the pool of blood I lay in while screaming for help. I try to shrug off the cries and pleads for help as I applied pressure to the wounds on Detective Strode. Shrugging slightly, I turn back to James who holds my gaze without blinking.

"I got into the passenger side of the car, and then all of a sudden, a car passed and started firing. I threw myself across the seats, my head in my hands as the endless bullets seemed to rain down over us." Swallowing hard, I continue. "Once they stopped, I think the car sped off. I remember hearing tyres screeching. When I threw open the car door, I fell into the road and landed in the blood. I knew it wasn't good." Wiping away a single tear, James places his hand over mine.

"Did the police take your statement?"

"Yes, I stupidly ran away from the hospital. I just couldn't be there; I went home and just stayed. The pissed-off detective eventually tracked me down and took the statement, but I didn't see anything of any use. It all happened so quickly."

James listens intently, but the warmth momentarily leaves his face. For a second, I almost feel like I'm being subtly interrogated. He clearly notices this and smiles, but it's forced this time, and I shift uncomfortably under his gaze.

"Sorry, Summer." He leans back in his chair, running a hand across his face. "I spent so many years prepping clients for trial, I've forgotten how to have a normal conversation with someone that doesn't end with me pulling answers from them."

"You were a prosecutor?" I ask, a little surprised by his comment.

"Once upon a time yeah." Hearing the relief in his voice, I'm unsure whether to ask why he changed his career path.

"What made you change?" I ask curiously, realizing my mouth engaged before my brain.

"I found that sometimes, no matter how hard you work to seek justice that sometimes the law isn't on your side. I realized there are just some truly bad people in the world that should never be allowed back onto the streets. I just couldn't carry on; it weighed too heavily on my moral compass, so I decided to leave." There's a solemness in James's words, unsure whether I want to ask more questions. After a moment, I decide against it, nodding my head in agreement I strangely understand what he means.

Studying James's face, I see that his features are sharp, and he has a strong jaw. But after his brief declaration, I can see how his previous job has taken a toll on him. On closer inspection, he looks tired and worn out, as though he's carried the world on his shoulders for a long time. I suppose a high-pressure job like that can do that to you, along with the long days and late nights.

The waitress eventually passes by and takes our order. Clearly, we're both starving and end up ordering the same thing. The conversation falls onto the funeral as a cold shudder rolls over me. Every now and then, the news of my dad's passing hits me like a runaway train; it's as though my mind is aware, but my heart is playing catch up all the time. But it's his murder that leaves me angry and fearful, with detective Strode in the hospital and Bhodi seems to have his mind elsewhere, I worry that it'll never get solved, and I'll never know why someone could be some heartless to a kind and loving man who never did a bad thing in his life.

Saying our goodbye's, James and I part ways. As he disappears out of sight, I feel my confidence falter a little as the afternoon sky appears to darken. Understanding I'm still in an unknown city, I opt for a taxi back home instead of the walk. I seem to walk into bad choices and regrettable decisions permanently, so maybe the walk home isn't a bright choice for me.

After the short drive home, I step into reception as the concierge nods to me. Offering a polite smile, I don't stop until I reach the elevator and the doors open immediately. Allowing me to step inside and hit the penthouse button, I feel my body sag against the mirror as my eyes watch the passing floor numbers. When the doors finally open, I reach the front door and punch in the new code, silently thanking Two/Face again for his awareness, even though I'd never fucking admit to it.

Pushing open the front door, I see that the apartment, like always, is dark. Locking the door behind me, I place my purse on the side table and allow my back to fall against the solid wood. When my head falls back, I take a deep inhale.

Oh shit...

As the adrenaline begins to pump through my body, my head snaps straight ahead to the living room as the end of a cigarette lights up, the smell wafting through the hall.

"Welcome home, Summer. Have a nice day?"

His words drip with a devilish sarcasm. I watch as the end of the cigarette lights up once again, but I can't move my feet. My brain is screaming to fucking run. If I run now, I'll likely get to the elevator in time, but I don't. Instead, I feel my body being pulled towards the dark reaper, walking into his darkness, and I do so without question.

Chapter Sixteen

TWO/FACE \

Exhaling the cigarette smoke and watching it disperse through the dark living room, my lips curl into a smile as Summer hesitantly moves towards me. I knew in that split second what she was thinking, the way her head dropped towards the open space, the wonder in her eyes when she could smell the cigarettes, and then came the initial panic. Her body went into a brief fight-flight mode. Her brain teased her, making her think there was a chance she could get away, but luckily, she chose wisely.

Laying her long coat on the back of the sofa, she stands a few feet from me. Sitting in the chair by the window, my legs splayed while I enjoy my cigarette. She doesn't speak, but the questions are written all over her beautiful face. But she's probably wondering what I have planned for her by now. That would be a great question, but not one I'm going to answer. That needs time and a little more work first, but when I'm finished, she can have exactly what she wants: a clean slate and the truth.

I'll at least have the decency to offer her everything, the truth she needs, and maybe some things she doesn't. The truth about her father, the kind of man he truly was, who killed him, and what we are going to do about that. It's common knowledge now the police are shit out of luck. With one of their own shot and the police captain nervous about pursuing Luca Bernardi, it's obviously up to me.

I've wanted a shot at Luca for a long time, but Michael was always very aware of how dangerous he was and how he was connected to many crime families here within the city. I didn't give a fuck, but that's why Michael was the sensible one.

"Don't be so fucking reckless Two. We've gotten away with this for so long because we're smart." He'd say more often than not.

That's why he was the brains and not me. Michael was clever and planned everything. He knew what we did had risks but did it anyway. He felt in some strange way, that he was doing some good in the world. I guess we were helping those who were failed by the justice system. Helping those who were ignored and cast aside, our own trauma of our pasts guiding us towards the bright light of redemption.

Lord knows we all fucking need it. This life isn't without sacrifices. Even if the way we go about it is twisted, I don't have any regrets.

"What do you want?" Summer's voice is irritated, and she keeps her distance, but the question is clipped.

I'm starting to feel her confidence coming back, and I like it. It's what I wanted, for her to become a human again, not some fucking shell of a side piece, accepting scraps off that cunt Harry and being grateful when he doesn't lay his hands on her.

Lifting my eyes to meet her accusatory glare, I see the hesitation flicker in hers. Her confidence faltering for a moment when she sees the mask, she knows why I'm here; I warned her, and she didn't listen, but she still has time in New York before she leaves forever.

"You didn't listen to me, Summer." I rise to my full height and watch as she lifts her chin to hold my gaze.

Summer swallows hard before looking away. Knowing she's been caught, she doesn't try to hide it. When she turns back to me, her face is unreadable. Tugging her teeth between her bottom lip, she slowly nods.

"I didn't."

"And why is that?" I cock my head to one side, speaking calmly. I lure her into a false sense of security.

Moving closer, she continues to hold my gaze. Her body sways seductively, her eyes filled with curiosity and wonder while she begins to play a game of her own. Pressing her body into mine, she waits for my reaction, a little disappointed when I don't step back. Raising slightly on her tiptoes, she speaks softly into my ear.

"Because, who I fuck, has nothing to do with you."

My hand is around her throat before she can back away, her nails clawing into my wrist as I slam her against the wall.

"Who you fuck is my business. It's my business when I fucking warned you, and it's certainly my business when you put people's lives in danger!" Her eyes widen in worry as I continue, "You think Harry and Luca won't go after Detective Grey now? They already got to Strode. From what I hear, he's barely holding on in that hospital."

Squeezing a little harder, I watch her pupils dilate, and the vein in her temple pulsate. Easing the pressure a little, I feel her body sag and pull her towards me.

"I told you; I don't like people touching what's mine." I search her curious eyes for a moment. "Eventually, Summer, I will fuck you. You'll beg me, those deep blue eyes will plead with mine, your breathy pleas will flood my ears, and I'll indulge your curiosity. I can't guarantee you'll like what you see, but I know when I sink my big cock into you over and over again and you writhe beneath me, you'll never forget me."

I hold her gaze. Her soft pink pouty lips let out a low breath, her body giving far too much away that her mind is kicking her for. I feel her thighs rub together. I know she hates herself for how much she wants me and how much her morbid curiosity towards me turns her on. I can almost see her soul trying to claw its way from her body.

I smirk beneath the darkness. Pushing away from the wall I release Summer's throat. She staggers slightly before bracing herself against the wall, coughing a couple of times.

"And what if I don't want that?" She stands defiantly, watching as I move towards the exit. I feel the grin spread across my face as I turn to face her.

"You will, when you see the lengths, I'll go to to protect you and keep you safe."

"Did you kill my dad?"

I halt at her question; it takes me by surprise as the chill rushes over me but it's soon replaced with hot rage. Clenching my fists, I take a deep breath, half turning my head towards her.

"No, but I knew him." I reply bluntly.

Summer 🖤

The door slams shut behind him, I clutch to the wall and refuse to allow my knees to give way. The dull ache between my thighs becomes unbearable as my lace thong clings to my skin.

That fucking bastard

I sigh. Yet again, our interaction just wields more questions than fucking answers. Do I believe he killed my dad? No, but he knows who did and is fucking toying with me. He never tells me what he wants, not really, and never tells me why he's here.

Moving to the sofa, my head falls into my palms while my mind whirls with all the fucking questions. Massaging my temples, I relieve some of the building pressure. I feel the frustration of being kept in the dark, which is beginning to chew away at my soul.

I jump to my feet as a harsh knock penetrates through the front door. With my eyes fixed on the figure underneath the door, I wait.

Two/Face wouldn't knock...

He'd just fucking appear like the ghost he is, no this isn't him, and it's not Bhodi. He somehow managed to get in last night without warning. Whoever is standing on the other side of the door isn't someone I have invited. Swallowing hard, I quickly realize.

Harry.

As my entire body deflates and the slow knocks continue, I cautiously step the door, making sure not to make any noise while I move closer to Harry. I freeze once I hear his voice taunting me through the door.

"Suuuuummmmeerrrrrr." He sings eerily through the door. "The funeral is in a couple of days, my love; I'll be seeing you real soon." He sniggers, and I watch as the shadow moves away from the door.

A cold sweat falls over my skin, and my stomach twists and turns with how relentless Harry truly is. I know he wants revenge because I fled to New York. I know he is the reason Detective Strode is lying in a hospital bed. I don't trust that he won't cause trouble at the funeral; hell, I don't even think he won't try and hurt someone else.

Shit.

Pulling my phone from my purse, I unlock it. Scrolling through looking for Bhodi's number, my finger hovers over the call button once it appears on the screen. I hesitate for a moment, unsure of what I'm meant to fucking say? I've never told him about Two/Face before or anything that's happened between us, probably because it sounds fucking insane, and I'm crazy for allowing it to continue.

Plus, it would then open up Bhodi to whatever Two/Face is into, and I can't have that. He's right. This won't end well. But if I stay away, that could ensure his safety. Throwing the phone back down onto the glass table in front of me, I allow my head to fall back onto the sofa. The silence in the apartment consuming me.

Chapter Seventeen

TWO/FACE ⚔

"Shit." Jimmy's muttering pulls my focus from the dive bar to him. Shooting him a questioning look, he sighs. Locking his phone and sliding it back into his pocket, he shakes his head. "Nothing, it's fine."

"If there's a fucking problem, Jimmy. Just say it. I don't have time for this shit." I spit out, feeling impatient and already pissed off.

I'm stuck out here in the freezing cold, picking up scum off the streets.

"Harry went to the apartment again. The alarm was triggered when he tried putting in an incorrect code, but don't worry. She didn't answer the door."

My head snaps to his, the seething anger beginning to pulse through me.

"What the fuck did you just say?"

"Look, it's fine, he left."

"Are you fucking kidding me? He's terrorizing her, yet we're stuck here dealing with this shit."

Jimmy turns to me, his usual calm demeanor changing in an instant. There's a chill to his voice, the weight, and risk of what we do continuing to have a hold over him.

"No one fucking begged you to be here, Two, we each have our reasons, and I'll be fucking damned if we let this piece of shit go home to his wife pissed and fucking rape her again." He gestures towards the dive bar entrance.

"Look, I can hear all the shit you're spouting from that van. Mind shutting the fuck up? Hard to concentrate when I have the nerd and the fucking cowboy complaining in my ear." Axe chimes through the earpiece.

Jimmy shakes his head, letting out a small sarcastic chuckle as I turn my attention back towards the bar. The street outside is quiet. The occasional engine backfiring and feral dogs is all that can be heard this time of night. Lucky for us, this bar stays open all hours. It's not exactly a salubrious establishment, so it's perfect to pick up this package.

"Just keep your eyes on the target, Axe."

"Not hard. He's been ploughing through a bottle of Jack since seven. I'll probably have to carry this fucking idiot out myself, that's if he doesn't start a fight beforehand."

"If he does, just pull him out, like the good Samaritan you are." I quip sarcastically.

"Pull him out by his fucking hair, maybe." He mumbles back.

Ignoring Axe, I settle into my seat. Knowing full well this could carry on for hours, this is probably the worst part of each job. Especially now I know that cunt Harry is lurking around the apartment again. This clown is fucking relentless with Summer. Part of me wonders if he's just torturing her because he can. He enjoys the terror he inflicts and the fear she feels whenever he's nearby.

I smile silently, knowing that's exactly what I've been doing. I had no intention of ever seeing Summer, but once I laid eyes on her, I just had to know her. I needed to meet her, speak to her, and listen to her voice. I had no idea why because this would never work. How could it? I'm a killer, and she's the unfortunate collateral in her father's murder.

Each time I enter that apartment, the air smells of her. I sit patiently in the armchair by the window. I smoke my cigarettes, knowing all too well she'll smell them. The smell will put her on high alert. The adrenaline will begin to pump through her body, her brain will begin to convince her she can escape. But we both know she doesn't want to; she wants to see what lurks beneath the mask.

Each interaction we have confuses her more, making her question what's right and wrong. I can't think about the future, likely because I have no intention of making it. This work is dangerous and dirty, with far too many risks.

"he's heading out the side door now. Keep an eye on him. I'm not far behind." As soon as I hear Axe's words, the door to the bar opens, and a dishevelled drunk stumbles out.

"Great, gotta deal with some fucking pissed moron." I mumble.

"Problem?" Jimmy quirks a brow.

"No, they just always think they're invincible after a couple of drinks."

"He's had more than a couple."

Switching on the ignition, the rickety van rumbles to life. Looking towards the target again, the noise of the van hasn't alerted him to our presence. Likely, he's paying no attention to what's happening around him.

"Sooooo..." I glance at Jimmy, who's running through the target file. "Finn Reid, thirty-seven years old. Just acquitted for the rape and violent assault against his wife Sarah, after she refused to testify in court."

I shake my head, trying not to let my eyes roll. It's not that I don't have empathy for victims because I do. It's the anger I feel towards people who prey on the vulnerable, manipulating them for their own gain, traumatizing them over and fucking over again because they're just shells. Shells waiting to be swept away, when the fucking predator has no use for them or finds a new victim to torment.

"How did we come by this one?"

"Our good friend at the women's shelter witnessed Finn hanging around but never saw him interact with Sarah. She refused to testify in court a day later and went back to him."

"Why are we here, though? We can't force her to testify. We usually only deal with victims who want justice?" I ask curiously.

"A week ago, she came back to the shelter. Sarah took another severe beating and ended up being taken to the hospital. When she was there, they told her she was pregnant." Jimmy answers solemnly.

"Fuck..." I mutter, keeping my eyes on Finn as he stumbles through the street.

"The baby is ok, but I guess that's the wakeup call she needed. She went to Pamela; Pamela came to me."

"Take it there's no chance he'll change?" I ask sarcastically, quirking a brow.

Jimmy shoots me a cold look. My humor isn't for everyone, and I know as well as anyone that violent and cruel bullies will never change. With a baby on the way, it just means a new victim is arriving for him.

"We'll head to the end of his street; Axe is following from here." Jimmy gestures towards Axe, who's silently following Finn through the badly lit street.

With his hood up concealing his face, from here, it looks like the devil himself is following him. Axe stands well over six feet and is as broad as he is tall. A former US marine, the discipline he was taught treats him well in this little hobby. His immense patience is something I should probably take notice of, but I'm too reckless and out of control for him. My anger clouds my judgement, I hoped it would subside in time, but it hasn't; if it hasn't by now, it likely never will.

"Axe, you good with that?" I speak via the radio.

"All good, Two. Take into account this guy is fucking rinsed. It could take a while. I'll call if there's an issue."

The van picks up the speed and heads towards Finn's house. As we pass the rundown property, I feel a shudder slither up my spine as we park on the quiet road. Luckily for us, the gardens are so unkempt and overgrown, this tatty van would go unnoticed.

Fuck, this looks like where I used to live...

As my eyes scan the dark street, an unnatural cold feeling begins to settle over me. The once white small houses are now falling apart, dirty and rotten. I swallow hard, knowing all too well the sadness that's likely going on behind each closed door. Kids watching their parents get high, begging them to stop, to pay them some attention, hell, even fucking feed them. The arguments turn violent, leaving the younger, smaller members in the home to pick up the fucking pieces of their lost hope.

Clenching my fists, I count to ten. As much as I want to walk into each home and kill every bad person in there and save the kids, I know I can't. I learned a very long time ago.

You can't save them all.

I can still smell the whisky and cigarette smoke from the back room of the bar. I can feel the sweat on my skin, and I can hear those words. The memory is so vivid, even now, eight years later, something I'll never allow myself to forget. The first time, I felt like I was doing some good, even if what was proposed on paper sounded wrong.

"How's things with Summer?" Jimmy asks, yet I hear the concern in his voice.

When I don't answer, he turns to me, letting out a heavy, frustrated sigh.

"Don't fucking start, Jimmy," I bite back.

"I'm meant to look out for her, and I know you're tormenting her." I feel him getting angry.

"You know shit!"

"You haven't removed those fucking cameras in the apartment. You're still going there and for what? To scare the poor girl even more?"

My jaw ticks, but I have no response. My gaze moves towards the opening of the street, but Jimmy has a valid point: I am tormenting her.

"If she knows I'm around, she'll feel safe." I reply blankly.

"Safe? Safe how?"

"She knows I'll never hurt her, but she needs to know I'm around and I'm fucking watching. Maybe then she'll stop letting her guard down and letting Harry continue to torture her."

"You can't be fucking serious? What you're doing is fucking dangerous and could get us all exposed. We agreed that once the funeral was over, we'd get her to leave and get rid of Harry once and for all. Give her a chance at a clean slate, but if you keep coming around, she might stay."

I know what we agreed. I don't need Jimmy's holier-than-thou attitude ringing in my ears right now. But I can't help myself. I want to protect her forever, but if she leaves, I lose that control.

"What's so wrong if she does stay?" I turn to Jimmy, but the question causes him to pale.

"If she does and something goes wrong, she could be a target. Michael could never forgive us for that, and we owe him that much."

Allowing my gaze to move back towards the street, his words rest heavily on my dark soul. He's right. The reason this works is because none of us have anything to lose. If a relationship developed, questions would eventually be asked, and everything we worked hard for could fall apart and cause undeniable damage to everyone.

"Sorry to break up the heart-to-heart ladies. He's turning the corner now." Axe's voice breaks the thick tension in the van. Looking in the side mirrors, I spot Finn approaching and Axe not far behind.

Sliding from my seat, I move to the back of the van. As the uneasy footsteps approach, I slide the door open. Initially, Finn jumps, but Axe is soon behind him, pushing him into the back.

"What the fuck?" Finn asks with a wide-eyed look as he spots the black mask looking back at him.

With one smack to the side of the head, he's out cold. Once the zip ties are secured around his wrists and feet, Jimmy wastes little time in tearing away from the street and heads off into the night.

Settling back into the passenger seat, I zone out for the drive back to the warehouse. Luckily, the drive isn't long, but I spend most of it thinking about Summer. For a moment, I let my mind wonder whether she could stay in New York and start a new life.

That would involve answering a lot of questions about me, her dad, and Jimmy.

That could complicate things in an instant. I fucking hate it, but Jimmy's right. At any time, this could blow up in our faces, and we understand that someone innocent getting hurt isn't what we stand for.

When the brakes screech, I feel my body wince at the whining sound coming from the vehicle. Looking up, the dark old warehouse stares back at me. The evil souls still lurk within the walls, but they can't hurt anyone anymore. Their torment on this world now ceases to exist.

Sliding open the rear door of the van, we bring Finn's limp body into the warehouse. As Axe ties him to the chair, I move into the side room with Finn's file in my hand, something Jimmy managed to obtain. Placing it onto the workbench, my eyes scan the words and photos attached. Shaking my head, I can't believe someone so violent and cruel has managed to evade a prison sentence.

Then again, after seeing the justice system's failings first hand, I can believe it. I follow each police report, each domestic violence call, each hospital report. Police officers, doctors and nurses seemed to offer all the help they could to Sarah, even offering her a protection order whilst he was out on bail, but it failed. She sadly caved every time and went home to the only thing she knew: abuse.

Her only glimmer in this dark world is her baby. Since she refused to testify, the police were likely concerned about the outcome of the arrest if she did decide to press charges this time round. Their concern would be that at any moment she would refuse, and the vicious circle would begin again.

On this occasion, I can't blame law enforcement, there are only so many resources, and even if convicted, Finn could still claim his parental rights to that child. Sarah may never escape him. We're the better option for a happy and healthy life for her and her child.

Not wanting to look at the countless images of the abuse suffered at the hands of her own husband, the man who swore to protect her, I drop the file onto an old workbench for later.

"I can't keep looking at this shit." I mutter, moving from the back room.

Sliding the mask back over my face, I feel the dark persona overtake me. Easing the building tension in my neck, I crack each side's joints. Releasing some of the building pressure, I stare down at Finn. Still unconscious, he's slumped in the chair with both his feet and hands securely held down.

As Axe approaches with a bucket of ice-cold water, he pours it over Finn. It takes a second, but he soon gasps, his wild, confused eyes scanning the unfamiliar room. Once he spots us, I can't help but smile. When the color drains from his face, he sobers up instantly.

"Where the fuck am I?" He bellows, "I'm going to fucking kill you!" The threats continue, but I ignore them, as does Axe and Jimmy.

Shaking my head, I roll my eyes and step closer. Kneeling on one knee, I cock my head to one side while he's making threats, I can smell the fear coming from him. His body begins to shake, and his teeth clattering.

"Do you know why you're here, Finn?" I ask calmly.

"My fucking whore wife complaining again?" He spits back.

"Ah, so you have an idea why you're here. That's something." I sarcastically respond, hearing a deep chuckle from behind me. Axe shakes his head.

"What the fuck do you want?"

"What I want is for you never to lay a hand on your wife again, but we both know someone like you can't control the sickness deep inside you." My response is blank, causing Finn to still.

Swallowing hard, he remains quiet for the moment.

"You see." I continue. "We only get called when someone like you manages to avoid justice, when we can all see what a piece of shit you are. We get involved because there's no rehabilitation for someone like you. No medication, no treatment plan, and certainly no remorse."

"What, so you're just gonna kill me?" Finn begins to laugh, his smart-ass comments being used to hide his guilt and fear.

"Yes." I answer his question bluntly.

"You can't fucking do that; I have a fucking kid on the way!"

"That's exactly why we're doing it. We have no intention of letting your innocent child grow up watching their mother suffer at the hands of her dead-beat husband. That child then grows up thinking that behavior is acceptable, not a fucking chance Finn."

He begins screaming for help and tugging at the restraints. Rising to my full height, I continue to stare down at him, pitying his pathetic attempts to set himself free. Even with what he knows, he's shown no remorse, apology, or even a fake promise that he'll never do it again.

Zoning out, I slowly move towards the tools placed along the worn workbench. Turning back to Finn momentarily, he stills as our eyes meet. The sweat drips from his forehead, and his breathing becomes shallow as the adrenaline begins pumping through his body. My gaze falls to his bruised and grazed knuckles. I blink a couple of times, trying not to allow my own memories to haunt my mind.

"HELP!!! SOMEONE FUCKING HELP!" The pleas continue, but I just shake my head. My attention turns back to the tools laid out in front of me.

"No one can hear you out here." I say, still making my weapon choice.

"I'll fucking find you, and I'll kill you all! I'll gut you! You won't get away with this. People will come looking for me." Finn continues to spit his poison. "You have no idea the people I know!"

Turning on my heels, I hold a large blade between my fingers, allowing the tip of the sharp blade to press into my thumb. I kneel in front of Finn again, allowing the blade to slowly glide across his cheek. Watching with intent as the burning pain rushes through his flesh.

"AH!" he spits out, the blood beginning to trickle down his cheek.

"Really? Well, in that case, maybe we should just let you go?" Another sarcastic remark of mine as Finn's face begins to contort with uncontrollable rage.

Rising to my feet again, I slam my fist into the side of his head. As the blood flies from his mouth and spatters across the concrete, he stays fixed in the chair. I guess it was a good idea of Jimmy's to nail it down after all.

"Thing is, Finn, you won't find us. No one will come looking for you because no one fucking wants you around." I shrug before delivering another blow to the face. This time I hear a crack as a tooth flies from his mouth along with more blood.

Footsteps coming from the separate room causes me to turn around, observing Axe walking back in, holding the case file in his hands. He shakes his head, reading the same reports I have. Pulling out the photos, he begins to pin them to the wall in front of Finn, images taken over a span of eight years. He displays it for all to see: each brutal attack Sarah received, each cut, each bruise, every stitch she required. He displays it as a sick timeline of abuse, documenting the suffering she endured.

"She knows her fucking place! she'll never get away, she fucking needs me!"

Continuing his delusional rant, I see movement in my peripheral. Glancing to my right, Jimmy passes me a machete. I lift it towards the light, checking the sharpness of the blade. Finn's words are caught in his throat as he watches the long blade shimmer slightly.

With the machete over my shoulder, I stride back over to face Finn. His eyes haven't moved from the machete placed over my right shoulder. Standing before him, I allow the silence to fall over the room before I speak.

"Are you right or left-handed?"

His brow furrows, "What the fuck does that have to do with anything?"

Studying both hands, I examine the scars and bruises that mark his skin. Spotting the deeper colored bruises on his right and how they're more scarred than the left, I already have my answer.

"Never mind." Taking a step forward, I slam my left hand down onto his right, holding it in place.

"Wh-what…" He's unable to get his words out.

As the machete rises above my head, I force it down hard. Once the blade connects and cuts through bone, the desperate maniacal screams bounce off every wall in the warehouse. I feel the blood splatter across my face as Finn cries out in agonizing pain, blood pooling at his feet. Holding his right hand in mine, I thrust it into his face as the sweat pours faster from his body.

"You don't need this now." I say before throwing it into his lap and heading outside.

Pulling out my cigarettes from my pocket, I lean against the exterior wall of the warehouse. Sliding the mask up, I light the cigarette and inhale deeply. My lips curl into a sinister smile as the sound of cries and retching fills the air around me.

That's the least that piece of shit deserves.

When my eyes wander towards the night sky, the stars sparkle, and the moon offers the only light around for miles. For somewhere so dark and eerie, it offers me some odd peace. Possibly because this is where a lot of the trauma ends for each victim, they'll never be terrorized by these people again and have their chance at a happy life.

"Gonna finish this?" Axe breaks the silence, taking a space next to me as I exhale.

"Yeah, eventually." I mumble. "Think this will ever end?"

"What, pieces of shit, stop being pieces of shit?" Axe asks, quirking a brow, knowing full well that I already know the answer. "Never."

"Didn't think so." I answer before stubbing out my cigarette and sliding the mask back over my face.

Jimmy leans up against the workbench, watching Finn as his body continues to writhe in pure agony. The blood continues to seep into the concrete as it pours from Finn's semi-conscious body. Dragging the machete blade across the floor, his head slowly lifts. The coldness in his stare tells me everything I need to know; he knows what's coming.

Standing behind him, I grab a fistful of hair, wrenching his head up. A garbled cry escapes his throat, my fingers pulling so tight, I can feel fear and pain radiating from him. Holding the blade to his throat, I lean in close, my lips lowering to his ear.

"I'll make sure your child never knows you." I speak through gritted teeth.

"I'll see you in hell, you fucking bastard."

"I'll look forward to it." I sneer.

Dragging the long blade across his throat, the blood sprays across the photos, still pinned to the wall. Releasing his head, Finn's body slumps forward in the chair as his lungs fight for breath. Stepping around the chair, I stand in front of him, the blade of the machete dripping over the floor as the blood pours from his neck. The only noise in the warehouse now is the garbled cries from the piece of shit who'll never hurt anyone again.

When his body finally stills, I look to his wide eyes. I feel a wave of satisfaction wash over me. Even now he's dead, I can still see the real, undeniable fear deep within his soul. Dropping the blade onto the floor, it clatters against the concrete as I walk through the separate room. Lifting a heavy kerosene bottle, I head outside.

"Let's clear up this shit." I bark as both Axe and Jimmy drag the body out towards the pit at the rear of the property.

Once the body is rolled into the pit, silence falls over the three of us. I pour over the kerosene, throwing in the case file and gloves. Lighting a match, I throw it over the body, destroying all the evidence, along with the majority of the body. As the flames lick higher, I sit on the log next to Axe and Jimmy. Taking a sip of my whiskey, we all watch as one more bad person leaves this earth, never to return.

Chapter Eighteen

Bhodi ⚥

The young nurse tending to Strode finally leaves the room. Closing the door behind her, she offers a polite smile before disappearing entirely. Sitting back in my chair, the beeps from the machines eventually just become background noise. Managing to block them out, I feel my hands begin to tremble. As my friend and mentor lie helpless in a hospital bed, revenge is the only thing on my mind.

I have no intention of letting Harry leave this city or Luca ever walk these streets again. I'll cut them into small pieces and dispose of them, and their names will eventually become a lost memory in the city of New York. No one will miss them, and no one will look for them, they'll become ghosts in a forgotten time.

I managed to get to the office this morning before abruptly being turned away by the captain. He advised I could do with a couple of days off after everything that's happened. There was no missing person's report for Alex that I could find anywhere, so it makes me think no one will look for a while and the trail will be long dead by the time they do.

Lost in thought, I feel a gentle nudge on my shoulder. Snapping my head around, my eyes soften as they land on a familiar face.

"Maggie?"

Standing abruptly, her soft eyes meet mine. She pulls me close, feeling her small frame tremble. I wrap my arms around her. Lifting her head from my chest, she gently wipes her eyes. Wearing her silver hair in a French pleat and her signature pearl necklace, her usual kind eyes look tired, and her skin dull.

"I came as soon as I could, Bhodi. How is he?" Maggie reaches for Strode's hand, giving it a gentle squeeze as she sits at his bedside.

Sitting beside her, I let out a sigh.

"They've managed to remove the bullets. Luckily, nothing vital was hit, but he lost a lot of blood. Surgery took quite a few hours, so he's been resting. He hasn't woken up yet."

"What happened? The captain wouldn't tell me over the phone." Her eyes plead with mine.

"We don't know who it was, but he was shot in a drive-by." I hate lying to Maggie, but I can't give too much away for now. She'll ask questions and demand answers.

Her shoulders sag, turning her attention back to Strode. Her thumb gently brushing over his hand as she speaks.

"I always worried when he was at work. The job is so dangerous, especially here." Wiping away a tear, she continues. "Probably why our marriage failed. I was always so worried. I hoped he would eventually retire."

"Strode's stubborn Maggie, we both know that." A small chuckle escapes her throat as she nods at my comment.

"Oh, Al, what have you gotten yourself into?" She gently shakes her head.

After a moment passes, I decide it's the best time to leave. Rising from my chair, Maggie turns to me. Her soft gaze holding mine.

"Dare I ask if you've found a nice you lady yet, Bhodi?" The words are warm and kind, something I'm still quite unfamiliar with.

I shrug, turning towards the door. Throwing her a quick smile over my shoulder, I lace my fingers around the door handle before turning back.

"Maybe, just seeing how it goes."

As her eyes widen with joy, I exit the room. I feel her gaze follow me until she can no longer see me. But her question is playing on my mind, heading for my car. I know exactly where I want to be, but it's the one place I need to fucking stay away from.

Sliding into my car, I breathe a sigh of relief when I see there are no messages or calls. For once in my life, I have nowhere to be or no one trying to get hold of me. The feeling makes me feel uneasy, but these last few months have been non-stop. I can feel my body beginning to cry out for sleep, but I know that's not a good idea.

Pulling out of the parking lot, the traffic is heavy as usual. Taking a different route, I soon realize where I'm heading. Refusing to stop myself, I head for Summer's. As her apartment nears, I begin to feel the weight of her reaction weighing me down. I wouldn't blame her if she slammed the door in my face. I haven't spoken to her since I left hers the other morning and I didn't speak much whilst I was there.

Once I'd killed Alex, I needed to be close to her, feel her body pressed into mine. I wanted to hear those soft moans as she bounced all over my cock, feel how her body reacts to me, the way her nails marked my skin. I wanted to feel less of a heartless monster. I wanted to feel human again, and, in that moment, she gave that to me.

And like the heartless prick I am, I just left once I was done. Letting out a frustrated huff, I run my hand over my face. With everything happening in such a short space of time, I feel my loss of control becoming a serious fucking problem.

As the approaching lights turn red, my car eventually stops. Watching the passing traffic, I try to focus on the next couple of days ahead. I know the funeral is tomorrow, and I have every intention of escorting Summer there and not letting her out of my sight, even if going to church makes my skin want to crawl off my body. People like me no longer have any faith. I lost that a very long time ago.

Just because Alex is gone doesn't mean Harry can't get to someone else just as easily. He has money, and there's little people won't do for cash if it's waved in their faces. I know he'll show up tomorrow. He wants Summer to know he's still around even if he hasn't done anything yet. He enjoys knowing she's always looking over her shoulder and living in fear that he can pounce at any time.

Murdering her father could have been a way for him to gain further control over her. I know it was him, via Luca, but there's still no proof. Harry knows that that's why he had no concerns about coming to New York. He's not afraid of being caught, he's paid for the best, and that's what he got. But he stupidly forgets how New York can swallow people like him.

Once the lights turn green, I slam the car into drive and speed off, my patience wearing thin. A few cars bounce on their horns, but I ignore it. They're clearly not on their way to see Summer, so they'll never understand the pull she has over me.

Summer ♥

Sitting on the end of the bed, I stare up at the black dress hanging on my closet door. After a week of turbulent hell, the funeral is tomorrow. It feels too soon, and everything feels like a blur, but James advised it was likely best to plan the funeral as soon as possible, else I could be here for a lot longer than anticipated.

I know he could sense my hesitation about staying, so he managed to speak with the police captain and medical examiner, and they agreed to release my dad's body for cremation. For a few days, I felt an unbearable guilt, like I was trying to get everything over and done as soon as possible, but that wasn't the case. The thought of my dad sitting in some cold fridge for longer than needed seemed cruel, even though I know his soul is now elsewhere.

Last night, I had a horrible nightmare. I was standing in the morgue surrounded by fridges. There was a loud, sharp banging that came from one of the doors, but when I approached, the knocking moved to another door, and then another. Pained screams followed, moving around different fridges. Each time I turned around, the noise moved to the opposite one. I could feel the terror in my body. I know it was a dream, but I couldn't seem to force myself awake and pull myself away from the horror. On the final turn, I saw Harry standing in front of me, his suit covered in blood. As he held a knife towards me, his lips turned upwards into a sinister smile, and his eyes were hollow and dead.

As he drove the knife into me, I could hear his crazed laugh echoing off the metal doors. I woke up in bed, sitting bolt upright and covered in cold sweat. My heart thundering in my chest. My eyes flashed around the empty room, and at that moment, I hoped to see him. The dark reaper that keeps me safe.

Pulling my large grey hoodie over my head, I step into my warm slippers. With the funeral approaching, I have no intention of going out today. If anything, I want to lay on the sofa, eat pizza, drink wine, and cry until the sun comes up. There's a heavy sadness hanging over this apartment today. For a moment, I could swear I heard my dad talking to me. I followed the voice and could smell his cologne in the empty kitchen.

I pull out a stool and lean against the marble island, shutting my eyes. The memories of cooking in the kitchen flooded my mind. Dad insisted he taught me how to cook and look after myself. The first dish I ever made was a Spaghetti Bolognaise, and I can still see the shock on his face as he took a spoonful, his face contorted almost in pain when he realized, I'd added a whole bottle of cooking wine.

Being a teenager, I assumed I knew better. I glanced over the recipe and that was about it. I misread one glass for one bottle and didn't even use a good wine. My god, it tasted terrible. We fell about laughing and ended up ordering a pizza. We ate it over the kitchen island as he quizzed me on my future career choices.

The conversation felt alien to me; Mom had never been interested in a career of any type. She had Eric, and he was rich, so why the hell would she work? But I could still see my dad wanted me to have good values, and he was right. He wanted me to be a respectable member of society who worked, contributed and never relied on a man to care of me. He guided me towards college, which I enjoyed, and I gained my degree in business, but soon after I met Harry, any career plans seemed difficult for me. Trying to maintain peace. I never pushed it.

What a fucking waste.

Leaning my elbows into the marble, my chin rests in my hands whilst I focus on the ticking of the large clock above the oven.

"One day, you'll find a purpose, Summer. It may not make sense to you initially, but in time, it'll be the best decision you ever made."

I can hear those words echoing in my memory, dad always seemed so happy with work. For a while, I wondered how you could enjoy running a couple of businesses but somehow, he did, and he thrived off it. Great working relationships with everyone he met. He was respected, fair, and incredibly generous to his hard-working employees. That's why I knew none of them could have done this. They were like his family.

I feel a pain in my heart thinking of other people being his family. But deep down, I know he didn't blame me for not being around as much as I wanted. But that still doesn't stop the hurt.

I still when a gentle knock taps on the front door of the apartment. It's not fear that passes over me this time. It's frustration. Frustration that whenever someone knocks on that door, I feel scared. I shouldn't fucking live like this. I'll admit with everything that's happened in such a short space of time, I'm likely living in a fight-or-flight state, but I'm starting to hate myself for it. I hate feeling weak and pathetic, but I know that only I can change that, and no one else can.

I can't rely on my masked hero. I don't even know what he fucking looks like or who he is. He just appeared in my life and continues to appear with no answers. Gnawing on my bottom lip, I feel my fists clench slightly as my deep sadness is soon replaced with anger.

When the knocking continues, I push from the bar stool. The legs screech across the tiles as I stomp towards the door.

"I'm coming!" I bite out as I swing the door open.

As the door opens, my anger washes away. Staring back at me are those deep emerald irises' that make my knees weak. A heavy sigh escapes my throat, taking in his broad frame. My mind flashes back to that night in the shower, each powerful thrust, his hands roaming my body, and the toe-curling orgasm that left my body limp as the shower poured over us.

Blinking a couple of times, I push those memories away for now. Swallowing hard, I take a hesitant step back.

"What are you doing here?" I ask coldly, unable to meet his eye.

"I wanted you to know detective Strode is out of surgery. He'll be ok, just needs rest for now."

I feel the tension move from my shoulders, and I slowly nod.

"I'm pleased to hear it. I'm glad he'll be okay." I force a smile, but Bhodi doesn't move away.

I crane my neck to look to him, I feel my chest rise and fall with each strained breath. My hard, tender nipples grazing across the fabric of my hoodie, the goosebumps rising all over my skin, followed by the chill of mystery as his gaze slowly travels the length of my body.

"I should probably get going. I'm heading out in a moment." As I go to close the door, I feel a palm braced firmly against it.

My eyes snap back to Bhodi's, cocking his head to one side, I see a smirk ghost across his lips.

"Are you lying, Summer?"

My eyes widen at his question. Still trying to close the door, he doesn't remove his hand. My jaw falls open for a moment as my mind reels with a good excuse.

"I..No...Why?" I manage to spit out.

Fucking great, now he does know I'm lying.

"Just felt like you're trying to get rid of me?"

Because I am!

"No."

"Then, what?"

Letting out a huff, I scratch my forehead for a moment, trying to work out how to respond and not sound like a complete bitch.

"It's probably for the best; we should forget whatever happened the other night. It shouldn't have happened, and I don't want to get in the way of your job."

"My job?" He asks.

"We shouldn't have crossed that line."

Bhodi takes a couple of steps closer. My grip on the door loosens as the rich scent of his cologne fills my senses. Standing a few inches away, he leans closer.

"We did cross that line, you and I." Sucking in a deep breath, my eyes flutter closed. "I have no fucking intention of forgetting the other night. I can still feel your body wrapped around mine, feel your skin beneath my grasp, and the way your tight pussy strangled and slid over my cock. I felt every moan, every contraction, and I felt your fucking soul leave your body."

I finally let out the breath I'd been holding in. My heart is screaming to break out of my chest, my entire body is shaking with anticipation, and my pussy drips at his sinful words. I feel my feet begin to move backward. As I do, Bhodi closes the gap between us and kicks the front door closed.

"I'm not willing to let you go just yet, Summer."

Chapter Nineteen

Summer♥

I feel as though I'm inhaling Bhodi's words, devouring them. Every sensible choice immediately leaves my mind. My body aches to feel him again, taste his skin, smell the sweat as it seeps from our pours while we lie in a heated mess of tangled limbs and euphoria.

Clutching the hem of my hoodie, I pull it over my body. Gently sinking my teeth into my bottom lip, I await Bhodi's reaction. Standing in a white lace thong, as the hoodie is lifted over my head, I feel my hair cascade over my shoulders and down my back. The cool breeze sweeps through the room and gently grazes across my bare skin. I see the desire swirl in his dark green iris's, I watch the short inhale of breath and eventually the curl of his lip into a half smile. I home in on that desire. I feel my body falling into the trap. Throwing the clothing onto the floor, I shift on my tiptoes as his eyes devour my semi-naked body.

I watch with intent, as his lips move. His tongue sweeping across his bottom lip, wetting it slightly. As he takes a couple of steps closer, the cool leather of his jacket runs against my hard, painful nipples. I'm unable to tear my eyes away from his. I feel the goosebumps all over my skin, followed by a chill. The chill of anticipation, as he reaches out, taking a lock of my hair between his fingers, he twirls the curl around his digits like silk. I feel my head lean towards his touch, as his eyes search mine.

"We're playing a dangerous game, aren't we?" Bhodi asks calmly. The ghost of a smirk glides over his calm expression.

I feel my eyes widen at his comment, how calm he appears, how little he seems bothered by the threats that do linger over us. My eyes narrow on his, his calmness, appears almost arrogant. The confidence he carries himself with almost makes me jealous. Allowing the lock of hair to fall back against my skin, I watch in wonder trying to work out his next move.

As the intensity feels like it's too much, my right hand shoots out to grab his jacket. As his hands snap around both wrists, the arrogant smirk appears a little bigger on his face, and my jaw falls open slightly. Bhodi pulls my body to his. Spinning me around, I gasp as my back hits his firm chest. The clinking sound of metal fills the room as he dangles the object in front of us both.

His lips lower to my ear as the shudder of wonder and intrigue dances right through me. The afternoon sunlight bouncing off the shiny metal handcuffs, the promise of something wild and animalistic.

"Today, we play by my rules, Summer. Are you ready?" His voice is low and mysterious, the handcuffs gently flickering in the light.

"Yes." I push the words out, the intrigue of the handcuffs outweighing any fear I have about being unable to fully move. But the truth is, I trust Bhodi.

I'm drawn to his mystery, the dark soul behind those beautiful eyes, the secrets he holds, and the way his body dominates mine. It's reckless. I've been warned, but right now that threat is nowhere to be seen. I refuse to have something or someone who hides behind a fucking mask dictate what I want. I'll get the answers I need, but I just want to forget right now.

I feel the amusement skate across my skin. As he sweeps away my hair from my shoulder, he inhales deeply.

"You smell like safety." There's a subtle pain in his words. For a moment I feel my brows pinch. Unable to understand the meaning behind it.

As his fingers stay laced around my left wrist, I feel his warm hand glide down my right shoulder and arm before securing my other wrist with his grasp. Taking a deep breath, the thundering in my ears, is the only thing I can concentrate on. The anticipation forming a tight knot deep within my body, as the long-drawn-out click can be heard as my hands are secured behind my back.

With my head bowed slightly, the excitement builds. As Bhodi's fingers hook into the band of my underwear, he slowly slides them down my thighs. I feel my arousal leave a cool trail down the inside of my legs as the lace eventually meets the floor. Feeling his hot breath against my ass, he moves between each cheek. I shudder, sucking in a strangled breath.

"Does danger turn you on, Summer?" His fingers skate up the back of my thighs, stopping just before the dip of my ass cheeks. His teeth gently dig into the left cheek, and my entire body reacts as a thrill pulses through me.

"Do you like being trapped with me?" My mind tries to process the second question as his lips move to the right cheek, his teeth gently clamping down into my sensitive skin.

A heavy moan escapes my throat, "Yes." I manage to force out as my eyes flutter closed.

As his teeth move away, I can feel a smile against my skin. Looking ahead, I can see Bhodi rise to his full height through the floor-to-ceiling window in front of us. His large frame swallows mine entirely, and his leather jacket slides from his shoulders as I watch in awe. The snapping of his belt causing my heart to jump and my throat to dry up entirely. As the sound the leather sliding across denim can be heard from behind me.

When the leather strap skates across the back of my thighs again, I feel myself shift on my feet and bracing myself for what's to come. I feel his eyes on me, staring back into our reflection, and I wait in heated anticipation.

"Did the blood scare you?" He asks curiously.

The image of him standing in front of me, dry blood soaked into his skin, the vacant look and vulnerability in his eyes.

It should have scared me, hell, it should have fucking petrified me. But it didn't. If anything, it made me dig deeper and unlock those feelings, I already knew I had. Bhodi made a decision. He made it, carried it out, and left no room for second-guessing. He did what all of us wanted to do when we were so cruelly wronged by someone else.

"No, it didn't." I whisper.

I feel him let out a low breath, a slight chuckle escaping his throat as all of a sudden, the belt is whipped across my ass cheek. The sharp thwack, causing me to jolt forward. My garbled cry of pleasure echoes off the walls, and my feet stumbling as I fight against the restraints. Throwing my head back, the already fading sting on my skin leaving nothing but the need for more.

"Why?" He asks.

The question swirls around in my mind. Since arriving in New York, nothing seems normal, nothing has gone to plan and quite frankly nothing surprises me anymore. In such a short time, it's opened my eyes to what people are capable of by their choices and what they're capable of when pushed.

The blood didn't scare me, Bhodi doesn't scare me. However, the fear of the unknown does, for the past couple weeks or so it feels like something is always waiting around the corner to test or punish me somehow. The intense way he stares at me, his eyes hold a darkness. Something so far, I've been unable to chip away at, unable to gain his trust and something he's never uttered a word about.

"Turn around and drop to your knees." The demand has a chill to it. Before turning, I take one last look into the window as Bhodi lifts his T-shirt off and discards it onto the floor.

Sinking to my knees, the hard wooden floor is uncomfortable. Parting my knees slightly, I try to gain some more balance as I'm at eye level with his crotch. I let out a low breath, faced with his large, clothed erection. Licking my lips, my pussy pulses with what's to come. His right-hand palms the fabric, and my eyes follow his movements, already lost in a trance.

"Eyes on me, Summer."

"Summer." This time, it's a demand. His tone is clipped.

Blinking a couple of times, I fight to pull myself out of my self-inflicted trance and force my eyes to meet his. When I do, the right side of his lip is curled into that arrogant smirk again. The same one I can't help but mimic. Sliding his zipper down, Bhodi slides his jeans and boxers down his firm, tanned thighs.

I suck in a breath as his large, firm, thick cock comes into view, holding himself in his right palm. The room feels like it's spinning.

There's something about being at eye level with a beautiful cock, it's erotic. Especially when you know what he's capable of with it.

My eyes flicker to the deep veins, the beading of pre-cum on the head, and the rich smell of arousal inches away from my nose. I feel my body beginning to lean forward, the urge to taste him becoming too much, the tension between us suffocating. Rising on my knees slightly, I catch Bhodi's gaze.

"Come here." His voice is low and husky. Leaning closer, I sweep my tongue against the head. I watch as his stomach muscles contract, and he hisses. "Fuuuuuck".

With a nudge of encouragement, I open my mouth wider. Taking him further and further each time. Settling lower on to my knees, the angle gives me full view. Bhodi's emerald eyes ablaze as they bore into mine. Each time I take him further down my throat, I see them flicker, the sweat forming on his brow and the way his muscles all over his body tense.

With tears pricking my eyes, I continue to suck hard, the salty taste hitting the back of my throat each time. Bhodi's hands travel to my neck, his palms placed over my skin, squeezing gently.

"Fuck, I can feel my cock down your throat..." His voice is exasperated, his breathing laboured, but it spurs me to continue.

Eventually, he pulls away, his chest heaves. Leaving my lips swollen, Bhodi takes a few steps back. I blink a couple of times as my eyes land on the small circular scars that mark his skin, a small cluster on his thigh, and an additional few scattered across his chest. Snapping his eyes back to his, there's a moment of silence between us. I refuse to let my eyes travel back to his scars, but I feel them demanding my gaze.

Shit, did he notice me looking?

I feel a blush creep up my chest, right to my cheeks. I feel like I've been caught doing something I shouldn't be.

He closes the space between us, circling around me, he pulls me to my feet. For a moment, I stagger, but he places his hands on my arms for support. Pulling my back into his chest, his erection nestled between my ass cheeks.

As Bhodi's fingertips gently graze down my skin, I can't help but allow mine to travel up and down his hard length. Sweeping my hair to one side, his lips find my neck again. Gently kissing and licking the sensitive skin, he fists my hair, pulling me to one side, exposing my neck further. His lips continue all the way up to my ear. His hot breath sends shudders all through me.

"Walk to the bedroom, stand on the bed, and face the headboard."

With his voice low and full of promise ringing in my right ear, the command sends excitement right to my core, I snap my thighs together hard, trying to relieve the dull ache.

Wetting my lips, he gently releases my hair, and I slowly nod, feeling him step away from me.

"Ok." My voice a whisper as I turn towards the bedroom. Bowing my head slightly, I can't hide the mischievous smile on my lips as I enter the room.

Placing one foot onto the chaise lounge at the bottom of the bed, I push off the ground with the opposite foot. The adrenaline must be helping since I manage not to fall face-first onto the bed. Shuffling along the mattress, I find myself a few inches from the headboard, facing the wall.

Taking a couple of deep breaths, I feel my hands shuffle slightly in the cuffs, the metal now beginning to feel warm against my skin. Hearing Bhodi's footsteps enter the room, I feel the bed shift behind me, moving closer towards me, his hands reaching for my wrists. Hearing the gentle clink of metal, one of my hands fall free.

"Turn around." Slowly turning, my hard nipples graze across Bhodi's chest, my eyes closer to the scars this time.

Remembering his words in the car.

"It's rude to stare Summer."

I crane my neck to look towards him.

Lifting his hand towards me, he twirls one of the loose curls between his fingers, his body moving closer to mine.

"I'll explain those another day." His voice softens.

Shaking my head, I try to avoid the explanation.

"No, you don't have to. I'm sorry, it was rude…"

Bhodi wraps his arms around my waist tight, pulling me tight towards him. Lifting my body, I wrap my legs tight around him, craving the closeness between us, kneading his palms against my ass, my nails skim over his shoulders, rolling my hips, seeking some friction.

He lets out a deep, throaty chuckle, his eyes sparkle when he feels what I'm doing. Lowering my head slightly, I bite my bottom lip trying to stifle my slight embarrassment.

Dropping to his knees, I feel my back pressed into the soft mattress. Bhodi reaches for my right wrist; his body moves up mine slightly. Before I realize what he's doing, I hear the distinctive metal clink as he loops the cuffs to the headboard and secures my left.

My jaw falls open as he hovers over me.

"I like control, Summer; you should know that by now." His tone is deliciously dark.

My breath catches in my throat, pulling on the restraints, but there's no chance of freeing myself without the key. Bhodi pushes himself back onto his knees, reaching for my ankles. He pulls me down the bed, spreading my legs.

Lowering himself between my thighs, instantly plunging a finger into my soaked, throbbing pussy.

"Fuck…" I cry out, my hips bucking off the bed.

"You're fucking dripping". He purrs against my thighs as his finger thrusts in and out.

I can feel my walls already clamping onto his single finger. Squeezing my eyes closed, I take a deep breath. Slowly sliding the finger out, he swirls it across my swollen clit before plunging it back in. I cry out, the deep tension building in my thighs, the rattling of metal on metal as I tug against the restraints.

Bhodi doesn't hesitate, sinking his tongue into my pussy as my ass lifts off the bed entirely. My utter desire to chase my orgasm is the only thought at the forefront of my mind. The rest is a hazy blur. Pressing the pad of his thumb to my throbbing core, flattening his thick tongue, he continues to lick and suck as my deep moans fill the room. The sensation is intense and fucking amazing, as the promise of a hard release beckons me further.

Bhodi's left hand dances over my hip, traveling further up my body. When his thumb and forefinger tweak and tug at my nipple, I sink further down the rabbit hole. With his whole mouth devouring my pussy, my eyes roll back into my head.

My head falls back into the pillow, I aggressively pull on the handcuffs. The hard metal clattering against the headboard as my soul leaves my body.

"OH FUCK!" Are the only garbled words I can fight out, and for a moment, I swear I have an out-of-body experience.

As his fingers slide out of me, Bhodi comes into view. Licking the glistening arousal from his lips, his body moved slowly up mine. His lips smearing my come over my skin the closer he gets. When his lips meet mine, I can finally taste myself. His tongue dips into my mouth as the kiss deepens. After a moment, he pulls away, wrapping his fingers around the chain of the handcuffs. I instinctively tug again.

Bhodi settles back into his knees, admiring the sated mess before him. Reaching for my thighs, he effortlessly flips me onto the front, wrenching my hips up. I grab onto the headboard for support.

In one swift motion, he thrusts deep inside me. His fingers dig deep into the flesh of my hips as he pulls all the way out before thrusting back into me hard. Throwing my head back, I cry out hard as he continues.

"Bhodi!" I cry out, the immense power behind each thrust, stars blurring my vision.

Shunting me further up the bed, he pulls my back into his chest. With my arms outstretched, he grabs a fistful of hair, exposing my neck again. His free hand slides slowly down my stomach, gently dancing between my parted thighs.

"I need to feel that tight cunt strangle my cock again, Summer, fuck....I can feel how close you are again." Between each thrust, Bhodi's husky voice fills my ears.

I can feel my entire body begin to shake again when his fingers connect with my aching sensitive clit, and my head flies back into his chest. I pull harder and harder against the headboard as the sensation continues to wrack my body, my thighs burn, my toes curl.

His thrusts become increasingly erratic as the sweat pours down my back. As my white knuckles clutch to the headboard, my entire body spasms as the intense orgasm drives through me hard. Sticking my ass out, I work my pussy over his cock, and he stills for a moment as my walls clamp down on him hard. His hands slam over my hips so hard, I cry out again. His fingers dig deep into my flesh as his head falls into my neck.

As a deep roar escapes his throat, I feel his cock pulsating deep inside of me. Our bodies fall forward into the soft bedding. He flips my limp body over, pulling me close to his chest. Catching my breath, I look up as the cuffs are unhooked, the rattling of the metal drowned out by the heavy breaths filling the space.

My heavy arms fall by my side. Looking at Bhodi through hooded eyes, he gently kisses each wrist, and I can't help but admire the red rings that now mark my skin.

Glancing over, my eyes land on the black dress which hangs on the closet door, the reminder of what tomorrow will bring. Letting out a heavy sigh, Bhodi pulls me closer. I look up at him as he offers me a small, sympathetic smile.

"It's ok you know, to forget sometimes." He presses his lips to my forehead, speaking softly.

My brows pinch at his comment, his soft voice offering some comfort.

"No, it's not." I reply, shaking my head.

"It is, you can't carry this sadness forever. It's not healthy."

"What if we never find out why he was murdered?" I feel my voice break at the question that's been weighing me down.

"We will, Summer. I promise you we will." Bhodi leans closer and speaks gently before pressing a gentle kiss to my forehead.

He pulls the duvet over me; I wrap my arms around his strong body as my head lays on his chest. I feel my eyes become heavy, Bhodi's fingertips gently grazing up and down my hip. I feel safe for the first time in days as sleep slowly takes over.

Chapter Twenty

Bhodi ⚧

When the bloodcurdling screams penetrate my ears, I begin to fight. The desperate plea I make with my body to wake up before the bitter memories flood my mind. Willing my mind to pull myself from this hell, I feel my hands begin to twitch, pleading with the paralysis to fuck off just one more time.

As though I'm being pulled from water, I finally feel myself gain control over my body. Jerking forward, my eyes fall onto the unfamiliar space as I push the sheets away from my waist, managing to get to my shaky legs before a voice pulls me back.

"Bhodi?" The soft voice pulls me back to reality immediately.

Snapping my eyes towards the bedroom doorway, Summer stands holding a glass of water, her hand trembling slightly as I blink. Taking a cautious step towards me, she places the drink onto the side. As she nears, the thundering in my chest slowly begins to subside. When her arms snake around my waist, she pulls me close. I feel her trepidation as her body shakes, but the tighter her embrace, the harder it is to allow the memories back in.

Wrapping my arms around her body, I inhale her sweet scent. After a moment, she pulls away, her caring eyes meeting mine as she swallows hard. Lacing her fingers around mine, she guides me back to bed. The adrenaline begins to wear off, as soon as my back connects with the mattress.

Summer lays her head on the pillow beside mine, and I stare at the ceiling. Taking a deep breath, I reach out and pull her body close to mine. When her head rests on my chest, I feel her nails slowly draw circles across my torso, instantly noticing how she keeps away from the small scars I know she spotted earlier.

She's never asked about my scars, likely because the first time I caught her staring, I snapped at her, something I instantly regretted. It's not her fault. I've learned to forget about them over time. Feeling a knot form in my throat, I count to ten, allowing my mind to process the words before I say them out loud.

From the moment I laid eyes on Summer, from the photo in her dad's office. I've been unable to fight the pull I have towards her. A bright warmth surrounds her and allows me to feel complete.

"The scar on my face happened when I was eleven." I feel her body freeze, and her eyelashes flutter a couple of times across my chest.

I know my words have woken her up instantly, but I've opened that door now. I can't just shove it closed and hope it'll go away.

"My mom was a drug addict, heroin mainly." I take another deep breath before continuing. "Her boyfriend Sam, was originally her dealer before he came in and took over our place."

As her head lifts off my chest, Summer looks at me. The night fell hours ago as little light fills the room, but I can see her sad eyes looking right into mine. I feel her hand clutch onto my torso a little tighter as she nods her head for me to carry on.

"They fought a lot. I used to avoid being at home as much as I could. I'd go to the library, walk the streets, and even go to church if it meant I'd be away from the toxic fights."

Reaching for my hand, she entwines her fingers with mine as the pad of her thumb gently caresses my palm. The small gesture offers me some calm while I pull the terrible memory into the forefront of my mind.

I hate appearing vulnerable, but I need to tell Summer. Maybe if I do, it'll offer me some redemption for the things I have done, and the dark cloud that permanently hangs over me may begin to fade.

"I came home late one night, and mom was furious that I had been out." I begin, allowing the words to fall from my mouth. "She didn't seem to care that I would leave the house to get away from her. For some reason, she turned to Sam, her boyfriend, and began berating him and blaming him for my behavior. They were both so high at the time, it turned into a shoving match. When Sam pushed my mom down hard to the ground, I got in his face and pushed him away. He staggered back and hit the wall. He just saw red. His temper was horrific anyway, but this time, he grabbed a heavy glass ashtray and swung it at me. It shattered."

Swallowing the thick knot in my throat, I feel my hand clutching onto Summers tighter as I allow the horrific memory to be told.

"I fell to the ground hard. I could feel the blood pouring down my face. I tried to touch my face, but all I could feel was the tough shards of glass stuck in my skin. Mom was screaming, and Sam ran out. All I can remember is the thudding of the footsteps as they both ran from the house. My mom was shouting and screaming bloody murder."

"What happened to you?" Summer asks softly, but I shrug.

"I managed to get up. Luckily, the neighbors came out when they heard mom and found me standing in the doorway. Luckily Mrs Wayne's husband was a former medic, and he managed to patch me up."

"Didn't they call the police?"

I shake my head no in response, quickly catching a tear before it falls past my cheek and wiping it away.

"No, this wasn't uncommon. If it wasn't me getting hurt, it was mom. Sam used violence to get what he wanted or to prove his point."

Summer swallows hard, slowly nodding her head. Her body moves closer to mine, so close I can feel her peaceful warmth on my skin. Pulling herself up from the bed, she holds me close. Gently stroking the back of my neck whilst the weight is slowly lifted from me.

Cupping my cheek, pulling my focus to her beautiful face, I see the tears welling in her eyes. Leaning into her warm embrace, she gently presses her lips to mine.

"You don't have to tell me everything tonight, Bhodi. I can see how hard this is for you." She speaks sincerely as I slowly nod.

With my arms wrapped around her tight, I hold her close.

Pushing the dark memory from my mind again, I know I'll have to tell Summer the rest. But for now, I'm content with what she knows so far.

Chapter Twenty-One
Summer ♥

The morning has been a blur so far. Sitting in the church, I've managed to keep it together for now. Occasionally, I pull my coat tighter around myself as the chills keep sweeping through my body. Bhodi's fingers link with mine, I lift my head slightly and side-eye him. He offers a quick wink and a smile whilst I try to remain strong.

As the coffin is placed at the front of the church, I try to remain focused on the spray of white Lillies which lay on the coffin. I feel the thick knot slowly forming in my throat as my hand begins to shake uncontrollably in Bhodi's.

As the tears blur my vision, the distant tapping of heels pulls my attention away. Slowly turning around in the church, I spot a familiar woman moving towards James Kressler. He offers her a small smile as she takes her seat next to him, I manage to catch her eye. My jaw falls open for a moment, and I blink a couple of times. But she merely offers a polite and sad half smile before focusing on the front of the church.

Pamela? The receptionist from the hotel?

Snapping my jaw shut, my brow furrows as she offers little else during this moment. Glancing around, the church is busier than I expected. I'd managed to avoid the pitiful gazes from the attendees and have been on autopilot since arriving. Swallowing hard, my eyes land on the four unwanted people nearing the back.

Shit…

Before I can catch their eye, I manage to turn back as my grip on Bhodi's hand tightens. He shoots me a questioning look as I hold his gaze. He leans in closer before whispering.

"What is it?" Clearly, the alarm is plastered all over my face. As the fear begins to swarm my body.

Swallowing hard, I try to keep my voice low and not allow my concern to show in case they're watching me.

"Don't turn around, but he's…. Harry is here." I manage to get the words out, but really, all I want to do is vomit all over the floor and run as far away as I can.

Anger flickers across Bhodi's face, his eyes stormy as his jaw tenses. He takes a deep breath before wrapping his arm around me and sliding me closer along the pew. His lips lower to my ear.

"Take a deep breath, he wouldn't dare fucking touch you, not while I'm here, ok?"

Drenched in dread, I manage to nod, holding back the tears as the service begins. My eyes fall onto the coffin once again. Swallowing hard, I don't hear the words which are spoken. I'm terrified that if I do, I'll fall apart. As my head falls to Bhodi's chest, I squeeze my eyes shut and allow myself to listen to the rhythm of his heartbeat.

All the hairs on the back of my neck rise, I know Harry, the stranger, Eric, and my mom have spotted me. I can feel their eyes burning holes into my skin, but I refuse to turn back around.

After a deep breath, I find my mind drifting off to a happier time. A time when my dad was alive and well, and I had just landed in New York for a summer trip. We'd headed out for lunch in the afternoon. I smile as I recall the burger sauce getting all over his shirt, the utter annoyance followed by humor due to his clumsy action. I replay us both doubled over laughing as the napkins on the table did nothing but smear it further into the fabric.

Every now and then, his murder seems to hit me hard in the chest. I know it happened, but it's as though I need a bigger reminder of what happened to him. I know it hasn't been long, but it feels like his killer has been out walking the streets for years. I know they haven't, and investigations don't just get solved overnight. But with everything that has happened so quickly, is someone watching us? Making sure we're always aware of the threat surrounding us.

I can't help but allow my body to shift, staring towards the back of the church. Eric and my mom appear to be watching the service. For a moment, she even looks a little sad as Eric keeps his arm around her. Narrowing my eyes, I feel anger wash through me, as the selfish bitch seems to be playing the part of the doting widow well, even if she made his life miserable along with mine.

This is an additional nail in the coffin that confirms I will never have a relationship with my mom again, not after her behavior. Money and status meant more to her than I ever did. She allowed me to fall into a trap with a monster and didn't care. She cast me aside to enjoy her perfect life with Eric. Even if it was built on corruption and possibly crime.

Swallowing hard, I try to push past the rage within me. Not allow it to ruin the send-off for my dad. However, as my eyes move to the side, I see Harry. His eyes narrow on me like I'm the prey he's been watching for hours, he's savouring the moment until he can pounce and tear me apart. His lips curl into a sinister smile. I hold his stare, refusing to show him weakness or fear.

I never thought I would see the day when I defied him, but the moment I hit him with the bottle and fled to New York, it was a slippery slope. I'd escaped Harry, and he didn't like it one fucking bit. This was on my terms and not his, so he's doing everything he can to let me know he isn't far away.

When my eyes finally land at the end pew, the dark-haired man stares ahead. He's staring directly at the back of Bhodi's head. His ice-cold eyes never flicker, never move, and certainly don't look my way. He's the same man who was at the bar the afternoon Bhodi and I went for a drink. I know he's a dangerous man, but Bhodi has never told me how he knows him, and it's likely because the story doesn't have a happy ending.

Turning to face the front, I try to take in the words being spoken, but the fact remains, gnawing at my gut like it has from the moment I heard the news.

Someone killed my dad, I still don't know who, and I don't know why.

An eerie thought shudders through my body, a flicker of chaos followed by a heavy wave of darkness as it descends over the service.

What if someone here did it? What if it was Harry?

My heartbeat intensifies and I feel the adrenaline pumping through my veins, telling me I need to run because it's clearly unsafe. But it feels as though in this city, nothing is.

We all stand up as the service finishes. I watch through teary eyes as the coffin disappears behind the curtain. Multiple footsteps begin shuffling towards the church's main door, but I take a moment to watch the curtain fully close before turning away.

Bhodi stands at the end of the pew as I turn to face him, holding out his hand. I take mine in his as he begins to lead me from the church. An undeniable sadness begins to consume me when it dawns on me: I'll never see my dad again.

"Are you ready? I can stay if you need a minute." Bhodi asks.

"Would you mind if I sat here for a moment alone?"

He gives me a half smile; his eyes quickly dart towards the exit of the church. I follow his eyesight as most attendees have left or are leaving. A few familiar faces seem to hang by the door, hoping to catch me on my way out, but I just need a moment.

"I'll be right by the door, ok?"

I nod as Bhodi moves towards the door. As he turns away, I can't help but admire his dark suit. The way it hugs his perfect body, how it's fitted so perfectly to each muscle, as he walks away, I can't help but let out a low breath. I know we'll have to part ways soon, because as of now, I have no reason to be in New York. There are no friends, no family, and no work for me, and with that, I feel my heart hurt.

"Excuse me, Miss Harper. Is everything ok?"

I move my focus towards the gentle voice. I throw my hand over my heart. I take a deep breath and shake my head.

"I'm so sorry Father Dudley, I..."

"Oh no, please, I apologize. I didn't mean to startle you." I can't help but smile at the worn denim blue eyes that are kindly looking at me right now.

"It was a lovely service, thank you, I know it would have made my dad happy." I feel my voice break as I fight to finish the sentence.

The priest gestures for me to sit. As I sit down, he sits beside me, looking towards the altar. As his shoulders sag, he bows his head slightly.

"Your father was a very good man, Miss Harper. I hope one day you'll be able to understand just how good he was."

I turn my head to face him, his comment causes my eyes to narrow slightly. I gently nod my head before looking back to the altar.

"I know how good he was, I just wish we could spend more time together."

"I'm sure you'll see him again." He offers me a kind smile before rising from the pew. "The ashes will be ready for collection in a few days. James gave me your number, but I'm happy to call him if you prefer?"

I blink a couple of times as I take in his question. Turning to the priest I nod.

"Thank you, please call me. I'll be here."

Standing from the pew, I take one final look at the altar before exiting the church. Walking past the empty pews, the short walk feels like a lifetime before I reach the door. Stepping back into the afternoon air, I glance up at the dark grey clouds that threaten to pour down.

I feel Bhodi's presence at my side. As I look towards him, he smiles, but the angry snap of his name soon pulls our focus to the angry balding man approaching us.

"Fuck sake." Bhodi mutters as I quickly shoot him a questioning look.

Once the man is in front of us, his angry features soften slightly when he sees me.

"Detective Grey, you aren't meant to be working today? I thought we agreed it was best you took a couple of days off." His tone is clipped, and I can tell he's pissed off.

Looking between the two men, I step away. I didn't know Bhodi wasn't working at the moment. It makes sense after Detective Strode was hurt that a few days away from the precinct could help.

After a couple minutes, I catch the man out of the corner of my eye heading back down the concrete steps and heading for a waiting car on the sidewalk. Turning to Bhodi, I quirk a brow.

"In trouble?"

He smirks, before sliding his arm around my shoulder and pulling me close. Placing a gentle kiss on my forehead, his lips linger against my skin when he speaks quietly.

"It's worth it for you."

I look towards him, his arrogant smirk plastered all over his face. I can't help but smile and shake my head at the same time, giving him a gentle nudge.

"I don't want you getting in trouble because of me."

"I `haven't, I explained to the captain I'm just here paying my respects, and if it helps keep Harry and Luca away from you, then it's a win-win." He shrugs.

I feel myself deflate when he mentions them, looking away briefly. I scan the surrounding area in case they could still be watching. Feeling Bhodi's warm hand on my chin, he pulls my focus back to him. For a moment, he searches my eyes.

Fear like that doesn't just go away, no matter how much I will it to or try to remain positive. I know it'll take time and a hell of a lot of distance before I stop looking over my shoulder.

"Is Luca the guy with Harry?" When I ask the question, I watch as Bhodi stiffens.

He delicately pushes my hair away from my face, his palm cupping my cheeks as his eyes soften.

"You don't have to worry about him. He won't be a problem soon."

I swallow hard at that statement. The bluntness of the comment tells me all I need to know.

"Who is he, Bhodi?"

"He's a dangerous man, the worst kind of person. He has no loyalty, no conscience, and will work for whoever is paying."

My eyes widen, processing Bhodi's words. Blinking a couple of times, I begin to choke on my words, a lump forming in my throat, trying to understand the hidden meaning behind the comment.

"Do you think he killed my dad?" Managing to speak, I hear my voice break.

Bhodi swallows hard, feeling his hand tense slightly against my cheek. My eyes dart around his face, looking for an answer.

"I believe it's possible, yes."

I immediately pull away, slapping his hand away as the rage and sadness begins to crawl over me.

"Then why has no one fucking arrested him then?" I spit out.

Shaking my head, I take a couple of steps back. Trying to create distance between us as my hands begin to tremble. The thought of the man who killed my dad, having the fucking audacity to attend the funeral of the man he killed, seems so fucking heartless and cruel, and Harry was there, waving it in my face. Taunting me with his smug fucking grin, knowing he knew something I didn't.

"We can't arrest someone with no fucking evidence, can we? If we did and the case was thrown out, it means we have nothing, and that bastard walks!"

Bhodi snaps back at me, the frustration clear in his voice. As my bottom lip begins to tremble and more tears threaten to fall, I try to move away. After a couple of steps, I feel his firm grasp around my wrist, tugging me towards him.

I brace my palms against his chest, refusing to fall into his warm embrace. As much as I need to, I just can't. Shaking my head, I push away again. Running a frustrated hand through my hair, I look towards the busy street.

Seeing all the yellow cabs driving by, I decide my best option is to head home. I feel the waves of sickness begin to wash over me, the exhaustion and the many questions swimming through my mind.

"I need to go home."

"I'll take you."

Taking a step forward, I put my hand out for Bhodi to stop. For a moment, I see a flicker of disappointment cross his face as he halts.

"I'll get a cab; I just want to be alone."

I turn away and proceed down the steps, refusing to look back. Stepping onto the curb, I hold out my hand, and within a few seconds, one pulls up. Sliding into the backseat, it pulls away and I allow my head to fall back into the headrest, hot tears streaming down my cheeks.

Chapter Twenty-Two

TWO/FACE

The funeral was tough, but it was made tougher by the appearance of Harry and Luca. With my fist clenched tight around the beer bottle, I feel the tremble and muscle tension running up and down my arm. My deep hatred for Luca currently overshadows the bitter resentment I have towards Harry.

"The police won't arrest Luca, will they?" Jimmy asks. Even though he's asked a question, I know it's more of a statement.

Taking a swig of beer, I slam the bottle down on the table, alerting the rest.

"Of course, they fucking won't. Nothing sticks. He's too fucking good." I spit out.

I look across the table as Pamela sits nursing a double whiskey, her fingers running up and down the glass. Her eyes fixed on the amber liquid as it gently rolls in the glass. As soon as Luca's name is mentioned, her body language shifts. She becomes rigid, and her eyes widen for a moment as she tries to control the deep resentment that's bubbling under the surface.

Axe shoots me a pissed-off look. Even the fact I've given Luca the accolade of being 'too good' causes waves of tension at the table.

"He's the reason we're all here." All eyes move to Pamela. Her statement rings true as the memories of how we all met washes over us. Along with the shame of how we initially all failed her.

"We're here because we've seen too often how victims don't get justice." I speak through gritted teeth.

"For fuck sake, Two, we fucking know he killed Michael. What's stopping us from just killing him?" Axe interjects.

"Oh...fucking do we Axe? And just like that, we'll just kill one of the most well-known men in the city and expect no repercussions?"

"Since when did you become all high and fucking mighty, huh?" Axe snipes back.

"Since we lost the fucking person that keeps us all in check!"

A silence falls amongst the table, the other three shifting uncomfortably.

Leaning back into my seat, I loosen my suffocating tie as the pressure from the group becomes almost unbearable.

"We can't wait for him to strike." Jimmy speaks, his calm voice bringing some reasoning back to us.

"I know that, but unless he tells us why he killed Michael, we don't know if it was something to do with us or Summer."

"It's Summer, it must be. It's hardly a coincidence that Harry followed her to New York and decided to align himself with Luca."

Pamela speaks softly, gently shrugging. "We've seen the lengths people will go to, to keep those they control in check."

"Was anything ever left to Michael's ex-wife in his will?" I turn to Jimmy.

"No, as soon as they divorced, it was all left to Summer. There was no mention of the ex."

"Could Harry have organised Michael's death, to stop Summer from leaving?" Axe shrugs.

"If he did, it didn't work. She left anyway?"

Sitting around the table, the four of us are falling further and further down a warped rabbit hole. Nothing makes sense, and in every scenario we come up with, we're able to counteract with a different argument.

"What if it was Luca, but Harry had nothing to do with it?"

We all turn to Jimmy, the confusion plastered over our expressions.

I feel my brows pinch, and I look at Jimmy; he nervously chews on the corner of his lip. I can see the cogs turning in his mind, his eyes darting between us, and he tries to piece together this riddle. But after a moment, he just shrugs, letting out a heavy, frustrated sigh.

"Fuck sake, I have no idea. But there's something off about Rachel and Eric turning up today. Harry, well, we knew he would show up to get under Summer's skin."

We all nod in agreement as the silence and emptiness take over again.

"Do you know where she is now?" Pamela asks, concerned, leaning closer to the table.

Pulling out my phone, I click on the app. My face softens for a moment, instantly spotting Summer laying on her couch. Seeing the flicker from the TV, she must be watching a crime documentary. She's engrossed in the screen.

"Yeah, she's at Michaels." Clicking on the separate camera in the hallway, I quickly scan the image, but it's all clear.

"You ever going to tell her the truth?" Pamela's eyes narrow on mine, her question thickening the tension further.

"No, Summer will leave New York soon anyway."

"Sure, about that? Seems like Bhodi Grey might have an issue with that. They looked cozy earlier." She raises an accusing eyebrow, her tone dripping with sarcasm.

My eyes narrow on Pamela. Both Jimmy and Axe look away their hesitation on the subject obvious, but she doesn't seem too bothered by bringing it up. Leaning forward, I place my palms firmly on the table, my eyes fixed on Pamela.

"That's my business, not yours, so keep the fuck out."

She scoffs, shaking her head, and rolls her eyes. Throwing her hands up in the air in an exasperated manner, I choose to leave. Rising from the table, I down the rest of my beer before leaving it on the table and heading out the door.

Slamming the door behind me, I make it a few feet outside before the door swings open and the sound of footsteps approaches, trying to catch up. I swing around when I feel a hand on my arm pulling me back.

Pamela's eyes search mine. For a moment, they soften when she sees the conflict in mine. Taking a step back, she runs her fingertips across her lower lip.

"Look, you know how much I cared about Michael, and by default, I care about Summer, too. But you're seriously messing with her head right now."

"I'm…" Before I can interject, she raises her hand and cuts me off.

"You're watching her when you're not at the apartment. You let yourself in…the poor girl is probably terrified, but deep down, you know she cares for you. You stopped her from getting hurt and protected her, but you've told her she needs to leave, and she likely will." She lets out a low breath, looking back at me. "But if I can see how you are around her, then so can everyone else."

Rolling my bottom lip between my teeth, I allow Pamela's words to soak in.

"Either you tell her everything, or you let her go and never contact her again. You're being cruel, and it's not fair on her." Her eyes well with tears as she speaks, but her statement hits me harder than I thought it would.

The guilt and resentment I carry around towards myself seems to come barrelling over the hill and hits me hard. Unable to form words, I nod and continue towards my car. Pamela's words play over and over in my head while my conscience begins to get the better of me.

Chapter Twenty-Three

Bhodi ⚥

It's been a strange forty-eight hours. After Summer's outburst at the church, I gave her a couple of days of space. The hurt in her eyes was too much to handle, but she didn't seem to understand the law, and as a detective, I can't just arrest someone on a whim, no matter how guilty I know they truly are.

I know her emotions were running incredibly high and no matter what I said, I would have just sounded like a condescending prick trying to reason with her. It's an argument I really didn't want to have, and If I'd followed her, there was a good chance it would have continued.

"Grey, my office now!" The captain hangs his head out of the office door before heading back inside.

Sliding a report to the side, I rise from my chair. Getting ready for another ass-chewing, I head inside. Surprisingly, I'm met with Captain Dean and a familiar detective from another precinct.

Entering the office, I idle in the doorway for a moment before the captain gestures for me to sit.

"This is Detective Daly; he's working a missing person case. A familiar name popped up in the investigation." He begins.

I turn to shake Detective Daly's hand before taking my seat.

"Sure." I shrug.

"Harry Maine." The captain speaks first.

"He's Summer Harper's former fiancé." I say without hesitation.

"Did you know he's here in the city?"

"I do. He flew in a day or so after Summer. He's been harassing her, but for now, she's just hoping he'll go away."

"And has he?"

"No, he's visited Michael Harper's apartment a couple of times, but she refused to let him in. She didn't want him arrested; she wants no contact with him." Looking between the two men, I finally ask the question. "What's this about anyway?"

"I got a call a couple of days back." Turning my attention to Detective Daly. "An Alex Crane was reported missing. He didn't turn up for his shift at O'Reilly's. When a colleague went to his place, it looked like a bloodbath, but no body."

I slowly nod, not allowing my eyes to give away any recognition. I slowly inhale and exhale subtly so they won't notice.

"Where does Harry Maine come into it?"

"Looks as though Alex called him just before Detective Strode was shot and then again around fifteen minutes after. There was a few back-and-forth phone calls for around an hour or so before all communication stopped, and no one has heard from Alex since. I managed to get to the bar and retrieve the security footage before it was wiped, it looks as though Alex grabbed Summer before she could leave. Within a minute, Strode comes in and pulls her away from the bar."

"That confirms Strode's version of events, too." My eyes shoot to the captain. "He's awake. I spoke to him an hour ago. He's off for physio, but you can head over after this."

I turn my attention back to the issue, running a hand over my mouth and contemplating my next move.

"And you don't think it was a coincidence the guy that works at the bar where Strode was shot called Harry within that time, and that disappeared?" I say nonchalantly.

"Definitely not."

"Did CSU find anything at Alex's apartment?" I ask.

Detective Daly shakes his head before his brows pinch, and he shrugs.

"They tested the blood. It was pigs, not Alex's."

I paint a confused expression on my face, looking between the two men. My facial features manage to mirror the captains.

"Could it have been a warning?"

"Possibly, but we don't know why. I've issued an arrest warrant for Harry Maine. But by the sounds, it may be best off sitting on Michael's apartment for now if that's where Summer is, he may turn up there."

I blink a couple of times; I don't like the idea of someone watching the building. Questions will be asked if they see me coming and going at different times, but that's something I can mull over later.

"Makes sense, but you should know Harry was spotted twice with Luca Bernardi. I haven't worked out their connection yet, but it's just a heads up."

Detective Daly pales slightly, swallowing hard. He looks between both the captain and me.

"Fuck sake." He mutters before turning his attention towards the open office door.

"What is it?" The captain asks, as Daly stands up and closes the door.

Sitting back down, he gives one final look to anyone passing the office before lowering his voice.

"Apparently, an investigation started around twelve months ago. The PC had a team put together to investigate the potential that cops and detectives on the inside may have been working for Luca."

"But this isn't confirmed?" I ask.

"No, it's only what I've heard from a confidential source at One PP."

"Why has this only just started? Luca's been around for years."

"This is only a rumor." Daly leans in closer. "The PC and a team reviewed all the case files related to Luca. They found that many previous associates that worked with Luca over a brace of years had all gone missing. Now don't get me wrong, these people were scum but they just vanished without a trace."

"The PC thinks some cops did this for Luca?" I ask, trying to understand why anyone would help that fucking bastard or how Daly has come to this pretty dumb conclusion.

"I find that hard to believe, son. Luca's a killer and a rapist, I don't see why anyone would help him." As the captain interjects, I can see he's not buying this shit either.

"Money." Daly shrugs, leaning back in his chair. "If he's willing to pay, sometimes the offer is hard to turn down."

Briefly looking away, I feel a pang of anger rush through me. After seeing what Alex was willing to do for five grand from Harry, it's now a little more believable that we could have dirty cops walking among us.

"Look, I get this could just be a rumor." Daly raises his hands in defense. "I don't want to believe anyone I work with could be taking backhanders from this guy, it's just what I've heard. The PC may be just trying to protect the NYPD and trying to quash anything before something concrete could hit the press."

"We think that Luca could have been the one who killed Michael Harper." I look to the captain, surprised he even said anything. Especially after he told me to let it go.

"Any motive?" Daly asks.

I shake my head no in response.

"Just that Summer was attacked her first night here. Harry arrives a couple of days later, and each time he's been seen, he's been with Luca. No evidence, but it looks suspicious."

"What do we know about Harry?" Daly turns to me.

"Not a lot. All his businesses with Eric Stanton are legit. No crim..."

"Eric Stanton? Daly jerks forward in his chair, alarmed.

"Yeah, Summer Harper's Stepfather."

"Shit, that can't be a coincidence." He mutters, lowering his gaze looks to the desk in front of him.

"You've heard of him before?" I ask.

Daly nods, swallowing hard. As though you can see the shiver running up his spine.

"About a year ago, a woman came into the precinct. Claimed they'd be raped and beaten by Eric Stanton. She went for a rape kit, but no DNA was recovered." Daly lets out a low breath as he continues. "Six months after that, a different woman came in with the same story. Both said they'd been kidnapped from Mexico, drove for days, and then ended up at a party. They claim Eric purchased them for the night, repeatedly raped them, beat them, but they'd managed to escape."

"What happened after that?" I ask, trying to keep my expression neutral.

"They just disappeared from their shelters. They had no papers, no passport, no money. Each within a few days of making the reports, they just vanished. Didn't leave a note or ever try to contact the police again."

"Did you ever speak with Eric about the accusation?"

"He went to his local precinct to make a statement back in L.A. But with no DNA, evidence, or record of him being in New York, there was little we could do."

"Could it have been a setup?" I hate myself for asking; no one should go through such a traumatic ordeal, but something about the story just isn't sitting well with me.

"Maybe, but without the two victims, it went cold. Plus, their legal status and the drugs in their system, they wouldn't have been reliable."

"Eric is here in the city. He was at Michael's funeral yesterday along with his wife, Harry, and Luca."

"What the hell? Why would they show up?" There's a flicker of anger in Daly's face, mirroring mine from Tuesday.

"Harry was there to torment Summer, But I'm not sure about the others."

Daly looks around the office momentarily, his eyes almost looking past the walls as he contemplates his next question.

"What if we had a surveillance team watching them?"

"How would we swing that?"

"All three of them could be in business together. We have the complaints about Eric for rape and battery. There could be something bigger at play here?"

"That's all circumstantial without the two victims. It just looks like a phishing expedition." I say hastily.

"True." Daly rises from his seat and straightens his suit before extending his hand to Captain Dean and myself. "If I hear anything, I'll call you. If it'll help put Luca behind bars for the rest of his life."

Exiting the room, he closes the door behind him. An odd silence falls in the office as the captain, and I look at each other with the same suspicious look.

"Something on your mind Grey?" The captain quirks a brow at me, a small smug smile creeps across his face.

He knows all too well there's something up with Detective Daly's story, but I won't accuse someone I hardly know of being a liar. Especially when I don't know the reasons behind it or have the proof to back my theory up.

"I'm gonna head over to see Strode." Pushing to my feet, captain nods before I head out of the office.

Luckily, the drive to the hospital isn't long, but Detective Daly's visit keeps me occupied. There are too many questions in my head right now, and luckily, the captain wasn't buying it either. This guy must have thought I was fucking born yesterday; however, I do need to see those two reports first before I jump to conclusions.

I don't knock, stepping into the hospital room. I raise an eyebrow at the bouquets scattered around the room. Raising a sarcastic eyebrow to Strode, he just shakes his head.

"Admirers Strode?" leaning into one of the bouquets, I smell the roses. "Red roses, fancy."

"Give it a rest, kid. It's too fucking early for your sarcasm." He jokes, rising in his bed slightly.

Walking over, I prop a pillow behind his back and hand him a glass of water before taking a seat.

"Captain told you I was awake, huh?" he asks, placing the water back on the side.

"Yeah, he said you were off trying out for the Olympic team first."

Both Strode and I break out into a hearty laughter, made even worse as his clutches his side in pain.

"Jesus fucking Christ, they throw you around. I don't know what they were expecting from me, but shit! I think that was worse than being shot." He jokes.

"Maggie been around?" I ask.

"Yeah, I told her to head home for some sleep. She looked tired, and I think we both needed some space from each other." He smiles.

"Think she'll stay this time?"

Strode gives me a small smile as he shrugs. The look in his eyes tells me he's hopeful. But we both know what he's like, and Maggie is a strong woman. She won't put up with his shit.

"Who knows? She offered to stay a few weeks at the house."

"That's a good start."

"Yeah." The hopeful looks passes over Strode's face, replaced with one of determination. "So, what's happened?"

I let out a heavy sigh, neglecting to tell him about my part in Alex's disappearance. I relay the story from earlier today with Detective Daly and the captain. As I do, his face pales, and an almost brooding look ghosts across his features. As I finish the story, he's silent and looks away.

"What is it?"

Strode's runs his hand across the white stubble on his chin. His shoulders sag slightly. He forgets he's been my partner for so long, I can tell when something is bothering him, so I ask again.

"Strode." His eyes finally meet mine. "What is it?"

I watch as his eyes flicker. Wetting his lips, he pulls himself a little higher in the bed, resting against the large pillow for support.

"Did you notice how Detective Daly was working sex crimes and now working missing persons?" He cocks his head to one side.

Sitting back in my seat, I mull over the question for a moment before answering with the most obvious answer.

"It's not for everyone. Most detectives only stay a couple of years or so. It's a tough gig." I say.

"It is, but Daly was only there nine months at the most."

My brow furrows, leaning forward in my chair. I eye Strode curiously.

"How do you know?"

"Cops talk, we both know that. I remember hearing about the case from a couple of buddies down at the bar one night. They thought it was odd: one detective catches both cases, both girls go missing, and it's the same story?" He quirks a brow, giving me a knowing look before continuing. "Some of the ones with a darker sense of humor started calling him the strangler, implying he got rid of them."

"But why would he do that?"

"Because people like to joke and assume the worst, but there was no proof, and it was all just an ugly rumor that spread across the precincts. Eventually, he was moved along to missing persons, but whether that was at his request of the brass, I'm not sure." Strode shrugs.

"Something doesn't feel right though, Strodey."

"I always said you're too good for this job, kid. You can spot something off a mile away."

"Isn't it a bit coincidental? Two women, same story, months apart, both go missing, and both..."

"Report the crime to the same detective that was on duty and accuse the same guy?" He interjects.

Blinking a couple of times, I slowly nod.

"Doesn't seem right and he makes a sudden appearance whilst I'm looking into both Harry and Luca."

"It doesn't, but if the captain is suspicious too, then Daly isn't as clever as he thinks he is."

"What would you suggest?"

Strode exhales, crossing his arms over his chest for a moment. Looking ahead to the wall in front. I watch as the cogs turn in his mind, contemplating how he would handle this.

"It depends, really." He finally says.

"Go on."

"If you're already suspicious of him, don't fall into the trap. However, if you believe this surveillance may pan out, always wear a wire and always let someone know where you are at all times."

"Just all seems a bit too convenient, you know?"

"I do, kid." Strode nods.

"I need to see those reports."

"Those reports will just confirm what you already think that it's all a little too convenient."

"Yeah, true. He wants to sit on Summer's apartment too, see if Harry shows up."

Strode raises a sarcastic brow towards me, a smirk pulling at the corner of his mouth as I shake my head.

"Really? That's probably a little inconvenient for you."

"Don't start."

"Kid, I'm not going to tell you what to do. I tried and it didn't work. Just be careful, ok?" Strode offers me a warm fatherly smile, knowing all too well I wouldn't have stayed away when he first told me to.

Chapter Twenty-Four
Summer ♥

With my finger hovering over the call button, I once again can find an excuse not to call Bhodi and apologize for my shitty outburst. I hate feeling stubborn, but for some reason, I just can't bring myself to roll over and apologize, even though I know it's the right thing to do.

Part of me feels apologizing is weak, and he'll believe anytime I get angry, I'll just apologize and that will be that. Catching myself, I inwardly mutter. I'm talking as though Bhodi and I will have the opportunity to have more arguments, but we both know that isn't the case.

I want to stay, but with Harry still around and now for some reason my mom and Eric have decided to show up too, I feel suffocated. As though they're all trying to make sure I know they're around, watching me, for whatever reason.

Surely mom and Eric wouldn't allow Harry to hurt me, would they? The thought worries me, mom and Eric both know Harry hits me, hell, my mom has seen the results, but they didn't seem to care. Unless they thought it was ….NO! Shaking my head, I catch myself and make excuses for them. They knew exactly what he was doing and did nothing to stop or even help. I owe them nothing and shouldn't be fucking defending them.

Turning my attention back to the laptop, I push the thoughts of them aside and continue to idly scroll through homes to rent for a few months on the West Coast, East Coast…Hell, anywhere right now looks better than being trapped here. My forefinger nervously picks at my thumb, looking at listing after listing of homes and apartments in each place. None jump out at me because it'll just be me. No friends, no family, and right now, no job to focus on.

With dad's ashes due to be collected tomorrow morning, I feel my time here is running out. I haven't heard from Father Dudley yet though, so I guess this could delay my escape from New York.

Reaching for the glass of red wine, I lift it to my lips and take a large gulp. As I do, the thoughts begin to whirl in my mind.

Why does he want me gone so badly?

Tasting the rich and warm vanilla tones, I sigh heavily. Placing the glass back down onto the marble counter. With my elbows placed on the surface, I aimlessly stare off into space. My eyes are fixed on the screen, but I know I'm not taking in any of the information. Nothing looks appealing. For the past few days, I've allowed myself to think about what life could be like in New York. However, in my fantasy Harry, Eric, and my mom are nowhere to be seen.

With my phone still placed on the breakfast bar, I jump as it begins to ring. 'Unknown Caller' lights up the screen as I sit frozen in place for a moment. Taking a deep breath, I answer softly.

"Hello?"

"You know you have a tell." That deep, husky voice speaks through the phone as the shudder runs over my skin. "When you're nervous, you pick at your thumb with your forefinger."

Clutching the phone in my hand, I glance at my thumb which I've managed to pick at enough to make sore. My eyes begin to slowly move around the room, looking to each corner as the deep chuckle crackles down the line.

"How long have you been watching me?" I turn around on my stool and look towards the living room.

"Does it matter?" He teases.

"Yes." I speak through gritted teeth, my frustration becoming more apparent with each passing second.

"Since the moment you moved in."

As my stomach drops, my mind flashes over the past few weeks in this apartment. The times I've been asleep, in the shower, and when Bhodi has been here. Me on my knees, handcuffed.

Fuck...

The deep, throaty laugh continues to taunt me. I feel a hot sweat fall over my entire body. The realization I've been watched during some of the most intimate moments, my privacy was fucking invaded, and my mind reels. I swipe the sweat from my brow, as my stomach feels like it wants to fall out of my ass.

Trying to control my breathing, I slowly inhale and exhale keeping my eyes fixed onto the living room. When my feet hit the cool tiles, I slowly walk into the living room, glancing around the walls, wondering how I could have missed a fucking camera.

Easy, because I wasn't fucking expecting to see one.

My heart begins to thunder in my chest, slowly moving in circles, hoping to see the obvious lens that's been watching me for weeks.

"What do you want from me?" My voice becoming louder. "You stalk me, you come here whenever you fucking want, you take what you want, you warn me to leave, and then you just fuck off and don't reappear for days? Seriously who the fuck are you?" I begin to feel lightheaded at my outburst. The burst of adrenaline leaves me shaking.

"You'd prefer I knocked?"

My face contorts with further rage at his poor attempt at humor, trying to ignore the fact he's been watching me.

The sarcasm in his tone, causing me to pinch the bridge of my nose. All this fucking time, I've felt that shudder up my spine, felt someone watching me, I thought I was fucking crazy, but it turns out I wasn't. He's been fucking watching me, tormenting me from a distance, all because he can.

With the tornado of scenarios spinning around in my head, I keep going to open my mouth, but no words come out. Everything I want to say is stuck in my throat. Eventually wiping the sweat pouring from my brow, I manage to spit out the only words I can form.

"Fuck you!" Mashing the buttons to end the call, my eyes frantically move around the room one more time before grabbing my purse and coat on the way out the door.

Bursting through the main doors of the building, I throw my hand out for a taxi. Luckily, the roads are busy. Within seconds, one pulls up, and I immediately hop in.

"Just drive!" I demand, letting out an exasperated breath.

Clearly, I'm not the first person to ask for this, the driver merely shoots me a look in the rearview mirror before shrugging and pulling out into the traffic. Passing by the tall buildings, I take deep breaths, trying to calm down and figure out my next step.

With the faint sound of ringing, from my purse the taxi driver pipes up, pulling me from my thoughts.

"Your phone's ringing."

I cock my head towards him, but once the noise registers, I let out a heavy sigh. Fumbling around in my purse, I finally find my phone.

Unknown Caller - Fucking great...

Knowing he can't see me now, I hit the accept button and pull the phone to my ear.

What now?" I answer, unenthused.

"Summer? Is that you? Thank god you answered" I know the voice immediately, but he sounds a little taken aback.

I purposely ignored all incoming calls from my mom and Eric and blocked Harry. They have no reason to contact me anymore.

"Eric?" I find myself straightening in my seat.

"I need to speak with you, Summer, it's urgent."

Before I protest, Eric speaks again. This time, his voice becomes lower, as though he's cautious as to who could be listening.

"It's about your father. I really need you to hear this."

His words grab my attention immediately but feeling torn between his loyalty to me and towards Harry, I bit my lower lip, unsure of how to answer.

"Just tell me, Eric." I feel my body shaking still, forcing the words out. I try to sound in control.

"I...I can't. I need to give you something."

"Fuck sake." I mutter, running my hand over my face. I glance out the window, thinking of a suitable place to meet. "Meet me at the church from my dad's service. I'll meet you inside as soon as I can."

Ending the call, I don't give Eric a chance to answer. I immediately regret my decision to meet him, but the sound in his voice wasn't something I can ignore. He genuinely sounded worried, which was unlike him. If he knows something about my dad, then I need to hear it, even if it's just him confirming what I already know. Harry was behind it all.

Once I've given the driver the address, I fall back into my seat and continue to pick at my thumb nervously. Catching myself, I sigh, glancing around for the obvious camera following me around. The street begins to look familiar, seeing the church in the distance. Twenty or so minutes have passed as the taxi has driven through the busy rush hour traffic, and the sun has already begun to set.

Once the car pulls up on the sidewalk, I pass the driver the money and slide out. Standing at the bottom of the steps, I look up. The church looks almost eerie in this light. I take a deep breath and kick myself for agreeing to meet here when it's getting dark.

Turning around, the street is busy. Smartly dressed men and women in suits finishing their hectic days, tourists snapping photos with their families and groups of friends heading to the local bars for a catch-up. I feel like a complete outsider as I suspiciously glare around the street, wondering if I'm still being watched or followed. Eventually I turn back to the church and roll my eyes.

He's hardly going to stand in a busy street masked up, where everyone can see what a fucking psycho he is.

Shaking my head, I ascend the steps to the church.

Chapter Twenty-Five
Summer ♥

Stepping into the church, I spot Eric sitting at the end of the pew halfway down the aisle. As he stares straight ahead, I feel myself begin to pick at my thumb again. Shaking my right hand, I glance around the quiet area as I approach. Hearing my footsteps, Eric snaps towards my direction, then looks around before facing forward again.

My brows pinch as he shuffles over, and I sit next to him. His knee nervously bounces, while he tries to steady his trembling hands.

Lowering my voice, I lean in. "Eric, what's this about? You're worrying me."

He refuses to meet my gaze, but I can see the sweat beading on his forehead. I find myself nervously glancing round, his entire demeanour is off. He's scared, but I have no idea what of.

"Has something happened?" I ask again.

I feel myself sink into the pew, spotting Father Dudley lighting candles at the altar. I try my best to avoid looking in his direction and turning my head slightly but as he turns, I can see him in my peripheral. My gaze burns holes into the side of Eric's head with my intense stare, hoping it won't prompt an unwanted guest to try to speak with me.

If he thinks we're in a deep conversation, he'll hopefully not interrupt. But with Eric refusing to look my way, I feel myself failing. Letting out a low breath, I feel the frustration building.

"You know something about my dad, now fucking tell me, Eric!" I speak through gritted teeth, hoping no one nearby can hear me swearing in church.

My entire body is tense, waiting for Eric to speak. The silence is killing me, like some god-awful medieval torture. Glancing around, there are a few people dotted around the large church but look as though they're far enough away to be unable to hear us speak.

"I want you to know how sorry I am, Summer." Eric finally turns to me. As I look around his face, I see an immense sadness deep within his eyes.

I shake my head slightly, unsure what he means.

"What do you mean?" My brow creases.

"For everything that's happened to you." He speaks in a low and solemn voice.

"I don't understand?"

I hear the sound of the large church door creaking open then closing, followed by the sound of heavy footsteps approaching. I feel a shudder run over my body. Eric looks past me, and his eyes follow the person heading towards us. My lips form a straight line when I quickly realize, he's sad because he's fucking set me up.

Inhaling a slow breath, I count to ten before turning around. Allowing the air to slowly leave my lungs, I steady the trembling that's currently running all over my body. The fear of who's there isn't what's bothering me. It's the confirmation of who's there.

"Hello, sweet girl." The voice is like slugs crawling all over my body whilst paralyzed.

Turning around in the pew, Harry stands in the aisle. His face cracks into a wicked, forced smile. He bares his teeth to me. His eyes flicker with the evil that lies deep within his rotten soul. My eyes dart around the large church, but it appears to only be the three of us now. I'm trapped between the two men, and I can only stare at the man I hate with a deep fucking passion.

Stepping away slightly from the pew, he gestures for me to stand. I look back to Eric, but he just stares ahead as the tears roll down his cheeks.

"Where are we going?" I ask dryly, refusing to look at Harry.

"Just for a drive, you know...catch up." His tone is strangely calm, even if the smile that's still painted on is maniacal.

I feel my teeth biting the dry skin on my lower lip, another bad habit I have when I'm anxious. My incisors are trying to draw blood, I don't know why. Maybe if I feel a little pain, I'll suddenly spring into action and escape this fucking beartrap, but I know that's not what's going to happen, and even if I do, I have no idea who's outside or what's going to happen once I set foot out those doors.

Looking back towards the altar, I don't see Father Dudley anywhere; all the people have left. I feel my forehead crease at the strangeness of it all. It's as though they all knew something bad was happening and moved away to protect themselves.

Wish I had that kind of fucking sixth sense.

My shoulders sag, and the only thought that comes to mind is to waste time. Looking to my left Eric has his head bowed slightly. When I nudge him, he jumps. Almost backing away from me.

"Can you move over a little, please?" I ask softly.

Eric's eyes dart between both Harry and me before he slides a seat over and I do the same. Turning to Harry, he looks confused for a moment before sliding into the pew. With the three of us sitting shoulder to shoulder, my eyes are fixed on the large burning candles at the altar. Focusing on the flames, I begin to speak.

"I don't know what Harry threatened you with, Eric, but I'm not angry with you." I keep my voice steady. "I know you're just protecting yourself, and no one should be punished for that."

Eric slowly nods, wiping the tears from his eyes. My focus turns to Harry, who seems unfazed by my request for him to sit with me.

"If I go with you, are you going to kill me?"

He lets out a small laugh, amused by the question put to him. His snake-like eyes turn towards me, and his lips curl into a slow smile. He doesn't answer my question, not verbally anyway but I know the answer by the flicker of amusement that dances across his expression. The thought of inflicting fear on me brings him a sick happiness. Like a child pulling the wings off a fly and looking in wonder at how it suffers.

Hearing footsteps towards the front of the church, I sit up in the pew craning my neck to see where they're coming from. Preying it's not Father Dudley. I doubt Harry would show mercy to someone in the wrong place at the wrong time. As the echoes get louder, I feel Harry and Eric shift in their seats, looking around as to who's approaching.

When a firm grasp grabs my arm and jerks me from the pew, a gunshot is fired. The bullet echoes through the church, causing

Harry to release his grip on me. I feel myself fall back into the pew as Harry lands in the aisle. With his gun raised and eyes wild, he frantically turns around, trying to spot the source of the noise.

"Get the fuck out here now!"

"If I do that, you're under arrest, Harry."

The breath I was holding in finally escapes my lungs, the familiar voice bringing hope as the footsteps near. A shadow flickers by the pillar. Harry catches my eyes and immediately turns around and fires four times. I slam my hands over my ears and duck behind the pew, pulling Eric with me.

"Fuck you, cop! I'll fucking kill you before you arrest me!" Harry's voice becoming frantic, behaving like a caged animal.

"Sure, about that?" The arrogance in Bhodi's voice is undeniable as he appears at the altar.

Stepping down, he keeps his gun trained on Harry, who finally turns around. The look of humor now replaced with horror as Bhodi has managed to move quickly through the church. Slowly rising to my feet, Bhodi looks at me before turning his attention back to Harry.

I scream loudly when Harry grabs a fistful of my hair, dragging me by the roots to use me as a human shield. Pulling my body to his, his grip on my hair causes my eyes to water. With the barrel of the gun pressed firmly to my temple, I can feel the anger radiating off Harry. I feel his breath on my neck before his voice bellows into my ear.

"I'll fucking shoot her, I'll blow her fucking brains all over this church."

Bhodi looks between us for a moment, his eyes flicking between us both.

"I wouldn't do that."

I feel my blood run cold, and my eyes fly open. A deep click is heard from behind. I look to Bhodi, but a smirk has now appeared on his face. When I'm forcefully jerked towards the exit of the church, two large men dressed in all black point their guns at Harry and me.

My jaw falls open. I can almost hear my own blood surging through my ears as I look between the two masked men.

"What the fuck?" Harry mutters.

The fear in his voice is almost beautiful; I can feel his heart trying to burst out of his chest when he realizes, he's fucking trapped.

I stare ahead, Harry is mumbling, but I've tuned him out. I can't tear my eyes away from Two/Face, the black matte mask staring back at me. The dark reaper stands in front of me, his weapon pointed at Harry's head.

"You have a choice, Harry." Bhodi's voice oozes confidence and sarcasm, causing Harry to spin us both around. "You either leave here with me, in handcuffs. Or you go with them." He gestures to Two/Face and the other masked man.

"But either way, you aren't leaving here a free man; at least I know what will happen to you in custody. I can't guarantee your safety with the other option."

He spins around again. Neither of the masked men has moved. However, the one standing on the right slowly nods. The sinister skull mark is dirty. Trying to focus, I can spot dried blood and dirt smeared over what was once probably a white mask.

Harry growls, and my body is shunted forward into the pew. Smacking my cheek onto the solid wood with a loud crunch, I cry out. Rolling onto my back, I feel Eric try to pull me close to protect me, but Harry now holds the gun to his own head.

"I'm not fucking going anywhere!" he screams.

His body turning, both exits are blocked, and he has nowhere to go. Holding the gun to his own head, the sweat pours from his skin. His eyes are wild, but a shot is fired once he turns to Bhodi again. Slapping my palms over my ears, I see Harry writhing on the floor as blood pools into the carpet, clutching onto his arm.

I feel the relief wash over me as the gun lays by his side. Scrambling to my feet, I grab it and stand over him, pointing it at his head. I feel my body shake and the anger clutching me tight. Harry's eyes widen in fear, but as a hand is placed over mine, he gently takes it from my grasp, which I don't protest.

"It's over, Summer." Bhodi's voice is quiet and soft as he leans in close to me.

The faint sound of sirens approaches, getting louder. Bhodi kicks Harry onto his front whilst he continues to cry in pain. Handcuffing him, he forcefully pulls him to his feet as the patrol and a couple of swat officers enter from both exits of the church.

I fall back hard into the pew, and with my head in my hands, I look at Eric. Still shaking in fear, he slowly nods towards me.

"Harry threatened to shoot you. That detective shot him in the arm to save you."

"You didn't see the other men?" I ask quietly.

"What men?"

He shrugs, and a knowing smile ghosts across his face before it's pushed away and replaced with shock.

Chapter Twenty-Six

Bhodi ⚥

"Grey, my office!"

The order pulls me back to the present, sliding my paperwork across the desk. My chair squeaks across the floor tiles. I feel my tense muscles stretch as the threat of exhaustion lingers over me. Running my hand over my tired face, I head for the captain's office. Already sitting at his desk, he gestures for me to sit.

Closing the door behind me, I fall into the opposite chair as the captain continues to study me.

"That was some good work out there today, Grey."

I nod slowly. "Thank you, sir."

"But I have one problem."

I cock my head to one side, gesturing for the captain to finish. "Ok?"

"Harry seems to be under the impression there were two masked men in that church also."

I can't help but scoff, running my hand over my face again. I smirk, cocking an eyebrow towards the captain, who merely mirrors my expression.

"I know, I know, son. The guys on some much coke, he'll be saying lilac unicorns shot him next."

"With no statements to verify his story, we'll have to let him detox for now and try to get a statement in a couple of days. Detective Daly will speak with him first about the disappearance of Alex Crane."

"Understood."

"Finish your reports and get home."

Pushing myself from the chair, I stride towards the door. As my fingers lace around the door handle, I turn back to the captain. Opening my mouth to speak, he looks up from his desk.

"What is it?"

"Did you ever get any confirmation on what Daly said the other day?"

The captain shakes his head in response.

"I didn't, but that doesn't mean anything. Sometimes One PP doesn't have leaky walls." He shrugs.

"Thanks."

Stepping back into the main office, I glance towards the clock. Midnight is fast approaching, and I have a couple of loose ends to sort out before the morning. Moving towards my desk, a bellowing unknown voice pulls my attention in the opposite direction.

"I want to see the captain now!" A tall man with dark greying hair, wearing an expensive grey suit with a black overcoat slung over his arm approaches me with his briefcase.

Fuck sake, this cunt.

I recognize him immediately; however, I don't think he recognizes me. We've only ever had one direct dealing, but I've seen him storm in and out of here enough times. A fucking slimy overpriced lawyer. When I go to speak, the captain's office door flies open, and they stare daggers at each other for around three seconds. There's an undeniable burning hatred between the two. The silence consumes the room as neither speak.

The captain turns his attention to me, "Go home."

"Elijah, my office now!" The captain barks his order to the lawyer.

Taking one final look at the glorified mouthpiece, his jaw ticks as he proceeds into the office without a word. Grabbing my keys off the desk, I waste no time in heading towards the exit. I take one final glance toward the captain's office. Elijah Elom stands in the office waving his arms around in a dramatic fashion. However, the captain seems to glaze over the tantrum while sitting behind his desk. My report on the event is solid, and both Eric's and Summer's statements match mine. For now, I have nothing to worry about, and for once, Harry's coke addiction has helped.

Sliding into my car, the engine roars to life. Adjusting the mirror, I glance around the quiet car park before pulling out and heading away from the precinct. I let out a low breath and feel my body going into autopilot. The only thing bugging me after tonight is weighing me down. I feel like I'm being pulled underwater with weights tied to my feet. No matter how hard I try to swim towards the surface, I'm drowning.

The way she looked at him.

I smack my fists hard into the steering wheel, hoping to relieve some of the burning tension burrowing through my body.

"AAAAAAAAAHHHHHHHHHHHHHHHHHHHHHHHHH FUCK SAKE!"

Screaming and white-knuckling the steering wheel, I try to let the rage out. The pent-up anger that I thought I had a handle on, but I know I fucking don't. The way she looked at him pulled my fucking heart from deep within my chest and fucking shattered it.

As soon as Harry was stuck between the two of us, she couldn't pull her eyes away. I saw the fucking hope, the want, and the fucking need.

She was never mine; I should have always known that.

Once the familiar houses come into view, I turn the corner and pull up in a quiet street. Killing the engine, I take a few deep breaths and watch my hands tremble. Running my hand over my mouth, I stare out the window, trying to work out my next steps.

Stepping out of the car, I glance around the street, but no one's around. The streetlights are dim, and all the windows' lights are out. Luckily, this residential area doesn't ever get very busy during this time. Pulling my leather jacket a little higher around my neck, the icy wind glides through the sparse street. Heading for the house, I begin to head up the stairs.

When the door flies open, I'm met with a glare. We stand a few feet away from each other, but I know I've crossed a fucking line. The rage coming off Jimmy is undeniable, and he's not someone who bites easily.

"Don't you ever fucking ask me to do that again!"

Jimmy moves from the doorway, and I follow, raising my hands in defense. Stepping into the brownstone, I follow him toward the living room where both Pamela and Axe sit. Their expressions match Jimmy's.

Axe stands. As he barrels over, Jimmy throws his arm out to stop him. I don't move. I stand my ground even though I know I've used them to my own advantage.

"What the fuck were you playing at out there? You could have got us cornered by the police," He spits out.

"That was never going to happen. Harry wouldn't have gone with you."

"Really?" Axe cocks his head to one side, speaking sarcastically.

"Yeah, really."

Jimmy's eyes narrow on mine. He looks between Axe and me, shaking his head.

"I don't fucking believe you!" He throws his hands in the air; he begins pacing the room. "You had me wear your fucking mask because you wanted to throw her off."

My jaw moves slightly from side to side when all eyes fly to mine.

"Jesus Christ, Bhodi, I saw how she reacted when she saw it! You can't hide that, she fucking cares about Two/Face, and you're continuing to mess with her fucking head!" Jimmy shouts, he never shouts, but right now, he's fucking livid with me.

Pamela shakes her head, and Axe runs his hand over his face before falling back into his chair.

"I had my reasons." I speak calmly.

"You had your reasons? Care to tell us your fucking reasons?" Axe speaks through gritted teeth.

Reaching for the bottle of Jameson's on the side table, I pour a glass. Taking a seat, I pass the bottle to Axe. As everyone takes a seat, I swirl the amber liquid in the tumbler before downing the measure in one.

"Detective Daly came by the precinct the other day and asked questions about Harry. I told him what I knew, what Detective Grey knew." I begin. "He told me he was investigating Alex Crane's disappearance, apparently, some colleagues were worried after he didn't turn up for his shift. The police went to his apartment, and the place was smeared in pigs' blood, and it was turned upside down."

Axe immediately shoots me a concerned look, to which I nod in response.

"I know. We picked him up off the streets and never set foot anywhere near his apartment. The police searched his call logs and found he'd been communicating with Harry and wanted to speak with him, but by this point, Harry conveniently couldn't be found."

A heavy silence falls over the room. Jimmy, Axe, and Pamela all look towards me to carry on.

"Father Dudley called when he saw Summer at the church. He described Eric, and I knew it was a trap. Harry still wants Summer for some reason, so that's why I called. You never had anything to worry about. I'd called in backup when I saw him panicking. He knows he's safer in custody."

"Why show Two/Face to Summer?" Jimmy asks.

Leaning back in the chair, I let out a low breath.

"I wanted to know if we can trust her. She still doesn't know about her dad's separate life, and she doesn't know about us. I wanted to see if she would say anything."

"And did she pass the test?" Pamela interjects, her face still unreadable.

"She did. She never said a word and has never even said anything to me." I confirm.

"Where do we go from here?" I turn to Axe when he asks the obvious question.

"Luca Bernardi's lawyer stormed into the precinct as I left. He'll likely represent Harry. We know he'll probably make bail. My report and the statements are sound, but that doesn't matter. Detective Daly mentioned a task force at One PP. The PC put it together to weed out the potential dirty cops working for Luca. So far, I can't find any proof on it."

"Who the fuck would help him?" Pamela spits out, her body almost trembling as Axe reaches for her hand.

"I don't know, Pam. Our only guess could be money, but I can't find any proof, and neither can the captain." I shrug. She shakes her head, but Axe pulls her close.

"For the last eight years, we've killed anyone working with Luca, are you sure the PC isn't just hunting us?" Axe speaks, almost amused by the whole thing.

"No, I think there's a lot more people than what we've removed." I shrug.

"Has Harry been interviewed yet?" Jimmy leans in.

"No, he'll need to be checked over by a doctor first. He tried to tell the police two masked men were also at the church, but because of the drugs, no one believes him."

"And Eric?"

"He didn't see enough."

"Something seemed off about him. He genuinely looked scared. Did we find out what Harry threatened him with?"

Looking at Jimmy, the realization hits me hard. Standing up, I begin pacing.

"Shit! The rapes!"

The group look at each other, confused by my outburst. Running from the house, I race towards my car. Unlocking it, I open the trunk and rummage through a box file. Once I've found what I need, I slam the trunk shut and lock it before rushing back up the stairs to the house.

Slapping the reports down on the table in front of everyone, Pam and Jimmy take one each before scanning their eyes over the statements. With his glasses balanced on the end of his nose, Jimmy peers over the rims.

"I hope these are copies."

"I'm not a fucking boy scout Jimmy."

Axe leans over Pam's shoulder as they both scan the report.

"He's been accused of rape?" Her brows shoot up.

"Twice." Jimmy says, his eyes still roaming the words on the page, while he gently bites his thumb.

"See an issue with it though?" I ask, gesturing further up the page.

As Jimmy leans towards Pam and reads her report, his eyes dart back and forth between the two documents. His eyes flash to mine, a puzzled look on his face.

"Same M.O, same detective, same person accused, six months apart, both victims are illegal, and both disappeared without a trace."

"Also, no proof and no DNA." I point out.

"Was Eric even here in the city at the time?"

"No record of him being here in New York. He went to the local precinct in L.A. to make a statement, but nothing happened after that." I shrug.

"You think he's being set up?"

"I do, and I think Detective Daly is working with Luca, or maybe being forced to."

"Because this all just seems far too convenient?"

"Exactly. Before he left the captain's office, he mentioned surveillance, too."

"Yeah, I get it." Pamelas looks between us all. "But why? If there's no evidence Eric was even around to commit those crimes, why would he be worried about being framed?"

"What if someone set up those women, to be killed?" Axe asks.

"So, the story about rape was made up? But they were eventually murdered and disposed of?" Running a hand over my face, the connection doesn't make sense to me.

"What if it's all connected? Eric is accused or a crime, and all of a sudden, the victims conveniently disappear. Harry and Luca are seen together as soon as Harry lands in New York and then Eric contacts Summer, luring her out in the open for Harry, we all saw how distraught he was over what he was being forced to do, What if it's all blackmail? With one person pulling the strings?" Jimmy speaks but he sounds uncertain, although something isn't adding up.

Replaying his words over, it doesn't make sense. It's not impossible but it's too messy.

"We need to go back to the very beginning." I say, placing my glass down on the table. "Someone murdered Michael, shot him in his office."

There's an uncomfortable silence filling the room, I look to Axe, Jimmy and Pam. They deflate, nodding at my comment.

"Why?" I ask. "What had him killed?"

"He was getting nervous; he had all his files removed from the apartment and we put them in storage like he requested. He had the cameras installed, changed to a pin code lock on the door instead of a key."

"And he wouldn't tell us why or what he was working on." I clarify.

"That didn't make sense, he'd never keep something from us." Axe points out. "Not in all the time we've worked together."

"Yeah, but he was careful too, if he was suspicious of something he'd investigate it first before sharing with us." Jimmy sips his drink, looking between us all.

"What did he ask you to remove from the apartment?" I ask.

Jimmy takes a moment, with the glass clasped between his hands. looking ahead before his eyes dart between us all.

"It was just personal documents, insurance documents for the clubs, ad hoc business statements and there was a camera."

"We need to go though it; he may have hidden something amongst it all."

"Fine, I'll dig it out tomorrow." Jimmy turns to me, his eyes narrow on mine. An overwhelming seriousness crosses his face. "You need to tell Summer the truth, Bhodi, all of it. We can handle the Daly stuff for now, but she deserves the truth. Even if it breaks her fucking heart, I trust her to keep the secret."

All the hairs rise on my body, that vulnerable shudder I fucking hate so much, crawling all over my skin. The three pairs of eyes all look towards me, Pam and Axe nod in subtle agreement.

Chapter Twenty-Seven
Summer ♥

"How are you feeling?" I clutch onto Detective Strode's hand as he smiles sweetly back to me.

"Well, if I'm honest. I look a little better than you." We both laugh as I lean back in my chair.

I gesture to the gash on my cheek, which has tiny stitches holding it all together. I wince slightly as even smiling hurts, causing it to feel like it's about to burst open.

"OW!" I continue to laugh.

"You know you didn't have to come visit. You should head home and get some rest."

I shake my head, not wanting to be alone in that apartment or to see anyone. Seeing Two/Face confirmed what I already knew: I have an undeniable pull toward him. I stood between the two men I care for and felt my heart crack.

It's morbid, it's wrong, but I can't help it.

"Something on your mind, kid?" Detective Strode leans in.

I blink a couple of times before shaking my head.

"No, no…I'm fine."

He quirks his brow towards me. He can see right through my small lie and I feel my shoulders drop, letting out a low breath.

"I thought Bhodi would be here that's all."

A small smile crosses the detective's face, causing the smile lines on his face to look more pronounced.

"Unfortunately, he can't for now. He'll have to give a statement about the shooting and what happened at the church. He can't be seen speaking to you in case you're seen to be getting your stories straight. It's just procedure."

"I know…"

"I can see how much he cares about you. Hell, I'd go even as far as to say he's in love with you."

My head snaps towards the detective, who merely smiles back at me. The softness in his eyes is inviting.

"I barely know him."

"But you know enough for now, else you wouldn't want him here."

"I guess." I blink a couple of times before speaking again. "Detective Strode?"

He laughs a little, waving his hand towards me.

"Summer, I think we're past the formalities. Just call me Al."

I smile at the kind gesture.

"Al…What do you know about Bhodi?"

"You mean personally?"

"Yeah."

Al leans against his pillow, his eye flicker slightly as he stares ahead. I feel myself slowly lean closer when he wets his lips, as though he's going to speak.

"That's not for me to discuss with you Summer. I can't."

"Can't or won't?" I feel my voice crack slightly.

"Both Summer, some things need to come from the person it concerns."

I try to understand his words, as though I'm trying to analyze the comment, but when I go to speak again, a knock at the door pulls our attention away.

When two patrol officers enter, Al politely greets them both.

"I guess your ride home is waiting, Summer." He places his hand over mine and gives it a light squeeze. "Thanks for dropping in."

Al's eyes are kind, but I feel he's trying to get rid of me.

Standing from the chair, I lean over and give him a light kiss on the cheek before a silent thank you in my smile as I leave.

Once I leave the hospital, the weather is bitter, and I feel my entire body shake with exhaustion and hunger. Sliding into the waiting police cruiser, I sag against the leather interior. Luckily, the officers are silent as I lean my elbow on the door and aimlessly stare out the window during the drive.

When the car pulls up onto the curb, I'm jolted awake, letting out a small gasp as my heavy eyes scan the area. The officer in the passenger seat turns around, and my mind catches up to where I am.

"Do you want us to escort you upstairs?" The young officer looks a little older than me. Her brown eyes are filled with kindness and warmth, instantly putting me back at ease.

"No, I'm ok thank you."

Opening the door, I slide out. Glancing around the street, but it's quiet currently. Rolling her window down, she passes me a card.

"That's the precinct number if you need anything ok?"

I take the card and nod. "Thank you."

Turning on my heels, I pick up the pace. Pushing the large glass door open, I stroll through the lobby, avoiding the night staff's gaze and head straight for the elevator. Pressing the button for my floor, the doors shut instantly. I allow my body to sag against the mirror momentarily, aimlessly staring up at the floor numbers as they climb towards home.

Once the door slides open, I find myself checking behind me as I punch in the code for the apartment. Once the door clicks open, I give it a hard shove before slamming it behind me. When my back presses into the solid wood, I allow my knees to give way and slide to the floor. Letting out a heavy sigh, my head falls back into the wood as my eyes become heavier.

That smell...

Slowly opening my eyes, I inhale again. Slowly rising to my feet, I pass the kitchen and drop my bag onto the breakfast bar. My heavy, tired feet drag along the wooden floor when I find myself standing in the living room's entrance.

A plume of cigarette smoke dances through the air. I spot the lit cherry immediately when it burns a deep shade of red. Leaning against the wall, I look at the table where the mask sits. My eyes roam the dark figure as he stands, staring out of the window. The moonlight of the city dancing off the large silhouette.

Moving through the living room, I see my reflection in the window as I approach. I know he can see it too. Pressing my chest into his back, I lace my arms around his torso, burying my nose into his clothes, and I inhale deeply. I feel his body stiffen for a moment before he relaxes and his shoulders sag slightly. His leather-gloved hand, glides over mine.

"Who are you?" I whisper softly.

Reaching for the mask, he slides it over his face before turning to me. Taking a couple of steps back, he gently reaches out and runs the back of his hand over my cheek. My eyes flutter close, whilst a single tear escapes.

His hand moves down my neck to my arm and eventually takes my hand and interlocking our fingers as he guides me towards the single armchair in the room. Taking a seat, I watch whilst he moves to the kitchen. After a moment and some light clicking, he re-enters with two glasses and a bottle of whiskey in his hands.

Pouring two generous measures, he passes one to me, before taking his own and moving back to the chair by the window. I sit silently, with my hands wrapped around the glass. I force down the knot in my throat, Two/Face places the tumbler on the table beside him, gently swirling the glass.

"Who are you?"

I force the words out again, as he stops whirling liquid in the glass. The dark mask turns to me, and I watch with bated breath, waiting for the answer I so desperately want.

Chapter Twenty-Eight

Bhodi ⚧

Eight years ago…

Each time I hear that fucking overpaid mouthpiece talk, I feel my entire jaw tense. I've been grinding my teeth for the entire trial. The only defense tactic that cunt can come up with is to blame the victims, paint them as whores and make sure their client is seen as an upstanding member of the community who often helps charities and the dispossessed.

Does he fuck, the guy is a fucking predator.

I feel the tension weighing my body down, the pressure building in my temples as though someone has my head in a fucking vice. Glancing along the row, I spot the case detective practically falling asleep. With him due to retire soon, he's barely fucking interested in this case. He showed little interest at the scene and has proven to be a useless piece of shit ever since.

As Elijah Elom delivers his closing argument, I watch the young red head turn around and look straight at me. Her light green eyes filled with sadness and lost of all hope, as they have been from the moment I first met her.

She's been painted as a liar, a whore, a gold digger, and they've even gone so far as to try and accuse her of extorting money out of Luca Bernardi. Apparently, asking for your wages from your employer is now extorting money. But as I look to the jury, I can see the admiration radiating off them as they gaze upon this fucking choir boy that sits at the defense table.

Pamela James was found, along with her friend Lisa, beaten, raped, and left in an abandoned pop-up brothel to die. Neighbors complained when water began to spill into the downstairs apartment. Pamela had managed to crawl towards the bathroom, block the plug, and let the water run free, her last-ditch attempt at calling for help.

As one the first responding officers, we entered the apartment with weapons and torches drawn. The thick stench of drugs and body odour was almost unbearable, as though it was woven into every fabric in the property. We went through each room, stepping over needles, debris, loose clothing, and blood spatter.

Stepping into the bathroom, I called for help and an ambulance immediately. I rolled Pamela over but was sure she'd already passed. Her face was so badly beaten, stained with blood, and swollen; I had no idea how she would have been able to breathe. Gently placing my fingertips on her neck, I felt my eyes widen when I felt a faint pulse.

"I need an ambulance in here now!" I repeatedly screamed the demand through the entire apartment until the paramedics arrived.

I cradled Pamela in my arms and kept talking to her, hoping she could hear my words and hold on for a little while longer. Once the paramedics arrived, I moved away and stepped outside as the detective assigned to the case arrived.

"Detective Donavon." The older man holds his hand out to me, while he smoked a cigarette. His appearance in that moment put me off striving towards my gold shield.

"Officer Grey, and this is Officer Randle." I gesture to my patrol partner as he walks out of the building, shaking his head.

"What have we got?" The detective looks between us, observing the Medical Examiner entering the apartment and the paramedics leaving with the young girl.

"Two girls found in the fourth-floor apartment, one dead, but the other is still holding on."

"Did she say anything?"

I shake my head, running a weary hand over my face. "No, she's in a really bad way."

"Any idea what went on here?"

"We're canvassing, but as you'd expect, no one wants to speak. The place has all the makings of a pop-up brothel, though."

"It looks like whoever was here left in a hurry." Officer Donavon interjects, and I just nod.

"Ok, get your reports typed up and on my desk."

The detective steps away. I quickly follow, grabbing his attention as he entered the apartment building.

"Excuse me, detective?"

When he turned around, he let out a small huff, instantly getting my back up. He's giving me the impression this is just all too inconvenient for him; you know his fucking job.

"Yes?" His tone was already impatient.

I blink a couple of times, trying to word my question in the best possible way.

"Would it be ok to head to the hospital? See how the victim is getting on?"

His brow creases, and he eyed me suspiciously. To my surprise, after a couple of seconds, he agreed.

"If she says anything, make sure you note it."

Turning on his heels, he headed up the stairs, eventually out of sight.

With my initial report typed out, I cleared it with the captain and headed to the hospital with officer Randle.

Stepping into the dimly lit hospital room, I immediately removed my hat. I found myself just staring down at her, my heart almost breaking at the unbelievable cruelty someone has inflicted on such a young girl. I couldn't tell you how long I was looking at her, but a nurse gently placed her hand on my shoulder, pulling me from my trance. As I jumped, she apologized.

"I'm terribly sorry officer. Are you ok?" Her kind eyes searched mine for a moment before looking back to Pamela. "She's going to make it. She's going to need surgery to repair the fractures to her face, her arm."

"The emotional fractures?" I whispered softly as the tears fill my eyes.

The nurse stepped aside, pulling a chair towards the bed, and gestured for me to sit. A warm smile spreading across her face.

"With kind officers like you, anything is possible."

I continued to visit Pamela each day through her recovery, even once she had been discharged from the hospital. I learned she was twenty-two from Baltimore, and her big dreams of becoming a Broadway star led her to New York. She told me her employer, Luca Bernardi, had led her to the apartment. She'd begun dancing at one of his clubs six months prior to earn some money while she auditioned for theatre work.

The night she was attacked, Luca had asked her to attend a party with him. She was so thrilled as he was such a well-known businessman, or so she thought at the time. She didn't learn about his connections to the crime world until after her attack. He hides it well in the beginning as not to scare vulnerable victims away.

But it turned out to be a lie. When she got there, she was force-fed drugs and shoved into a room, Luca repeatedly raped her, and when she tried to get away, he beat her. Several other men were there, but she couldn't identify them. By this point, she was in and out of consciousness. She'd been put through that hell for three days before they all up and left.

When one of them realized they had killed Lisa, they all fled. They didn't even bother to check Pamela. Either they didn't care or just assumed she would eventually die anyway. Once she'd been found, the crime scene reckoned it had been seventy-two hours since the property had been abandoned, but there was no DNA, all those people in and out, and not one scrap of DNA to be found.

The entire thing never sat well with me; it gnawed away like a disease eating away at my insides. It was then I realized, no matter how much you abide by the law, how hard you try to serve and protect those around you. Sometimes, that just isn't enough.

The trial was horrendous, but I went to support my friend, and I had to give evidence as the first officer on the scene. Luca's mouthpiece began to try and spin it that I was sleeping with Pamela and that somehow this was all some conspiracy to frame him, but no one bought it. Firstly, it wasn't true and second, there was no motive for either of us.

Each time Luca looked over to Pamela, and that snake-like smirk slithered over his face, it took everything in me not to walk over and put a bullet right between his eyes in front of everyone. Each passing day, I hated him more and more, but I knew revenge would need to be down the line. Anything so soon after his acquittal would be suspicious, and accusations would be flying through the NYPD like fireworks on the fourth of July.

Unfortunately for us, Luca had so many brushes with the law, that killing him would be too suspicious. For a while, I wondered whether he fucking knew someone was plotting to kill him, so with his constant arrests, he would be visible to everyone looking into each accusation of prostitution, drugs, racketeering, and the NYPD couldn't just forget about him. He was like a disease that wouldn't go away.

Forcing myself into the moment, I step back inside the courtroom. Glancing to my left, I spot Luca and Elijah deep in conversation. However, neither look fazed. They're smiling and laughing with each other, and I feel my teeth begin to grind again. Flexing my hands, I slide into a seat at the back.

With my eyes focused on the judge's chair, I take a deep inhale, trying to calm the erratic beating of my heart. The time feels like it's being dragged through the mud, but as soon as those words are uttered, the gasps and shock spread through the courtroom.

"Not guilty"

My head falls against the wall, and I stare at the ceiling. Bracing myself forward, I hold my head in my hands when my arms eventually fall into my lap. I watch as Pamela is escorted out of the room by her friend. She doesn't look my way, the tears streak down her face, and she shakes with uncontrollable rage in that moment, I truly feel I and the rest of the NYPD have let her down.

I watch Luca and Elijah congratulate each other, huge grins plastered across their faces as they leave the courtroom and likely out towards the waiting press. Luca flashes a smirk my way as he strides out the door.

Once the room clears, sat in the same seat, and I'm unable to move. This was my first time in a courtroom as a cop. We did everything right, and still, he wasn't convicted. Instead, Pamela was practically carried out by her friend in tears, whilst the criminal walked out of here a free man. A free man who can carry on as though nothing ever happened, and he can start all over again.

Feeling a vibration from my pocket, I slide my phone out. Eyeing a message from an unknown number, I enter my passcode before studying the message further.

Meet me at Blue Bar ASAP.

The Blue Bar is a small cop car about five minutes from here, I can't say I've ever been there, but I know it's quite popular amongst the local precincts.

I stare down at the message, before snapping my head around to see if anyone is watching me. But my curiosity gets the better of me, walking with a purpose out of the courthouse and into the street.

Approaching the bar, I push the doors open to find a quiet bar. Spotting a familiar face from the courthouse, he turns to me and gestures to the stool next to him.

I glance around the bar for a moment before pulling out the stool and taking a seat. When the bartender approaches, he's about six foot five and is as wide as he is tall, his forearms covered in tattoos, his hair styled in a short buzzcut, and a jaw that could break fucking glass.

As I open my mouth, the man next to me interrupts.

"Three double Jamesons's Axe."

Axe? He fucking looks like a bulldozer.

He grunts. Placing three tumblers on the bar, he pours three large measures before sliding one to me, one to the man next to me, and keeping one for himself.

"I'm Michael Harper, by the way." Turning to face me, he extends his hand.

"Bhodi Grey." I say, shaking his hand.

"Yeah, the officer. Pam says you were really nice to her."

Nodding slowly, I find my eyes scanning the room once again. The whole interaction feels like some strange trap. When the door opens again, in walks ADA James Kressler. I look between the three men with confusion curling the right corner of my top lip.

"Jimmy, drink?" Michael holds the bottle of Jamesons up to him.

"Make it a fucking triple." He mumbles, draping his coat over the back of his stool.

Axe pours a fourth drink and slides it over to James. When he leans across the bar, he catches my eye, and the confusion falls over his face, too. Before he can speak, Michael glances around the empty bar and nods his head to Axe. The big guy heads towards the door, locks it, and gives it a final nudge before heading back to the bar.

Michael downs his drink in one before slamming the empty glass back down on the bar.

"So, what are we going to do about this complete fuck up?" He asks, looking between the three of us.

Chapter Twenty-Nine
Summer ♥

The air has been sucked from the room. My eyes are lasered onto the large window, hoping that if I ran with enough force, I could fucking fly out and plummet to the ground hard, wake up, and this would all have been a fucking nightmare. My hands squeeze the glass tumbler so hard that I feel it could crack within my grasp.

"Summer?"

His voice penetrates my ears, but I can't look at him. Tears cling to my cheeks. Everything he's told me feels like too much to take in. Rising from his seat, he slides the mask off. The moonlight catches his gorgeous face, his tanned skin, and those beautiful sparkling eyes. I shake my head in disbelief as a sob escapes my throat.

Slapping my hand over my mouth to stifle the noise, I just shake my head.

"It can't be." My words choke out, "Why would you....Why?"

Forcing myself to my feet, I slap my hand onto the arm of the chair to steady myself, and waves of dizziness run through my body. When I manage to stand up straight, I look at the glass still in my hand before launching it hard at the window.

Bhodi ducks out of the way, luckily. Still, part of me hoped he fucking hadn't. Spinning on my heels, I run for the door, but the heavy boots aren't far behind. Managing to snatch onto the door handle, it only opens a couple of centimetres before it's forcefully shoved shut. I look at the large hand on the door. I feel his body pressed firmly into mine, the smell of his cologne, the sound of his voice.

How could I have missed all this? I'm so fucking stupid.

"Let me explain, please?" His lips lower to my ear. Even though I want to kill him right now, his voice is quiet and still sends a shiver of want right up my spine.

My fingers are still locked around the door handle, and I continue to pull, but he won't let up. I shake my head when he places his hand over mine, breaking my grasp with the handle before spinning me around and pinning my arm above my head. When I go to slap him, he grabs my other hand.

"I fucking hate you! You lied to me. You got what you wanted and left! Then came back as someone else!" I spit out, the anger pouring from my words.

Tears and rage blur my vision. I try to shake from his firm grip, but it's no use. He's too fucking strong, and I'm too angry to even think properly.

"You can hate me, Fine! But don't you dare say I fucking used you! Everything we did, we both fucking wanted, whether it was me or him!"

Bhodi snaps back, before letting out a heavy sigh.

"I had no fucking clue when I walked into that crime scene what I was dealing with, I barely knew anything about you...But fuck, when I saw your photo, I knew I had to see you, even just a glimpse. I had no idea how this would all turn out."

My teeth gently gnaw on my lower lip, his statement rings true. I used him like he used me, whether it was for intense sex or because I wanted to feel safe.

"This is so fucked." I mutter.

"I know, I only ever wanted to keep you safe."

There's no denying the warmth and sincerity in his words. Blinking away the thick tears from my eyes, I begin to feel my teeth digging harder into my lower lip.

I eventually force my body to relax. When Bhodi's grip on me loosens, he eventually takes a couple of steps back, letting me go completely. Only leaving the ghost of his touch on my skin, and as soon as it disappears, I need to feel it again.

My chest heaves while we both stare at each other. My eyes penetrate his. I want more answers, but they can wait. Pushing my body from the door, I take Bhodi's face in my hands, reaching up onto my tiptoes. For a moment, his eyes flicker with concern, but as the smirk pulls at my lips, I see his expression relax.

Closing my eyes, I lean in close, my lips almost touching his.

"You're going to explain this fucked up situation to me tomorrow." I whisper. Opening my eyes slowly, I search his. "But for now, I just want you to fuck me."

His palms skim down my back, over my ass, before gripping onto my thighs and lifting me. Wrapping my legs around him, I can feel his hard cock rubbing over my pussy. I moan, sinking my nails into the back of his neck when his lips crash to mine. I open wide, allowing his tongue to devour mine.

The kiss deepens and becomes frantic as he moves toward the bedroom. Kicking open the door, we land on the bed. Frantically scrabbling for Bhodi's belt, I slide his jeans halfway down his thighs before forcing him onto his back. Straddling his lap, I grind down hard, seeking the friction I so desperately need.

With my fists bunching at his hoodie, my lips find his again. Glancing across to the bedside drawer, my left hand slowly slides across, as my fingers gently tug on the handle, I reach inside and gently reveal the shiny metal.

He shouldn't have left these...

As one cuff snaps around his wrist, I feel his body tense. In an instant, I clasp the second cuff around the bedpost. As Bhodi's eyes snap to the headboard, he tugs at his right wrist before his eyes flash to mine. As I push myself from the bed, the sound of clattering metal fills the room.

Standing at the foot of the bed, Bhodi's eyes darken. I see the flicker of amusement creep across his face before he leans back and shrugs.

"Fine, you have the control." The confidence glides over his face. Wetting his lips slightly, he shrugs.

"I know." I smile sweetly before turning away.

I can feel the confusion fill the room as I exit. A thrill is pumping through me, and any exhaustion or fatigue I was feeling is long gone. Glancing at the mask lying on the coffee table, I pick it up. The light from outside the window dances across the black matte surface. Seeing it in my hands, feels strange. For weeks, I've seen that mask up close, felt his breath on me, and felt his body pressed into mine. Each time I closed my eyes, I wondered what was underneath it all. What his body looked like, his eyes, how he tasted.

Now I know....

Holding the mask down by my side, I head towards the kitchen. Sliding open the drawer, my gaze lands on the sharp knives in the butcher's block. Reaching for the sharpest, I pull it from the block and hold the blade to the light. As it glistens, an idea comes to mind.

Sliding my jeans down, I kick them to one side before pulling my top over my head. Catching a glimpse of myself in my reflection as I head back towards the bedroom, my black lace thong and bra seem to match the mask in my hands well.

Reaching for the bottle of Jameson's, I hold the three objects in my hands as I enter the room. Adding a sway to my hips, I place the knife and bottle on the side. Holding the mask towards my face, I saunter towards the edge of the bed.

"Did you enjoy watching me?" My voice is soft as I peek around the side of the mask.

"I did." Bhodi straightens against the headboard, the handcuff laced onto his right wrist, jingling slightly.

"What did you enjoy most?" I ask, cocking my head to one side.

His breath catches in his throat. My eyes roam his body as his stomach muscles tense, and he wets his lips. I smile when his pupils dilate, reliving the memories of each time he watched me.

"The shower." He swallows hard. "The way the water falls over your body glides over your ass, slides over those perfect round tits."

I take a heavy inhale, his sinful words dripping all over my body. Reaching for the clasp of my bra, I allow it to fall to the ground. Taking a couple steps closer, my knees hit the foot of the bed. Running my hands over my hips, my stomach, then eventually allowing my fingers to pinch my already hard nipples, I let out a soft moan before they glide up my neck and through my hair, ruffling my loose waves.

Bhodi's eyes narrow on mine, they darken as I can't pull the smirk from my lips. Reaching behind me, I slide the large knife from the side. As I press my fingertip to the point, the sharp blade drags along the wood. Snatching the whiskey, I lurch it onto the bed along with the mask.

Straddling his lap again, I slide back and forth a couple of times. Feeling his thick cock still restricted by his underwear, I moan again, throwing my head back, pinching both nipples hard. I feel my pussy throb harder, my thighs aching with each tug and pinch.

I see Bhodi's self-control begin to falter, his left fist clenched by his side, his knuckles turning white and almost trembling. Reaching for the mask, I lean forward, sliding it over his face. I place a gentle kiss on its lips.

"I always wanted Two/Face to fuck me, Bhodi." I whisper.

Tugging at the zipper of his hoodie, I slide it down. Allowing the fabric to separate and fall on either side of his body. Reaching for the knife, I hold the blade against the fabric of his T-shirt before slicing it all the way through. The satisfying sheer sends a shudder through me as I push the fabric away, revealing his powerful body, my fingertips gently dancing over his tanned skin. I feel his heart thundering in his chest whilst his muscles flex under my touch.

Lifting the bottle of whiskey, I twist the cap, tugging it with my teeth. I spit it out onto the floor. The tin bounces off the wooden floor before disappearing completely. Tilting the bottle, I watch as the amber liquid drips across his skin before leaning down and licking it all up. The warmth of the drink, feeding my courage to carry on.

My tongue softly glides lower down his body. Looking through my thick lashes, I feel his eyes penetrating me, watching with intent while I hook my fingers under his boxers, slowly gliding them down. When his hard thick cock springs free, I feel my mouth water. I lick my lips before flattening my tongue and gliding from the base to the tip.

I feel his entire body tense beneath me. A sharp hiss escapes his mouth when his head falls back into the pillow. I look up to him once again. Lifting the knife off the bed, I reach for the band of my thong, slicing through the lace. It slides down my thigh, feeling my arousal down the inside of my legs.

Allowing my fingertips to glide over my nipples again. My head falls back while I tug and pinch, biting my lip, soft moans escape my mouth. Slipping my middle finger into my mouth, I slide it down my body. I hold Bhodi's gaze as it glides down my skin and connects with my clit.

"Oh...Fuck." I spit out, plunging my finger into my wet pussy before circling my clit again.

Circling my hips, my fingers go back and forth as my eyes roll into the back of my head. I grind against my own finger, feeling the heat spreading through my entire body. Bhodi's chest rises and falls, spurring me to carry on, spreading my wetness over my swollen clit. I feel my body begin to spasm. Sinking lower to my knees, I feel my release fast approaching, plunging my fingers deep one final time, I feel my pussy spasm and jerk around my fingers.

"OH, FUCK BHODI!" Throwing my head back, I cry out as the sweat pours down my body.

My head eventually falls forward, panting heavily as the waves of pleasure still surge around me. I lean forward, my left hand braced onto Bhodi's chest. Bringing my right hand to my lips, I gently suck on my middle finger. Looking into his eyes, I press another small kiss to the lips of the mask.

"Liars don't get rewards." The satisfied smug expression painted across my entire face.

The mask cocks to one side. I can still feel his body shaking beneath mine. But I can't hide the satisfaction, of using his own words against him.

"Well, that's lucky."

My eyes search the mask, my brows lazily pinch. The noise of the metal on the headboard pulls my attention away. As the cuff falls open my eyes widen.

Shit.

Bhodi's hand surges for my throat, my back hits the mattress, and his body rolls onto mine.

"Because I'm not a liar, Summer, but if you want Two/Face to fuck you, then I will."

My entire body tenses, and I feel the shudder of the promise of domination rush through me. My breath catches in my throat, wetting my lips, and I nod my head, but Bhodi shakes his.

"I need you to say it."

"Fuck me." My voice is breathy and needy.

Bhodi pushes himself from the bed, discarding his sliced clothes to the side, he kicks his jeans and boxers away. Adjusting the mask, he stands tall at the foot of the bed. My gaze roams his entire body. He's strong, powerful, and sinfully gorgeous.

Pulling my ankles, he shunts me further down the bed. When his body climbs over mine, I shudder when his thick cock drags across my pussy before settling between my thighs. Reaching between us, he plunges his fingers deep inside me, causing my hips to buck and a strained moan to escape my throat.

I feel his smirk from behind the mask, his fingers sliding in and out of me before placing them against my lips.

"Nothing is sweeter than watching you make yourself come."

My tongue sweeps across his fingertips, tasting myself on his skin before opening my mouth fully and sucking hard.

"Or watching you taste yourself."

He fists the duvet tightly with his palms, braced either side of my head. With one thrust of his hips, I cry out, a guttural moan escaping my throat as Bhodi fills me completely. My hands fly to his shoulders, my nails digging into his skin as he withdraws before driving into me harder.

Hooking my legs tight around his waist, I feel his palm glide up my thigh before squeezing my flesh hard. Rolling onto his back, he pulls me with him. My palms are braced on his chest, with his hands firmly around my waist, rocking me back and forth.

"Fuck my cock. I need to see the look on your face again."

My eyes begin to roll as the sensation and desire of a second orgasm threatens to take hold. Pressing my palms further into his chest, I hang on, rolling my hips over and over, grinding hard over his cock, I feel the pressure building all through my body, but he doesn't let up. His palms squeeze tighter, jerking me back and forth, his cock rubbing where I need it most.

"FUCK! BHODI." The words fall from my mouth, as my walls clamp down on him hard, I manage to grind over him twice more before my orgasm takes over my entire body.

My back hits the bed. I swipe the mask away, revealing that gorgeous face I've missed. My lips crash to his, wrapping my legs tight around him. Each thrust is hard and brutal. Our garbled moans of pleasure fill the room. My nails dig into his firm ass, holding him in place. My heels dig into the bed, grinding my pussy over his cock. He stills, his lips parted as I continue to grind and thrust, swallowing his cock, over and over. I know he's close. I can feel Bhodi's body tremble, his pupils have dilated, and I can feel the sweat pouring down his back.

"Summer..I...I'm." His words are barely audible.

I pull my lips to his, I feel the muscles in my stomach strain, but his moans push me to keep going.

"FUCK!!!" He cries out, throwing his head into my neck.

A strained roar fills the room as he comes hard. Feeling his cock twitching deep inside me, his entire body collapsing onto mine. I can feel our hearts thundering in unison as we both quiver and shake from the intensity.

Rolling me onto my side, Bhodi places a gentle kiss on my forehead as he pushes my hair from my face. His eyes lazily search mine, running his knuckles across my cheek.

"Whatever happens, I need you to know how much I care about you."

Hooking my thigh over his waist, my head falls onto his chest, concentrating on the sound of his heart, his fingertips gently run up and down the back of my thigh as I hold him close.

"I love you" I whisper gently, my eyes becoming heavy. I feel the exhaustion consume me, pulling me towards the promise of safety.

Chapter Thirty

Bhodi ⚥

I've been lying in the same position for what feels like hours. Summer sleeps peacefully on my chest whilst I gently run my fingers through her hair. Looking down her long lashes lay on her cheeks, her soft breaths and gentle twitching bringing me so much solace.

But her words are running repeatedly in my head.

"I love you."

It was so sincere and so beautiful, but it fucking terrified me, I felt my entire body tense, and my mind began to spin. After everything I told her, she should fucking despise me, push me out of her life, and never look back, but she hasn't? Instead, she pulled me closer, embraced my darker side, and, in the end, said those three words that no one ever uttered.

This is the second time I've laid in this bed with her and the second time in a long while that I've felt some peace and not hated myself. I know when she wakes up, the reality of what I have told her may hit harder than it did a couple of hours ago, but this time, I'll be ready. I'll give her the answers she needs, but I can't stop. Not with my all those unanswered questions still lingering. There's still too much to do, and too many people still walking free.

I feel Summer's hand twitch, her nails digging into my chest. She begins to shake slightly, gently rolling her over onto her back, and her soft moans become haunted and scared. Her face contorts as though she's fighting something.

"Shhhhh, it's ok baby." I whisper gently, but her eyes fly open. A panicked look streaked across her face before she blinks a couple of times, and her fear slowly fades away.

Pushing herself up in bed, she leans forward and runs her hand through her hair. Taking a couple deep breaths, she turns to me.

"Sorry, I think I had a nightmare." Her head fall into her hands, her words sorrowful.

Placing my arm around her, I pull her close. My palm gently running up and down her back.

"It's ok, do you remember it?"

I feel her body go rigid for a couple of seconds before shaking her head. Immediately, I know she isn't being truthful when she doesn't look my way, but I decide against asking her again. The pressure she's been under for weeks will eventually take its toll, and I know if I push too hard, she'll close up entirely.

"Was my dad a bad man?" The question surprises me, but she sounds almost numb when she asks.

My hand freezes halfway up her back. When she finally turns to me, I see the sparkles of tears in her eyes when they trickle down her cheeks. Letting out a low breath, I pull myself up in the bed, leaning against the headboard I hold my arm out to Summer, who leans against my chest. Pulling the duvet over us both, I hold her in my arms. When her arm wraps around me, she pulls me tight, and her body quivers.

"No, he wasn't a bad man. He was never a bad man, baby."

"What did you all do?" She sniffs, and I feel her tears on my skin.

"We did what the police and lawyers couldn't. We got rid of bad people."

She raises her head; her eyes meet mine. Her stare is blank; her gaze is searching mine with questions, but I know she already has her answers.

"You kill people?"

"We kill bad people. We get rid of the people when law enforcement can't."

"Is that why my dad's dead?" Her voice breaks slightly.

"I don't know, Summer. We were always very careful."

"Harry?"

I feel the shudder roll across my skin, I'd never let on about my suspicions, but Summer has now seen for herself the lengths he'll go to, to get what he wants, but she has already experienced his anger for herself, he's become more unhinged and even going so far as to turn on Eric. I believe he did organise Michael's murder, but as to why, is still unanswered between us all.

"I think so, but since he wasn't here at the time. I think it was Luca who did it at Harry's request."

"The man who raped and hurt Pamela?" Her brows crease at the question, rising into a sitting position and crossing her legs before her head falls into her hands again.

Reaching out to lace my fingers around hers, I gently tug her hands from her face. The unbelievable sadness and confusion in her eyes breaks my heart, but she just shakes her head, swiping the tears from her eyes.

"I can't do this, Bhodi, I...I just can't."

Leaning closer, I cup her cheek, gently wiping her tears away.

"What do you mean?" I ask, running my thumb across her cheek. My heart jumps into my throat, fearful of what she'll say next.

"I need to leave; I can't stay here." She looks away, the sadness stitched into her voice.

"You can. I'd never let anything bad happen to you." I plead.

"Bad things already have happened to me, to Al, and they've threatened you too!"

Swallowing hard, I have no idea how to respond. She's right; bad things have happened, and more bad things will happen, too. But the thought of her leaving kills me, not being able to see her, hold her close, inhale her scent. I feel a lead weight has been dropped into my stomach.

"Please...Don't." The words are caught in my throat, but my eyes continue to plead with hers.

Tugging at her wrists, I pull Summer towards me. Laying in the bed, I wrap my arms tight around her, placing my lips and nose into her hair. I kiss her gently before inhaling her scent. I bunch the duvet around us, cocooning our bodies within the warmth and safety of the soft bed. Feeling her fingertips gently skim across my shoulder, I focus on her touch.

With my beating heart, erratic mind, and the waves of fear that keep washing over me, I refuse to let her go. Clutching onto her body, I focus on the ceiling above. With no secrets between us, I look to our tomorrow.

"Come out to dinner with me tomorrow night?" I whisper into her hair.

Her head rises from my chest, and her eyes soften on mine.

"Like normal people?"

She chuckles slightly, wiping away the stray tears. The moment of humour, bringing balance to the chaos.

"Yeah, like normal people."

I feel her smile as she places a kiss on my lips.

"I'd like that."

Laying her head back onto my chest, I run my fingers up and down her arm as we hold each other close.

"I'll answer any questions you have. But if you wake up in the morning and decide you never want to see me again, please just tell me."

I fight to keep my voice from breaking, I hold Summer close as a single tear trickles down my cheek.

I love you, so much. Please don't give up on me.

Chapter Thirty-One
Summer ♥

"I'll see you tonight. I'll pick you up around seven, ok?" Bhodi presses his lips to mine.

My hands cup his cheeks, and I feel my body leaning back onto the bed. Bhodi lets out a low growl before pulling away and standing tall, sliding his hands into the pockets of his jeans. His eyes sparkle, and that beautiful smirk pulls at his full lips.

"I really need to get going. You're making me late." He shrugs, but the smirk stays in place.

Pushing the duvet away from my body, I rise to my knees on the bed. I feel my heavy tits and hard nipples brush against the cotton when it slides away, goosebumps rising on my skin. Rolling my bottom lip between my teeth, I can't help but smile. Bhodi's eyes darken as he shakes his head, leaning in once more, his hand around the back of my head, he pulls me close.

"You're making me late; I'll see you in twelve hours." His voice is dominating, pulling me in for one final kiss.

I fall back into bed, letting out a heavy sigh. I watch as Bhodi leaves, his footsteps moving through the apartment before reaching the door. Once the door closes behind him, I pull the duvet back over my head, inhaling his woodsy cologne. Stretching, I feel my muscles ache, but I can't help but smile, as the memories flood my mind. His smile, his eyes, how his body and soul connects with mine, and how I react to his touch.

The silence in the apartment is strange; the sun has already risen, revealing a clear blue sky for the day, but I don't want to move just yet. Glancing towards the clock I see a couple hours have already passed.

I must have fallen asleep.

Rolling back over, I gaze out the window as I relive last night. I know how angry I should be right now, but I'm not.

The story about Pamela broke my heart. All those involved had seen firsthand how she was let down, made to feel worthless, and further humiliated by Luca and his lawyer. She was nothing more than a plaything for them to taunt, but my dad made sure she felt safe and cared for along with Bhodi. How could I ever be angry at that?

The mask is a different story for now, but I must assume it was meant to protect us both. Harry has been able to find me, which means I'm not too hard to track down, and it's not like I was hiding. This was my dad's home, after all.

This was my dad's home...

Kicking off the duvet, I step through the apartment, sliding my hoodie over my head and adjusting the clothing as I begin to make a much-needed coffee. Sliding the bar stool out, I prop my elbows onto the marble top, propping my chin on my hand as the rich, earthy scent fills the room. The apartment feels empty. I've spent the last couple of weeks aimlessly wandering the space with no purpose or plan.

Glancing around the walls, they're stark and bare. For a moment, I allow myself to wonder what the place would look like with a feminine touch, but soon, the idea becomes stale. This will always be my dad's home, not mine. It was a place I stayed and never lived, but these past couple of weeks have left an odd yearning to start fresh. Escaping Harry definitely gave me hope, but meeting Bhodi gave me so much more.

I feel safe with him, cared for, and needed. For once in my life, someone needs me, and I need him too. I know I told him last night that I love him. For the first time, I said it to someone I cared for, and I meant it. I felt his body tense, and I could feel him lying uncomfortably in my bed, but I wanted him to know, to know that he is loved.

He promised tonight to answer any questions I have. There's a fear deep within me, that I could be told secrets that make me look at him in a different way, it could cause me to run as far away as I possibly can. But something tells me, that won't happen. I need to have trust in my dad and hold onto the good person he was and always will be in my heart. His decision wasn't taken lightly and everything they have done was to protect those who couldn't protect themselves.

The beeping from the coffee machine causes me to jump slightly, sliding from the stool. I pour the steamy coffee into a mug along with cream and a single sugar. Cupping my hands around the mug, I inhale deeply, enjoying the rich, nutty aroma. Stepping out of the kitchen with the mug placed to my lips, I stare at my dad's bedroom door.

Pulling the mug away from my lips, I feel my body becoming heavy from sadness. My eyes land on the door handle. I've been here for days and haven't set foot into that room yet. Each time I find myself looking to the door, I've managed to force myself away, making up some silly excuse that I was busy with the funeral or something, but now that's not the case.

Lacing my fingers around the door handle, I slowly push it open. Standing at the threshold, I lean in slightly as the lingering scent of his cologne hits me. Closing my eyes, the scent fills my nostrils, and the tears threaten to fall. As I gasp for breath, sitting on the edge of the bed, I try to steady my breathing. I count to ten before opening them again.

The décor is stark, much like the rest of the apartment's muted grey, black, and white tones. If I didn't know this was my dad's room, you'd think it was a show home. There's little in the room that adds any personal touches, no photos, no small Nik-naks. Turning around and spotting the walk-in wardrobe, I pull the door open, revealing racks of suits, some formal, some informal, and on the opposite side of the space, a few casual t-shirts, sweatpants, and some gym gear hang on their racks.

Placing my coffee on the side, I step inside. Brushing my hand across the jackets. The thought of having to eventually bag all his clothing up sends a cold shiver through me. I hate how final it feels. It's as though stripping every memory away and having nothing left. Walking through the small space, one of the jackets feels heavier than the rest. Turning to inspect the bulk in one of the pockets, I smile.

Reaching inside, I pull out a pile of pictures. In an instant, my brow creases. Flicking through the images, my heart rate picks up and I feel my knees wobble.

"What the fuck?" I mutter.

Squinting my eyes, I pull the photo closer, trying to make out the image. Glancing around the room, I don't spot a light. Moving back into the bedroom, I spread the photos across the floor. My gaze darts between the different images; all look to be taken at different times, and I spot Luca immediately. The same man from my dad's funeral and the same man who Bhodi told me hurt his friend.

Why the fuck was my dad following him?

Bhodi never mentioned any of this.

The fear that he could be lying to me slithers over my body. Nervously chewing on my thumb, I scatter the photos wider on the carpet, hoping to see why dad was following him. The photos show Luca speaking with different men, shaking hands and then entering an apartment. I don't recognize anyone, not what I would have any reason to.

"Shit." My hand flies to my mouth when I finally spot the reason. "Oh god, no."

Falling back onto my ass hard, I crawl backward before my back collides sharply with the wall. Frantically shaking my head, I feel my eyes fill with tears, blurring my vision along with the thick knot forming in my throat.

Unable to think clearly, I scramble to my feet, thundering to my bedroom. I grab my phone off the bedside table, my fingers trembling as I try to unlock it. Hitting the call button, I hold the phone to my ear, my heartbeat storming through my ears, as the call eventually goes to voicemail.

"Shit, shit, shit!"

Scrolling to the next contact, I hit call as the ringing begins. I can feel myself willing James to answer my call. Hearing a knock at the door, I poke my head around the corner. With the phone still in my hand, it falls to my side as the persistent knocking continues.

I eye the door suspiciously. The sequence of knocking is strange, it's almost frantic.

"Who's there?" I call out.

Eyeing the phone in my hand, I hold it close to my ear again. Listening to the end of the voicemail, I go to speak but slam my hands over my ears as a loud bang goes off.

"OW!" I cry out.

My body falls onto the floor hard, throwing my hand over my arm. I feel the warmth beneath my palm. Pulling it away, the blood pools in my hand. My eyes fly towards the door again, and more shots ring out. Frantically crawling towards the bathroom and pushing the door open, I lean back against it, forcing the lock shut.

I hold my breath as the front door is kicked open and bounces off the wall. I freeze, hearing footsteps through the main hall, and faint whispers merely a foot away from me.

"She's in there." One whispers.

They're right outside the bathroom door. Gripping my nails onto the floor, I force my body away. Sliding away from the door and trying to hold in my cries of pain. Leaning against the wall, I let out a heavy breath. My eyes scan the room, but there's nothing here to help me.

Spotting the blood pooling on the floor, my eyes widen. Gripping my hoodie, I pull it up. Spotting the blood pouring from my right hip, I feel the panic further settling in.

How did I not feel that?

The footsteps eventually move away. I try to play it out to see whether I could escape, but it's unlikely. As my body slumps lower to the ground, I feel the waves of dizziness wash through me, my vision becoming blurry and jumpy.

My head falls back against the wall. I can feel it beginning to roll. Inhaling deeply, I clutch onto the bloody wound. Each breath feels like a knife being driven through me. My eyes become heavy, but the smell pulls me from my weak descent.

Smoke.

Chapter Thirty-Two

Bhodi ⚭⚭

Earlier that morning...

Stepping into the precinct, it's chaos. Moving past officers and detectives, I eventually reach my desk before I hear my name being barked through the office. Turning to see captain Dean standing in the doorway, his face is focused and showing no emotion.

Stepping inside his office, I close the door behind me as he falls into his chair. The familiar figure sitting opposite him doesn't turn, but I already know who it is. I feel my spine stiffen at his presence. I watch as he taps his fingers impatiently on the arm of the chair.

"What is it?" I finally ask.

"Harry is dead." The captain shakes his head.

Stepping further into the office, I slam my fists onto the desk. When the captain leans back, he shoots me a warning glare.

Turning to see Bernardi's lawyer shooting me a death glare, I look between both men, straightening my back.

"What happened?"

"You tell me, he was killed in custody." Elijah shrugs.

My eyes narrow on his, usually he comes in barking orders, demanding to speak with the highest authority and throwing his weight around. But he doesn't seem too fazed for someone who's just lost a client.

Turning back to the captain, I shoot him a questioning look.

"Someone in custody killed him." He lifts a file from the drawer and slides it across the desk.

Pulling it open my eyes land on some scrawny kid. His mug shot shows his hollow cheekbones and eyes. The scabs on his skin confirm what I already know before reading his sheet.

"This kids a fucking junkie." I say, throwing it back onto the desk. "What happened?"

"They were both in holding, a fight broke out, and he slit Harry's throat."

"How the fuck did he get a weapon? Everything should have been taken off him?" The frustration in my voice evident from my wide eyes and trembling hands.

Elijah rises from his seat; the blank expression remains on his face. He refuses to look my way. Instead, he turns toward the captain.

"I expect a full investigation. That junkie shouldn't have been able to smuggle a weapon into the precinct and it not be found." He speaks calmly before stepping away from the office, shooting one final look at me before disappearing altogether.

His words leave an uneasy feeling in the room. The captain shakes his head.

"He's waiting in the interview room. See what you can find out."

Nodding, I leave the room. Taking a deep breath, the chaos seems to have subsided slightly, but glancing around, everyone looks on edge. Whoever didn't process this kid properly, won't skate on this colossal fuck up.

Wasting no time, I push open the interview room door with Detective Callaghan on my heels. A keen new detective who just got his gold shield, feeling him bump into me from behind, I shoot him a warning glare to tone down the eager puppy act.

Pulling out the chair, I take a seat. Flipping open the file, I look between this kid and his sheet, studying the list as long as my arm. I immediately close the file and rest my arms on the desk.

"Brent Mason, twenty-six years old, parents live on the Upper East Side. You've been arrested for possession of drugs, selling, buying, hell, even petty theft. Yet you've never killed anyone until now."

I speak calmly and stare into his eyes, watching him twitch and pick at his face. His eyes flicker to mine, but he can barely hold my gaze for more than a few seconds. The sweat forming at his brow and the shakes leads me to believe he hasn't had a fix for a while.

"So, what made you do it? As far as I know, you've never met Harry until today."

Brent keeps looking away, his eyes momentarily dart between Detective Callaghan and me, but he chooses to chew on his fingernails instead.

"You're looking at twenty-five years for murder, Brent. If you tell us why, we can speak with the D.A. Did Harry threaten you at all?" Callaghan interjects.

Brent's eyes widen for a second, the fear threatening to show at the thought of being locked away. No matter how Callaghan tries to spin this, he's going to prison for a long time. He murdered someone. There were witnesses, and right now, no apparent motive.

"I can't go to prison!" Brent leaps to his feet, the chair clattering on the floor. Backing into the corner, he begins to rant incoherently. "I'm not going! They said I wouldn't!"

My eyes narrow on him, rising from my chair. I keep my distance as Brent begins to sob, cowering in the corner. I slowly step closer. Dropping to one knee, I lean in.

"Who said you wouldn't go to prison, Brent?"

"The man! The man who gave me the money!" He sobs.

"What money? Where is it?"

"I needed the money. They said they wouldn't give me anymore."

"Who wouldn't give you any more?"

"My mom….she cut me off." He rubs his eyes while more tears fall.

I can feel my limited patience begin to drain away. Turning to Callagham, he merely shrugs. I gesture for him to follow me from the room, closing the door behind us.

"Did he have money on him when he was arrested?" I ask.

Callagham flips through the log but shakes his head.

"Just a phone, his wallet and cocaine. But there was no cash."

"Why was he arrested?"

"Anonymous call came in last night; someone was complaining about a drug deal outside their apartment. Brent was picked up by patrol a little later."

I look back through the window, Brent pacing the room, scratching at his skin, but it's not the scratching and continued picking that draws my attention. It's the numerous track marks that mar his skin, some older and some new, but he's covered, which are the signs of a constant user.

Snatching the file from Callaghan, I continue reading through the reports of each arrest, my eyes scanning page after page. He shoots me a questioning look, leaning in closer, trying to read, but I just take a step back.

"Shit." I mutter.

Moving with a purpose, I storm through the office and back into the captain's office without knocking. As the door swings open, he holds his coffee halfway to his mouth. Ignoring the anger blooming across his face, I slam the report down onto his desk.

"It's a setup." I protest.

"What?"

"The arrest, the whole thing, someone wanted Harry dead."

"What makes you so sure?"

Opening the report, I slide it over to the captain. His eyes scan the pages for a moment before he looks at me. His eyes are wide, he leans back in his chair, running a hand over his stubble.

"Cocaine, he's a heroin user. But could he be selling?" He asks.

"Why have cocaine in the first place if you can have heroin instead?" I ask. "Because they wanted Harry dead, they knew he was here. They knew the junkie kid was an easy target. All they had to do was get him arrested." I protest.

Captain Dean slumps into his chair.

"But the blade wasn't on him. He was searched?"

My blood runs cold. Straightening up, my gaze roams across the busy office, watching everyone go about their day.

"Someone here gave it to him." I mutter.

"Grey, you can't be fucking serious. Do you have any idea what you're accusing somebody of?"

"Luca." I let out a heavy sigh. "Harry has been arrested, and if the right deal is offered, he may spill his guts. Tell us everything.

"Shit." The captain mumbles, leaning back in his chair he studies the ceiling for a moment.

My phone begins to ring, immediately sliding it from my pocket, I see Summer's name fill the screen. For a moment, I just stare, but I can't answer her call here. Tapping ignore, I slide it back into my jeans and turn to the captain.

"I need the security footage from the office captain."

"Fine, I'll call down now."

Nodding, I leave the office. Keeping my head down, I step through the main office and head towards the main doors and outside. Glancing around first, I pull my phone out and hit call. Holding it to my ear, I let out a heavy sigh when it goes straight to voicemail.

"Come on, answer baby."

Ending the call, I lean against the precinct wall. I take a deep breath and try to figure out what to do next. If the security footage shows a cop passing this kid the blade, it means they knew what was going to happen, and they went along with it.

I guess Luca really has an influence within the NYPD.

This just confirms what I already fucking knew. He and Harry were clearly into something that he didn't want us to discover. He couldn't trust him enough not to cave under pressure, and it must be big if he's willing to trust a junkie kid to do the deed.

But what?

I feel the disappointment rain down on me hard, pissed off I couldn't kill Harry myself. Take my time, slice off his fingers, followed by his hands, take each arm…..

Mulling it over in my head, my phone rings, pulling me from my thoughts.

Summer?

Glancing at the screen, I see Jimmy's name. A flicker of disappointment runs through me, but I hit answer.

Letting out a heavy breath, I hold the phone to my ear.

"Jimmy, it's…"

"Bhodi, the fucking apartment is on fire."

The statement paralyzes me. I can feel the blood draining from my body.

"What?" I bite back.

"Summer called me. It went to voicemail. I heard gunshots and got a call from the security company. The fucking place is on fire, Bhodi! They've called 911, but I'm heading there now."

I can hear Jimmy running through his apartment, the door slamming behind him as he heads to Summers. But I can't move,

I'm fucking drowning. I can hear my heart thundering in my ears, anger clouding my vision. I try to force my feet to move, but they won't. The only thought running through my mind continues to cruelly taunt me.

You should have answered the call.

See you soon for part two.

Lucy x

@L.Williams_Author – IG – Keep up to date with future work

(My only social media)

AKNOWLEDGEMENTS

My wonderful husband Frank, for the many days you'd come in from work and find me still hunched over the laptop staring at a blank screen. You never told me to give up, even if on occasions I felt like I should. You'll never know how much I love you and thank my lucky stars each day that our paths crossed. You continually support me and that means the world to me.

Thank you to my readers and fellow authors, who have become friends. Thank you for your kind words, continuous support and love. You'll never know the feeling I get when I see someone has shared my work, liked or commented on my posts or even sent a reaction, it fills me with a sense of accomplishment and the determination to carry on.

Thank you to my very own "Breakfast Club". My close friends who have listened to me talk about this book after a few glasses of wine and yet, have still promised to act surprised when they read it.

Ashley O! Thank you will never come close, and I know that. Your encouraging words of feedback and support, the horror movie memes and long discussions about our collab have helped in more ways than you can ever know. You've stuck with me through this new and wild ride of self-publishing and yes you already know the ending....so don't tell anyone! (lol) Thank you for being a true friend, a wonderful and kind person but best of all, a complete horror movie nerd like me!

Printed in Great Britain
by Amazon